ONE MORE MADE UP LOVE SONG

ONE MORE MADE UP LOVE SONG

JENNY PROCTOR

ISBN: 978-1-967500-01-7

For the Ivy who inspired Freddie's Ivy.

You amaze me every day.
Please don't kiss like the fictional Ivy
until you're older. Love, Mom

A NOTE FROM THE AUTHOR

This book contains a storyline that involves a sister who was lost in a tragic drunk-driving accident. The event happened many years before the present action of the story, but one of the main characters does spend some time reflecting on how the loss has impacted her life. I did my best to handle the topic of loss delicately. If you have endured such a loss in your life, I had you in my heart as I wrote.

Having said that, the book is still a romantic comedy, full of fun and laughter and swoony kisses. A lot of kisses, if I'm honest. The circumstances demanded it, and who am I to say no to a kissing scene? Happy reading, friends.

CHAPTER ONE

Ivy

IT'S NOT LOST ON ME THAT AT LEAST HALF OF ALL SINGLE women between the ages of eighteen and thirty would probably kill to have my job.

As they should. It's a good job. The pay is great. Benefits are comprehensive. It includes a lot of travel to destinations all over the world, and I meet famous people on a regular basis.

But it is not all glitz and glamour.

A lot of my job is ridiculous. Tedious. Exhausting in the worst way possible.

I do not have regular work hours. I basically have no work hours. My entire life is just...work.

Twenty-four hours a day, seven days a week, three hundred and sixty-five days a year.

I live in my boss's house. I sleep on his tour bus. I manage every single detail of his life with what, I am proud to say, is exceptional precision.

And, because I am not at all recognizable and my boss is recognized by almost everyone, I'm the one who has to go inside the twenty-four-hour drugstore even though it's well past two a.m. just to hunt for Freddie Ridgefield's favorite flavor of Starburst Minis.

I glance at my watch as I steer my shopping cart into the candy aisle. "FaveReds," I say to myself as I scan the numerous colorful bags decorating the shelves. "Come on. You have to be here somewhere."

There are plenty of other Starburst variations. Starburst Gummies, original Starburst, Starburst Jellybeans…seriously? Jellybeans? How many different ways can we eat a Starburst? And why are there no Starburst Minis here? Everyone knows they're the best kind.

I crouch down to look on a lower shelf, my muscles groaning in protest. Twenty-six feels much too young for groaning muscles. Then again, I have been awake for almost twenty-four hours. Maybe I should cut my muscles some slack.

"Found you!" I say as I reach to the back of the shelf. The bag of Starburst Minis isn't the FaveReds variety, but it's better than nothing. I'll eat all the yellow and orange ones if Freddie really cares that much.

I toss the candy into the cart, then wheel toward the back of the store where I pick up tampons, the cinnamon toothpaste I like so much, and some curl cream that should not work so well for how inexpensive it is.

No matter how many fancy creams and serums and sprays I've tried, I always come back to the one my older sister taught me to use.

"Ivy, you're a teenager now," Daphne said the night before my thirteenth birthday. She guided me to the edge of the bathtub and sat me down, then raked her fingers through my shower-damp hair. "You have to start acting like you care about your hair."

For the next twenty minutes, she scrunched and shaped and tamed my curls until they looked as good as hers, talking the whole time, teaching me all the methods she'd learned from online tutorials and curly hair guides.

It felt very ceremonial, this process, like she'd specifically waited until the eve of my thirteenth birthday to bestow the wisdom and knowledge of curly-haired goddesses.

I don't always remember everything Daphne taught me. The list is way too long.

But I do have really exceptional curls—and that's all thanks to her.

I drop the curl cream next to Freddie's candy as a sharp pang of longing cuts across my chest. I rub at my sternum, like I'm rubbing the ache away, but mostly I just need something to do with my hands. Some action to remind me that I'm still here, still living...and that's exactly what Daphne would want me to do. Live.

Even if she couldn't.

At the end of the aisle, a couple of women break into giggles. I look up, immediately noting their attire. Sparkles, glitter, stars on their cheeks, and yep, they're both wearing Freddie Ridgefield t-shirts. Well, one of them is wearing a Midnight Rush t-shirt, a throwback to Freddie's boyband days before he went solo, but it's clear these women were just at Freddie's concert.

I duck into the next aisle and head toward the self-checkout at the front of the store, hoping I haven't taken so long that Freddie comes in looking for me. It's exactly the kind of thing he would do—despite Wayne's constant efforts to keep him in check.

After last year, when Freddie rented a black sedan and drove himself from his home in Nashville over to North Carolina to visit Adam, one of his Midnight Rush bandmates —totally alone—his head of security has been a lot more serious about his responsibility to keep Freddie safe.

The fact that Freddie even made it out of his house without alerting Wayne was, in the security guard's mind, a personal failure on his part.

But Freddie is too charming for his own good. Whether it's Wayne or me or the entire global female population, he just has a way of winning people over. And that usually means he gets what he wants.

"Did you find them?" A deep voice asks right next to my ear.

I startle and spin around to see Freddie smirking at me, face shaded by a turquoise Appies Hockey baseball cap.

My eyes widen as I look past him and down the aisle to where his fans are still trying on sunglasses. If they look this way, they'll absolutely see him.

I abandon my cart and grab Freddie's arm, tugging him to the opposite side of the store. I don't stop until we're standing between the condoms and the adult diapers. Perfect.

"What are we doing?" Freddie says, his voice at full volume. "Did you forget something?"

"Can you please stop talking?" I whisper-yell. "What are you doing in here?"

"Looking for you," he says. "What's taking so long?"

"I was searching every stupid aisle for your stupid candy," I say. "Also there are two women four aisles over who were at your concert. Feel like chatting with them right now?" I give him a pointed expression, and his face immediately shifts.

"Definitely not," he says, his voice finally at a volume to match mine.

"Then stop talking," I whisper, but it might already be too late.

"Are you serious?" a woman's voice says. "Could it really be him?"

Freddie winces. He's honestly so great with his fans. But he's been on all night. He shouldn't have to interact with anyone at two a.m., let alone women he doesn't even know.

I breathe out a sigh and tug him toward me, backing us directly into the wall of diapers. "Please don't hate me for this," I say. Then I hook one hand around him and pull his head into the crook of my neck, twisting our bodies so his back faces out.

"What are we doing?" Freddie whispers, his mouth close enough for his breath to tickle my earlobe.

Goosebumps skitter across my skin, and I bite my lip, willing myself to think of something, anything, besides how good it feels to be this close to him.

I've got years of practice ignoring my feelings for Freddie, but this is a lot, even for me.

"Just play along," I whisper back. Then I pitch my voice high enough that I hope the approaching women can hear me.

"Here, Johnny? You want to kiss me here?!"

Freddie practically snorts, his body shaking with suppressed laughter. "Johnny?" he whispers. "Is it 1967?"

"Shut up," I say through clenched teeth. "Hug me a little closer."

Freddie's arms tighten, his body curling around me as he tucks me closer to his chest. "You know, this could backfire."

Ha. He has no idea. It's already backfiring because I can't stop thinking about unzipping his hoodie and crawling inside, latching myself onto his body like a baby koala.

I knew going in that a tour would be tough.

So. Much. Togetherness. Time on the bus and time in his dressing room and time hanging out after concerts.

I prepared myself mentally. Made a commitment to minimize touching as much as possible. Promised myself I would set clear boundaries and handle Freddie's *Living Out Loud* Tour with the utmost professionalism.

Doesn't exactly sound like pretend make-out sessions in drugstore diaper aisles, but Freddie is the one who came in here in the first place. This is on him.

Or so I will tell myself.

And if I happen to enjoy the physical contact, well, I'll at least never admit it out loud.

"Freddie Ridgefield caught making out with unknown woman in the diaper aisle," Freddie continues. "It's a good headline."

"It isn't going to backfire," I say, but I tug him a little closer anyway, letting one hand skim up and down his back. "Just don't look up."

He nestles even closer. "You smell good," he says into my hair.

His words send an immediate, pulsing heat racing through my body, but no, nope. No heat allowed. I force my brain to think of ice water. Buckets and buckets of dousing cold water raining down onto me, cooling whatever fire this man triggers.

Except, now I'm wondering what it would be like to kiss

him in the rain, so I'm not sure if my mental gymnastics are helping or hurting.

"You smell like sweat," I say, even though it isn't true. Freddie showered after his show, and he smells amazing. Like the orange and oatmeal goat milk soap he always makes me order from Stonebrook Farm.

He chuckles. "I do not."

For a split second, I wonder if he knows what I'm doing. Deflecting. Refusing to accept his compliment. Holding us firmly in the friend zone.

Not that he should question. He was the one who made it clear how important it is that I not fall in love with him. He might as well have written it into my contract.

When I don't hear the women talking, I peek an eye over Freddie's shoulder to see if they've left, but they're standing directly at the end of the aisle, looking our way with curious expressions.

I lift an eyebrow in challenge, then I pointedly turn my face and tilt it toward Freddie's, hoping against hope that the way we're angled, my hair falling just so, it looks like we're kissing. In reality, my lips are pressed against the side of his jaw just below his ear. I slide my hand up and tangle it in the hair at his nape.

"Johnny, they're watching us," I say. "Isn't that weird?"

One of the women breathes out a huff. "Let's go," she says. "It definitely isn't him."

"I know what I saw," the other woman says, "and there's a bus in the parking lot."

"The bus could belong to anyone," the first woman says, their voices growing quieter as they walk away. "Besides, that guy isn't nearly as hot as Freddie Ridgefield."

Freddie huffs out a laugh. "Should I feel insulted?" he whispers, his lips torturously close to my mouth.

I could turn my head a matter of centimeters, and we'd be kissing. Instead, I force myself to think about the time Freddie got food poisoning from a post-concert burger and fries and spent the next three hours holed up in the bathroom of his tour bus. Anything to break the spell he's casting over me right now.

"That you aren't as hot as yourself?" I finally manage to say. "I don't think so."

Based on the sounds floating back from the front of the store, the women are checking out, but Freddie and I don't move. At least not completely. We do relax a little, shifting into what feels more like a regular hug than an actual performance.

He lifts his head, and mine falls onto his chest before he drops his cheek to the top of my hair. It's easy, comfortable in a way I don't expect, and we stand like that until the women have left the store. It's not like Freddie and I have never hugged before. I'm sure we have. But we don't do it often enough for this to feel natural, which is why it's so disconcerting that it does.

Finally, Freddie takes a deep breath and steps back, letting his arms fall from my shoulders. "Close call," he says, a softness to his words that makes me suddenly incapable of meeting his eyes.

After years of working for Freddie, I know exactly what will happen if we make eye contact. He will see me, just like he always sees me, and he'll know there is something up. Then he'll push because he cares, and he'll want to make sure I'm okay.

But there is no way I'll admit the problem is that hugging him in the diaper aisle at two a.m. felt really good—good enough that I didn't want it to stop.

I haven't been hugged like that in a really long time.

A sudden wave of emotion makes my throat tighten, and the threat of tears builds behind my eyes.

What is wrong with me?

It was just a hug.

But then, who do I ever hug? My life is all work, all the time. Everyone I spend any amount of time with also works for Freddie. Tour managers. Caterers. Drivers. Sound technicians. Crew members.

I tend to keep my work relationships as professional as possible. I need people to take me seriously when I'm running Freddie's life, and hugging doesn't help with that.

But in general, I am a hugger. I like the contact. The connection.

It occurs to me that might be the real reason it felt so good to hug Freddie. It wasn't my feelings—it was just human connection.

The realization makes me sad. Honestly, how out of balance is my life right now?

"It *was* a close call," I say, agreeing with his assessment. My voice comes out a little harsher than it needs to be, but I can't seem to rein it in. "And it could have ended really badly."

Freddie frowns. "Relax. Worst-case scenario, I would have just talked to them. Taken a few pictures. It wouldn't have been a big deal."

"You don't know that it wouldn't have been a big deal," I say. "You've dealt with unpredictable fans before."

I'm not being fair to him.

I know I'm not.

I mean, things really could have gone sideways—they sometimes do—but I'm self-aware enough to recognize that's not why I'm being so hard on him.

"Just stay here, okay? I'm going to go check out. Then I'll ask the employee if she can let us out the back door. I'll text Wayne and have them pull around to meet us there."

"Ivy, I really don't think—" Freddie starts.

"Don't move," I say, cutting him off, then I turn and head toward the front of the store. At the end of the aisle, I look back and whisper-yell, "And put your hood up!"

Freddie scowls, but he does as I ask and pulls his hood over the top of his hat.

I'm probably being ridiculous, but the whole encounter has me flustered and off balance, and neither of those are feelings I can afford right now. I have a job to do, and while keeping Freddie safe isn't my primary responsibility and he is a grown man accountable for his own actions, I'm also responsible for *my* actions.

In that regard, I probably shouldn't have pretended to make out with my boss. But it was an extenuating circumstance. A spur-of-the-moment emergency situation. And it worked. I saved Freddie from curious fans, and everything is fine.

At least on the surface, anyway.

I reach my abandoned cart and wheel it up to the lone worker at the front of the store. I was hoping for self-checkout, but the kiosk is closed, so I dump my purchases onto the counter and do my best to avoid eye contact.

"Did you find everything you need?" the employee asks as she rings up Freddie's Starburst.

I force myself to smile. "Sure did," I say, but the answer isn't even a little bit true.

I didn't even come close.

CHAPTER TWO

Freddie

I POUR A HANDFUL OF STARBURST MINIS INTO MY HAND AND sort out the yellow and orange from the pink and red. Ivy wordlessly holds out her palm to collect the unwanted colors.

"I don't know how you eat that stuff," Wayne says from the couch across from us. We're in the lounge space at the front of the tour bus on parallel bench seats under the windows on either side.

"I don't know how you don't," I say to my very grouchy security guard.

"Sorry, Wayne," Ivy says as she tosses back a handful. "I'm with Freddie on this one."

It's nice to hear Ivy say something positive. For the last half hour, ever since we left CVS, she's been cagey and more defensive than usual. I realize I made her job harder by wandering inside when she and Wayne both told me to stay on the bus. But it was two a.m., and the parking lot was empty. How was I supposed to know a couple of fans were wandering the aisles?

"Can we stock up then?" Wayne asks. "To avoid late-night snack runs?"

"Not a bad idea," I say as I toss back another handful. "Though I can't promise I won't crave something else next time." I nudge Ivy's knee. "It'll be fine. Ivy's quick thinking saved me tonight. It will next time too." It's a little pointed, as far as compliments go, but I want more evidence that Ivy is okay—that she isn't still upset with me. As much as we tease and banter and joke about getting on each other's nerves, I care about what Ivy thinks.

"What does that mean?" Wayne asks before Ivy can respond. "Quick thinking? I thought you just hid in the diaper aisle until the fans left."

I grin. "*We* hid. Both of us together," I say, watching Ivy, who seems much too focused on her phone. "And pretended to make out to throw them off our trail."

"Okay," Ivy finally says, dropping her phone onto the cushion beside her. "Do we really have to talk about it? I did what I had to do, and it wasn't a big deal because you and me would never actually work."

"What? Why?" I ask, suddenly feeling defensive. Not that it truly matters. I don't have feelings for Ivy—we've only ever been friends. But I'm weirdly insulted that she's so sure we couldn't be more, even in a hypothetical sense.

"Because I know too much about you," Ivy says, though she's acting weirdly cagey, like she's intentionally avoiding eye contact. "Plus, you're completely insufferable."

"I am not," I say as I pour another handful of Starburst into Ivy's hands. "Oh, wait...you got two red ones. I want those back."

She lifts her eyebrows, giving me a pointed look, and I grimace.

"Okay, bad timing. But you agreed to give me all the red and pink. If you want them, you can totally have them."

Wayne chuckles. "You walked right into that one."

I frown into my hand of color-sorted Starburst. An unfortunate side effect of my celebrity status is that most of the time, I don't even have to ask to get what I want. People are lined up to give me things, to make my life easier, to smooth every wrinkle and eliminate every possible roadblock.

It's probably good I have people in my life who bring me back down to earth when all that attention goes to my head.

But it still stings to hear Ivy's assessment.

Even if I'm fully aware that we would be a very bad idea —because we would—for a split second in CVS tonight, holding Ivy in my arms felt...good. It's not like I expect her to be as moved by all the friendly touching as I was, but she could at least not be repulsed by it.

My tour manager appears from the back of the bus looking tired to the bone, the bags under his eyes framed by deep creases in his sun-worn skin. Even though Seth *looks* like a retired cattle rancher who spent his days on horseback, baking himself under an Arizona sky, that's not anywhere close to the truth.

Seth grew up in Beverly Hills with parents who both worked in show business. The Wranglers and cowboy boots he wears are more fashion accessories than practical choices, but man, can he sell the look.

Last time I was in LA to film a couple of talk shows, we lost Seth for almost three hours because someone mistook him for an extra on a Western filming nearby and shuttled him to the *wrong* sound stage.

We still like to tease him about that one.

"You should get some sleep," Seth says, using a fatherly tone that only he can get away with. "We all should."

Ivy yawns beside me. "He's right. You have an early start tomorrow." She glances at her watch. "Or, today, really. In just a few hours."

"Do I? What am I doing early?"

"A radio interview," she says. "But you'll be done by nine if you want to sleep a little more before soundcheck."

I breathe out a sigh. Soundcheck, then *another* concert.

I love what I do, but this late in the tour, back-to-back shows are pretty draining.

Ivy nudges my knee. "Ten more days," she says, reading me as well as she always does. "Then you'll get a break."

I run a hand through my hair. "Hardly a break," I say, though that's not entirely true.

In ten days, I'll be back home in Nashville for two months.

No tour bus.

No traveling at all.

At the end of the break, we'll kick off the second leg of the tour with a show in Nashville before hitting seventeen more cities in the eastern half of the United States. Then we'll head to Europe for ten more concerts there. I'm looking forward to the Nashville show—I love performing to a home crowd. Well, *sort of* home crowd. I grew up in Seattle, but my roots feel a lot deeper in Nashville than they do in Washington, even with my family still living there.

The point is, I'm supposed to use the two months we

aren't traveling to record my next album. And that's the last thing I feel like doing.

Mostly because I don't have a single new song I like singing. I have dozens I *could* record. But none that feel like what I *want* to record right now.

Ivy keeps telling me to trust the process. I've been in this position before, and inspiration has always found me. But something is missing this time.

I can sense it, even if I can't quite put my finger on what it is.

Maybe I'm just tired.

Tired of gas station candy and tour buses.

Tired of made-up songs about made-up emotions.

How am I supposed to write about love when I have no idea what it feels like?

"Come on," Ivy says. "Sleep. You'll feel better in the morning."

I let her tug me to my feet and guide me toward the back of the bus. We shuffle past a set of bunks where Ivy, Seth, and Wayne will sleep tonight. My band and the rest of the crew are on another bus somewhere up ahead, but I like to have Ivy and Seth close, and I've had enough run-ins with fans to know it's best to have security *on* my bus at all times.

Ivy reaches around me and opens my bedroom door. Even months into the tour, I still feel twitchy about having a private bedroom when everyone else has to sleep in the bunks. Seth keeps saying it's my right, since I'm the one paying the bills—including everyone's salaries. And Ivy insists the bunks are comfortable.

But I still don't like it.

"Dude. Why are you dragging your feet?" Ivy whispers.

"Your bed is right there. You can literally just collapse into it."

She tugs the bag of Starburst out of my hands and gives me a gentle shove toward the bed before turning away.

"Ivy, wait."

She pauses and looks back, brown eyes wide. "What?"

"Nothing. Just—thanks for tonight. Sorry I made things hard on you."

Her expression softens, her lips ticking up into a subtle smile. "Don't worry about it. I'm used to it. And everything turned out okay in the end."

I push my hands into the pockets of my hoodie. "Do you really think I'm insufferable?"

She breathes out a sigh like me asking the question only builds her case against me. "Yes," she says. "But it's actually kind of endearing."

"Endearing?"

She leans against the wall. "The way you always assume that everyone already loves you. Or you trust that everything will *always* work out. I envy it, honestly. I tend to plan my way into feeling confident, which requires a lot more stress."

"So...when you say I'm insufferable, you actually mean... I'm amazing?"

She rolls her eyes, then reaches out and pats me on the chest. "Sure, Freddie," she says with a grin. "That's exactly what I mean."

"For real though," I say, not wanting her to walk away just yet. "I probably wouldn't be so confident that everything will always work out if I didn't have you planning for me. So maybe the right conclusion here is that we make a really good team."

Something flickers behind Ivy's expression that I can't

quite read. "Yeah, I guess we do," she says. "Now go to bed. Seth already took off his boots. That means it's time to sleep."

"I thought I smelled something," I say.

"I heard that," Seth calls, his voice muffled by the privacy curtain in front of his bunk.

I watch from my bedroom door as Ivy walks to her bunk. She reaches in and pulls out a small zippered pouch, then crosses to the bathroom. When she turns and sees me still standing there, she shakes her head, giving me an exasperated look before she picks up her hand, using two fingers to mime walking as she tilts her head toward my room.

As tired as I am, I don't know why I'm so restless—why I'm resisting going to bed in the first place. If I were smart, I would have been asleep an hour ago. But after what happened in CVS, or maybe just after the conversation we had, I'm craving validation like I haven't before.

From Ivy, specifically.

She was so quick to say that we would never work.

Why does that bother me so much?

When Ivy disappears into the bathroom, I finally turn and shut my bedroom door, sighing before I kick off my shoes and collapse onto my bed.

I tug my phone out of my back pocket, then scroll through a dozen new text messages. I pull up the group chat with my former Midnight Rush bandmates, where several new messages are waiting for me. We were only a boyband for just shy of three years, and that was over eight years ago. But we recently reconnected for a one-time reunion show just before my tour, and we've been talking on a more regular basis ever since.

The first message is from Adam, a picture of him with his

arms full of what look like golden retriever puppies. The message under the picture reads, *One for each of you.*

It's exactly the kind of dog I would want if I could have a dog, but something like that feels a long way off. Like a thing that will happen when my real life starts.

I know a lot of people would kill to make music for a living. To tour like I'm touring. To fill stadiums with fans. I love that I get to do it. But when I crashed at Adam's farm for a weekend and watched him living his life, something in me shifted, and I haven't been the same since.

Adam isn't in the music business anymore, though he's been writing again, which is amazing. One of the only songs I'm actually excited about recording is his.

But most of his time is dedicated to his dog rescue. He spends his days covered in dog hair, scrubbing out kennels, and somehow, I'm jealous of the guy.

I zoom in on the pictures of the puppies. The one on the left has one of its ears turned inside out, its tongue lolling to the side in a way that makes me grin. That's a dog with personality.

I quickly read through the other guys' responses to Adam's picture before adding my own reply.

> JACE
>
> Sure. A puppy is exactly what I need to make my life easier.

I chuckle. Poor Jace. His son was born four months ago, and since his marriage ended two months before that, he's parenting on his own. His ex-wife hung around long enough to have their second baby, then she flew home to Australia to "recover," leaving Jace to do the single dad thing.

If her Instagram feed is any indication, recovering looks

a lot like hanging out on the beach with her pro-surfer brother and all his friends.

Jace is better off without her, but I can't imagine what he's up against raising two kids on his own.

Leo's reply is next.

LEO

Golden retriever? I had one of those as a kid.

ADAM

Not sure about the dad, but the mom is purebred golden.

He follows this message with a second photo of a fully grown golden retriever with white-blond fur.

There's something so grounding about this conversation. Because it doesn't really matter. We aren't talking about anything important. But we're *talking*. Staying connected.

A little piece of the loneliness that's been chasing me all night slips away as I add my reply to the text thread.

FREDDIE

You know I'd take one if I could. The one on the left looks ready for a good time.

The rest of my text messages I pointedly ignore. One from my new agent, asking about an update on the album and if I feel ready to record. I'm booked in Leo's studio in Nashville for nearly all of my two-month vacation, and the album is supposed to be fully recorded before we start the next leg of the tour. I'm happy it's Leo who will be working with me—he's an incredible producer—but working with him also feels like pressure. I don't want to waste his time.

22   JENNY PROCTOR

And if I can't figure myself out, that's exactly what I'm going to do.

And finally, a message from Mira Stapleton, hoping we can sync up when I'm in LA for the last show on this leg of the tour.

Mira is an actress I've gone out with a few times. She's beautiful and smart too, though you wouldn't know it by the way she plays it in interviews. But she's also *very* famous. Dealing with my own fame is difficult enough. I'm not sure we have sparks enough to justify dealing with her fame on top of mine.

It can't be a good sign that thinking about seeing her again mostly just makes me tired. But the more I think about the *real life* I'm not living, the more certain I am that Mira is not the woman I'm looking for.

Once I've read all my new messages, I scroll down to find the text thread with my mom. We don't communicate all that often, but I've got a show in Seattle next week. It's one of the last ones before the second leg of the tour takes me back to the east coast, so if my family would like to come to a show, now is the time.

I type out a message to my mom and schedule it to send first thing tomorrow morning. She wouldn't get the message in the middle of the night, even if I sent it, because Ridgefields are not the kind of people who sleep with their phones by their beds. But she wouldn't appreciate seeing a timestamp that reads 2:33 a.m. regardless.

FREDDIE

Any thoughts on the Seattle show? You won't have to deal with the crowds. VIP treatment, a private box. Let me know.

I toss my phone onto the nightstand and sit up before unzipping my hoodie and shrugging it off, then I tug my shirt over my head.

I'm not even sure why I'm sending my mom a message.

It's not that we don't get along. My parents are good people who did a decent job raising me. But we are...what's the best way to say it? Very *different* kinds of people.

They're both college professors in the mathematics department at the University of Washington, and while I hate to define anyone using stereotypes, they are everything you might expect math professors to be. They love classical music. They do crossword puzzles. Their after-dinner activity is to drink a glass of wine while trying to stump each other with calculus problems.

They do not have any tattoos, nor do they care for mine. They wear a lot of sweaters and a lot of corduroy and shirts buttoned all the way to the collar. They don't yell. They rarely get upset. They never bark at the television during a sporting event or do anything but applaud politely at concerts.

After years of believing they would never have children, I was a surprise, born three days before my mother's forty-first birthday, followed by my little brother, Harold, who was born two years later. They gave us everything they could with a practical, methodical approach to their parenting.

Even when I wanted to fly to Nashville and audition for Midnight Rush, they treated it like an equation, measuring what they called my natural aptitude against the potential risks. Lucky for me, when they solved for x, it equaled a trip to try for the future I knew I was destined to have.

Honestly, when I got the gig and moved to Nashville full-time, living with a host family until I turned eighteen, I think my parents were relieved to have my very noisy presence out of the house.

Harold is a much better fit for their personality. He's also a mathematician, currently working on his PhD, and he has a closet full of sweater vests and a cabinet full of quiz bowl ribbons and chess trophies.

That sort of thing is much more their speed. Not stadium concerts full of screaming fans and music they once said seemed "much too loud."

I pull on a pair of pajama bottoms, though by this point, it almost feels stupid to sleep when I only have a couple hours before I need to be awake again.

I check my phone one last time and find a new text message, this one from Ivy.

> **IVY**
>
> Hey, just wanted to give you a heads-up that as soon as we're back in Nashville, I think I'm going to get my own place. Nothing will change about work. I'll still be close by. But I'd like to set a regular work schedule so I can occasionally have some non-working hours too. We can talk details once we're home. I just wanted you to know I'm thinking about it so you don't freak out if you see me hunting for apartments.

I read the text all the way through three times before I sink onto the edge of my bed.

There is nothing about this message that should upset me. I'm well aware how lucky I am to have Ivy. She's a logistical genius, managing every aspect of my life with enviable precision, and she's become a really close friend. It's been amazing having her live with me, and not just because it means she's always around when I need her. I also really like her company.

I wrack my brain for anything that's happened in the past few weeks that might have prompted her decision. I know I frustrated her tonight, but not enough to have triggered something like this. It was just normal stuff. And she was fine when we said good night.

But am I missing something? Did I inadvertently offend her in some way? Hurt her feelings? Take advantage?

I wince at that last question, all too aware that the answer might be yes simply because she *does* live with me. But I pay Ivy well. And my house is enormous. It's not like we're sharing a bathroom. She has her own entrance, and she's living rent free.

It's hard for me to wrap my head around her wanting her own place when she already has such a sweet setup.

Without really thinking about what I'm doing, I stand and open my bedroom door, tiptoeing down the narrow hallway to Ivy's bunk. Wayne and Seth are on the right side of the narrow hall, but Ivy sleeps on the left side alone.

I yank back the privacy curtain of the upper bunk, and she jumps, her phone flying into the air before it lands back on her blankets with a thump. The height of her bunk makes us eye level.

"What is this about?" I say, holding up my phone.

She rolls her eyes. "Seriously, Freddie? You just scared me half to death. What if I'd been naked?" Her eyes drop to my bare chest, and her cheeks turn the slightest shade of pink, just visible in the dim light of her bunk.

"Why would you be naked?" I ask.

"Maybe I sleep naked," she says. "Some people do. The

point is, just because I don't have a door doesn't mean you don't have to knock."

I grin. "If you sleep naked when Seth is asleep less than four feet away, you're braver than I am."

"I don't *actually* sleep naked," she whisper-yells. "I'm just saying. You still have to knock."

"You're right," I say, conceding the point. "I should have knocked." I hold up my phone one more time. "Now tell me why you're moving out."

She sighs. "Can we please talk about this tomorrow?"

"If you wanted to talk about it tomorrow, you should have texted me tomorrow. You texted me tonight, and now I'm not going to be able to sleep because I'm worried I'm a bad boss."

"You aren't a bad boss," Ivy says, "but Seth and Wayne are both asleep, as you already pointed out, less than four feet away."

"They can't hear over the sound of the engine," I say.

"Yes, we can," Seth says from his bunk. "But do carry on. I'm curious how this will pan out."

Ivy gives me a look that says *I told you so*, but I'm too far in to turn back, so I scowl right back, then climb up the ladder at the foot of her bunk and drop myself onto her bunk, pulling the privacy curtain closed behind me.

"Oh my gosh," Ivy says as she shifts closer to the wall. "Are you serious right now?"

"I'm just going to sit right here," I say as I try to angle my long legs into a comfortable position in the small space. My knee knocks against the wall, then my head bumps against a different wall. "Oof," I grunt as I rub at the spot on my head. "This was probably a bad idea."

"You think?" Ivy says, then she sighs. "Here, just stretch

out this way. These bunks really aren't meant for sitting, so if you're staying, you're just going to have to lie down." It takes some maneuvering and more than a few grunts and grumbles from Ivy, but I finally manage to stretch out beside her, head propped up on my elbow. I catch the faint scent of Ivy's hair, and a sudden wave of uncertainty washes over me.

We are *close*. Really close. We aren't touching, but I can smell her. Feel her body heat. Hear the soft inhale of her breath.

It's not like Ivy and I never touch. Our friendship is casual. Easy. But we aren't hugging every day. We've only hugged a few times, actually. Once when I got the news of my latest Grammy nomination. Once after the Midnight Rush reunion show when emotions were high for everyone. Once when I was stressed about a particularly brutal stretch of tabloid gossip that was entirely fictional. Well, and tonight, I guess.

I've always gotten the sense Ivy isn't much of a hugger, which is why it feels so notable that twice in one night, I've found myself this close to her.

Admittedly, I am the one who wandered into CVS and created a situation in which she had to save me, and I am *also* the one who just climbed into her bed.

Come to think of it, maybe I *shouldn't* be so surprised she wants to move out.

"You're ridiculous," Ivy whispers.

"Yes," I say, ignoring my insecurities. "You know this about me. Now, tell me the truth. Why are you moving out?"

She sighs, then she reaches up and turns off the light.

When she doesn't say anything, I ask, "Is that a sign you aren't willing to talk?"

She huffs out a sigh. "It's a sign that if we're going to talk about this, it will be easier in the dark."

My eyebrows lift. "Okay. That's fair."

She's quiet for a long beat before she finally says, "I don't have a life, Freddie." The words are quiet, her tone soft, maybe even a little wistful. "I mean, I have a life. And it's a good one. I love working for you. But...it's *your* life, you know?"

Her words aren't an exact echo of the thoughts I was wrestling with earlier, but they're close. Here lately, it hasn't felt like I've had much of a life either. At least not the kind I want.

"I don't have my own friends," Ivy continues. "I don't have my own apartment. I haven't been on a date in who knows how long. I'm not sure that's normal."

"You date?" I ask. A knot tightens in my gut at the thought. It isn't discomfort, exactly. Just an uneasiness I don't expect. In the five-plus years she's been working for me, if Ivy has ever gone on a date, she hasn't talked to me about it.

She scoffs. "Yes, I date."

"When?"

"I went out with the pilot who flew us to Paris. Blake."

"That was two years ago."

"Which only illustrates my point," she says. "I *want* to date, and I can't when I'm living in your house."

"I don't understand why you can't just date living where you live. Does it really make a difference?"

"Of course it makes a difference," she says. "Your house is amazing. But it's a little intimidating. If I want a guy to pick me up at my doorstep, I have to give him a five-step checklist on how to get through Wayne."

"I could talk to Wayne about that," I say.

"But it's not just that," Ivy says. "When people know I work for you, all they want to talk about is *you*. I just think a little bit of distance would be good for me."

"If that's true, then you're dating the wrong guys. They should only want to talk about you, and that shouldn't be hard because you're one of the most interesting people I know," I say, but I can't fault her. Fame can be isolating, and as close as Ivy is to my life, there's no way she hasn't felt the impact of that.

"Thank you," she says. "And you're probably right. But I'd still like to give myself a fighting chance."

Something about her words or maybe the way she's holding herself, like she won't let herself take a deep breath, makes me think there's more to this situation than what she's telling me. I can't see her, but I can *feel* her next to me, and she's radiating tension.

I slide my foot over and nudge hers. "Hey," I say. "It's just me. You can tell me if there's more to this. If there's anything you want me to do differently—"

"It's not you," she says, cutting me off. "I promise it's not."

I don't believe her, but I won't push her more than I already have. "Okay," I say instead. "Well, you know I support you. Let me know if there's anything you need. I'm good at carrying moving boxes."

She lets out a little chuckle. "Thanks."

I should go. Let her sleep and try to get some sleep myself, but then Ivy shifts, and I catch the scent of her one more time. I feel a sudden impulse to move closer, but that would be crazy.

This is *Ivy*. My assistant. A woman who just told me she wants to move out because she'd like to date more. There is no reason why I should enjoy being close to her. "So...do I just roll out of this thing?"

She reaches over, her hand landing on my bare chest. Her palm is soft and warm, and it's all I can do not to suck in a breath at the contact.

"Where's your hand?" she asks.

I move my hand and press it on top of hers. "Right here."

She takes my hand and wraps it in hers, then lifts it like she's bracing herself. "Now roll," she says. "It's easier if you have something to stabilize you on the way down."

I hang on, then slide the curtain back and roll out of her bunk, landing on my bare feet. "What do you hold onto when you get out?"

"Nothing," she says, "but I've got a lot more practice than you." She reaches for the curtain and closes it, pausing before it covers the last few inches of space and hides her from view. "Good night, Freddie," she says, then she closes the curtain the rest of the way.

I slowly make my way back to my room, strangely unsettled by the whole conversation. When I close my door and finally collapse into bed for good, I reach up and rub a hand over my chest. There's a dull ache behind my ribs, the same one that was triggered when I first read Ivy's text.

I don't know what it means. And I don't know if my conversation with Ivy made things better or worse.

I just know I don't like feeling this way. About my life. About Ivy. About anything. And I don't know what I'm supposed to do to fix it.

CHAPTER THREE

Ivy

I GLANCE UP AT THE GLOWING RED LIGHT ABOVE THE STUDIO door, an indication that the radio show currently interviewing Freddie is live on the air. He's visible through a large glass window, sitting across from a balding guy in his forties, who the station calls Captain Stan for reasons I haven't yet figured out.

There's a set of headphones sitting on the desk next to me, in case I want to listen in, but I've heard Freddie answer these questions a million times. After this past year, when two different PR crises threatened his career, he knows better than to go off-script. Not that he ever truly has before.

Both times he wound up in the press with unflattering headlines, he wasn't at fault.

The first time, he was having dinner with his parents, who were visiting him in New York, and a fan and her daughter wouldn't leave him alone until Freddie very sternly asked them to back away from his table. The second time, he was defending *me,* when a guy at a bar got a little too handsy, and some idiot took video, editing it just enough to make it look like Freddie was drunk and in an angry bar fight.

Freddie doesn't drink, and he only punched the guy once.

I still feel a little guilty about that one.

I saw the red flags. I should have backed away from the guy a lot sooner than I did.

I lift my eyes to Freddie, who is smiling at the radio host, green eyes sparkling, and a twist of gratitude makes my heart feel tight.

He might drive me up the wall and push my buttons and do ridiculous things like climb into my bunk uninvited. But he's still a good man. Maybe the best man I know.

Which is precisely why I need some space. All the touching that happened yesterday made it painfully clear.

If you had asked me yesterday what the cruelest form of torture would be, I would not have conjured up a shirtless Freddie crawling into my very tiny bunk to have a heart-to-heart about my living situation.

But after last night? My answer has definitely changed.

There is nothing Freddie could do that would be more torturous than that. The way he smelled, clean and fresh, the way his skin felt under my palm when I went searching for his hand.

I turned the light off because I couldn't trust myself not to stare at his body, to study the many, *many* tattoos that decorate his torso. But I didn't account for the unexpected intimacy created by talking—*in the dark.*

I texted him about moving out for my own peace of mind, but I had no clue he would charge in like Sherlock Holmes, ready to ask me all the hard questions. That was a miscalculation I shouldn't have made. I know Freddie better than anyone. I should have guessed he would have reacted like he did. Nothing gets to him more than the knowledge that someone he cares about isn't happy.

To be in Freddie's inner circle is truly amazing. He's so good to his friends. Good to me.

And I don't want that to stop.

But if I'm going to keep my heart from cracking open, I have to do it on my own terms. From my *own* apartment.

My phone buzzes in my hand, and I glance down to see a text from Mira Stapleton.

> MIRA
>
> Hey Ivy! Long time, no see. My messages aren't getting through to Freddie. Did his number change?

I tap my phone onto my palm and debate whether I should respond. Despite my annoyance that Mira is the only woman who has actually managed to get Freddie on a date the past few years, I can't truly hate her. Mostly because she's one of the nicest people I've ever met—genuine and funny and real—and she talks to me like I'm a real person and not just hired help.

But I also can't hate her because I'm pretty confident Freddie doesn't like her as much as she likes him. They don't have a ton of chemistry, and he's never seemed all that excited about going out with her. She's an easy date when his publicist wants him to make a public appearance, but I know him well enough to pick up on his lack of enthusiasm.

It's selfish of me to think it, but if I *have* to watch Freddie date another woman, I'd rather it be someone like Mira— someone he doesn't actually like.

Honestly, I probably would have quit by now if he made a habit of dating people for real. He goes out plenty, but rarely more than once with the same person. And it's never been more than twice with anyone but Mira.

I pocket my phone without responding to Mira's message. I'm pretty sure she doesn't actually think Freddie's number changed. She's just hoping I'll nudge him to respond to what I'm guessing was an unanswered text she sent to him.

I'll ask him about it later. It's probably time he put the poor woman out of her misery and tell her he doesn't have feelings for her.

"How's he doing?" a voice asks from behind me.

I swivel around, one hand flying to my chest. As far as I knew, I was alone in the control room opposite the recording studio.

"Sloane," I say to Freddie's agent. "What are you doing here?"

"I flew in for a meeting with another client," she says. "Figured it wouldn't hurt to check in while I'm in town."

Sloane Mercer is a million times better than Freddie's old agent, mostly because she's *honest*. But she's also slightly terrifying.

She's gorgeous, for one. Tall and sleek and business-professional, with a polish to her appearance I could never dream of achieving. Somehow, she is both nurturing, like the best kind of mom—she has two grown children, so she has some experience on that front—and unflinchingly firm. She made it very clear in her first meetings with Freddie that if he does what she says, she will always steer him toward success. But he has to trust her.

It's a relief, honestly, to be working with her. After so

many years with Kevin, Freddie's old agent, I got really good at recognizing his lies. But it was always work to get Freddie to see them. Kevin was the agent for Midnight Rush, the boyband that launched Freddie's career, so there was probably some measure of nostalgia or misdirected loyalty that kept Freddie hanging on to Kevin for so long.

But Sloane, in the nine months since Freddie hired her, has already proven her worth.

That doesn't mean I'm not surprised to see her.

It isn't *that* strange that Sloane is in Chicago to meet with another client. It's a big city. But I'm still guessing this is more than just a casual drop-in.

With how little progress Freddie has made on his album, she has to be feeling the stress of his looming deadline as much as he is.

"He's doing great," I say, trying to keep my voice chill. "He's a natural in interviews."

Sloane steps closer to the giant window looking into the recording booth and folds her arms.

Freddie looks up, eyes widening as he processes her presence, then lifts his head in acknowledgement.

Sloane waves, then turns back to face me.

"And the music?" she asks. "Any progress on that front?"

My phone buzzes in my hand, and I look at the screen, relief washing through me as I see a call coming in from my mom.

"I'm sorry, I need to take this. It's my mom," I say as I stand. I tilt my head toward Freddie. "He should be done in just a few minutes. I'm sure he'll be happy to fill you in."

As I duck out of the control room and into the hallway, it feels a little like I'm throwing Freddie under the bus, but honestly, Sloane will get her answers one way or another, and Freddie is the only one who can give her what she wants.

At least in this regard, I'm happy to just be the assistant and not the one responsible for making music. Or any other kind of creative decisions. I know my strengths—I'm a problem solver, a task manager, an organizer of things and people and priorities. I should not be trusted with anything else.

"Hey, Mom," I answer. "What's up?"

"Oh, I'm so glad you answered," Mom says, the tone of her voice immediately setting me on edge. Mom and I are close enough that she often calls just to say hi. Sometimes she wants to give me updates on Dad's tree farm. He's shifting to Japanese maples in the east field, or he just got a new contract to provide crepe myrtle trees for Lowe's Home Improvement stores.

Other times, she wants to tell me about the latest addition to the donkey sanctuary she's been building over the last few years. I shouldn't just call it a donkey sanctuary. She has other animals too. A peacock, several llamas, a couple of pot-bellied pigs a family across town bought as pets but surrendered when they grew to be well over a hundred pounds each. Last week, she texted me pictures of a baby donkey she picked up in Asheville. She named him Pirate because he was born with only one eye.

But Mom doesn't want to talk about donkeys today. I can already tell. "What's wrong? What is it?" I ask.

She breathes out the kind of sigh I recognize, and I know, before she says anything else, what she's about to tell me.

"It's Carina," she says. "She's gone again."

I lean against a vending machine in the hallway and pinch the bridge of my nose. I am getting very tired of worrying about my little sister. "Gone where? Did she tell you anything this time?"

"Not a thing. She at least left a note, but it was vague. *Chasing something big. Be back soon. Don't worry about me!*" Mom says. "But how am I supposed to not worry? She's only twenty-one years old."

The tension in my shoulders eases the slightest bit. I get why Mom's upset, but if Carina left a note, I'm not as concerned. This isn't the first time she's gotten a wild hair and taken off on an unplanned trip. She always responds to Mom's texts eventually. I'm sure she will this time too.

"I know, but Mom, twenty-one means she *is* a legal adult. Maybe you really *shouldn't* worry about her."

Mom huffs. "You know it isn't that easy."

"Carina's smart, Mom. And the note's an improvement over the last time she took off."

I'm not sure it's helping my cause to remind Mom of the time Carina jumped in a van with people she'd *just* met to attend a music festival on the other side of the country, but that's just how Carina is. It's maddening how quickly she trusts people, but most of the time, it's also pretty amazing. No one can see the good in a person like Carina can. I wish she were *slightly* better at picking up on the bad in people, but there's no good wishing for something that isn't going to happen. Carina is who she is—who she's always been.

"I'll text her to check in, okay?" I say to Mom.

"Maybe she'll respond to you," Mom says. "My phone says my messages have been delivered, but so far, I haven't heard back."

"How long has she been gone?" I say.

"Only four days. But that's a long time to ignore your

mother. I promise my messages haven't been pushy. I just want to know she's okay."

"Can you see her location?"

"I tried, but it wouldn't pull up. The app keeps telling me my username is invalid, which is dumb because I never changed it."

Sometimes it feels like a lot that, even though my sister and I are fully grown adults, my mother still uses an app to track our locations. After losing Daphne, I can't truly fault her wanting to hold us close—figuratively, if not literally—but I sometimes wonder if it makes her worry *more*. If it's created an unreasonable expectation.

"We can FaceTime later, and I'll help you figure it out, okay?" I say. "But I really don't think you need to worry. I'm sure Carina is fine."

"But you'll check on her?" Mom asks. "See if you can get through to her? I know you don't think I should worry, but I swear, something was different this time. She was off before she left. Like she'd lost her sparkle."

"What do you mean? How did she lose her sparkle?" I switch Mom's call over to speaker phone and pull up my sister's Instagram account. I doubt Mom has checked, but it wouldn't surprise me if Carina has posted something about where she is or at least who she's with.

I scroll through the last few posts on her feed, but she hasn't posted anything new in a couple of weeks.

"I don't know," Mom says. "She just seemed moodier somehow. Call it mother's intuition. I just think something's going on with her. I don't know where she came from, Ivy. She's nothing like you and Daphne."

My heart pinches at the mention of my older sister. I like that Mom mentions her, that she isn't afraid to say her name.

For a long time, she couldn't bring herself to bring her up in casual conversation because she knew she'd cry if she did. But those words, the way she mentioned me and Daphne in one breath, grouping us together, saying we're different than Carina. It almost feels like Daphne's still here, like Mom has some idea of what she would be like if she'd lived past her eighteenth birthday.

But Mom's got it wrong. I'm not like Daphne at all. I might have her confidence, her pragmatic mind, but Carina is the one who sparkles like she did.

"Could she just be discouraged about the job hunt? It's been almost two months since she graduated. It has to be annoying that she still hasn't found something."

"She hasn't even been looking," Mom says. "So that could for sure have something to do with it. But to just disappear? That's the last thing that's going to get her a job. You know what she said to me the last time we talked about it? She said maybe she'd forget her nonprofit goals and just run the tree farm with Dad."

I huff out a laugh. "I'll believe it when I see it."

"That's exactly what I said," Mom says. "I can feel it, Ivy. She's running from something."

"Okay," I say to Mom. "I hear you. I'll do some digging and see what I can find out."

She breathes out a sigh, like she's physically lighter for having transferred her worries about Carina to me. "Good. Now that we've got that settled, how are you? How's work?"

I glance over my shoulder, catching a glimpse of Sloane's form standing beneath the red "Recording" light over the studio door. "Busy," I say. "But good. Things are good."

"Did you ever go to that interview you told me about?"

My eyes widen as I scramble to switch Mom off speaker,

then move a few feet farther down the hallway. "Um, yeah," I say, my tone low. "That didn't work out."

Mom's quiet for a beat before she says, "Because you didn't go? Or because you went and you didn't get the job?"

I clench my jaw, hating how easily she reads me, even over the phone. I never should have told her about the stupid job listing. I didn't end up applying—one, because I can't imagine ever telling Freddie I'm leaving him, and two, this is the only industry job I've ever had. I'm not sure how well it qualifies me to work for a record label.

That was always the plan, before I started working for Freddie. To turn my degree in music business into an internship with a record label, then into an actual job through which I could work my way up to being an artist relations manager. I'm good with people. With details. And my organizational skills are next level. Working with artists, building careers, building bridges between creative types and executive types—I'm made for that kind of work.

"I'm taking your silence to mean you didn't apply," Mom says, and I huff.

"It's not that simple," I say. "A job like that, you have to know someone. You need connections."

"Ivy," Mom says dryly. "You work for Freddie Ridgefield. He's one of the biggest names in the music business. You don't think he has connections? You don't think *his* name on your resume would catch some attention?"

"I'm his assistant, Mom. You don't need a degree to be someone's assistant. You just need to know how to Door-Dash and fight off paparazzi."

She huffs out a laugh. "Ivy Conway. You do a lot more than that, and you know it. You run that man's life. You legitimately manage *all* his relationships. If that doesn't make you an artist relations manager, I don't know what does. If you have reasons for not applying, then fine. But lack of qualifications should not be on the list."

I clench my jaw, wrapping one arm around my stomach. Mom's right. I know she's right. At least on the surface. I might have started as Freddie's assistant, but over the past few years, more and more responsibility has been shifted to me. It might say assistant on my paystub, but I'm more of a manager, and Freddie would probably admit that.

But how do I explain that my biggest reason for wanting a new job is the same reason I don't think I can quit? I only ever search job listings when my heart feels particularly pinched—when the inevitability of my own heartbreak feels too much to bear.

But I've never actually applied for anything.

"It's not that simple," I say, but the argument sounds weak even to my ears. It always will if I won't admit my feelings.

I tell my mom a lot. Almost everything. But I can't tell her this.

Saying it out loud will make it too real, and right now, denial is my only coping mechanism.

"I'm not saying you have to get a new job, Ivy," Mom says, her tone gentler now. "I know you love what you do. I'm just saying I don't want you to forget why you got that fancy degree in the first place. Make sure you're living *all* your dreams. Know what I mean?"

I breathe out a sigh. "Yeah, I do. Thanks for the reminder."

Before we hang up, Mom gives me an update about Pirate, and she sends me a couple of pictures of his cute donkey nose draped over her shoulder like he's her literal baby. I'm happy for the distraction—I will talk about baby donkeys all day long if it means not talking about my unrequited feelings—but I still can't shake the sense of unease taking root in my belly.

Am I living all my dreams?

Or am I just living Freddie's?

I reassure Mom one more time that I'll let her know as soon as I hear from Carina—assuming I *do* hear from Carina—then we finally say goodbye.

I take a second to forward Mom's Pirate photos to Freddie—he's completely enamored with Mom's donkeys, and he'll love Pirate because of how tiny he is—then I key out a text to my sister.

IVY

Hey! Just checking in. How are you?

I debate whether I should mention my conversation with Mom, but I don't want to put Carina on the defensive, so I leave the message as is and send it, then shift back to her Instagram.

My little sister has always been more than a little enamored by my connection to Freddie, and she's used that connection to ingratiate herself to several people in the industry. Which...I shouldn't be surprised it's worked. She's gorgeous and charming and always up for a good time, so people are usually happy to have her around.

But it still feels startling to me when I'm scrolling her Instagram feed seeing images of her posing next to celebrities or influencers I've never met.

Once, right before Freddie's tour started, I attended an industry event with him in Nashville, and Carina happened to be there. I'd had no idea she was even in town, but she'd somehow become "best friends" with a country music artist who'd just made it big on one of those talent search TV competitions and was attending the event with her.

When she ran into us, Carina talked to Freddie like he was an old friend, even though they'd only met a handful of times, then gave me a crushing hug like it was perfectly normal for her to run into me, like she had just as much right to be there as I did.

Which, honestly, I *hate* attending industry events. I will only go if it *isn't* black tie, and I will only stay as long as I absolutely have to. So it's not like I cared that Carina was there.

But I do remember wondering if she was in over her head.

If the industry has taught me anything, it's that it will chew you up and spit you out no matter how sweet and charming you are.

Behind me, a door creaks, and Freddie appears in the hallway, his jaw tight. "Hey," he says as he approaches. "You okay?"

I slip my phone into my pocket. "Yep. Just talking to my mom. How was your conversation with Sloane?"

He frowns. "Super," he says dryly, and I press my lips together.

"She was tough on you?"

"Only as tough as I need to be," Sloane says, as she steps out of the control room.

I look at Freddie, eyes wide. "How did she hear me?" I ask under my breath.

Sloane stops and drops a hand onto each of our shoulders. "I hear everything, children." She looks at Freddie. "I believe in you, all right? I respect the creative process, but I also respect your contract—a contract I really *don't* want to renegotiate. You know I will. I work for you, not them. But trust me when I tell you they'll ask for more than you want to give. Your life will be easier if you can record something and meet this deadline."

Freddie nods. "I know. I hear you."

Sloane nods, her expression softening. "Good. Now take care of yourself. And put on a good show tonight."

Freddie's eyebrows lift. "Why? Are you coming?"

Sloane purses her lips, like she hates playing into Freddie's charm. "I'm bringing my niece," she finally says.

"You have a niece?" Freddie asks, and Sloane nods.

"My brother lives in Chicago. His daughter is fifteen, and it's her birthday." She sighs like it pains her to admit this out loud. "She's a fan. I'm currently staying in her bedroom, which means I get to wake up to a hundred different renditions of your face."

I fight a grin. It's not unusual for agents to be at the concerts of the musical artists they represent, but somehow, this feels different. Like we're catching a glimpse of Sloane's softer side.

Her eyes dart to me. "If you laugh, I promise you will live to regret it."

"Not laughing," I say, eyes wide, though the idea of Freddie's very professional agent sleeping under a Freddie Ridgefield duvet is almost more than I can handle.

"Bring her backstage," Freddie says. "I'd love to meet her."

After Sloane says goodbye, Freddie and I follow Wayne outside to the SUV waiting to drive us to a hotel near the stadium where tonight's concert will happen. There's a crowd of fans gathered on the sidewalk, and they erupt into cheers and screams as soon as we emerge. I walk directly to the car and wait. Wayne shadows Freddie as he greets a few of the fans and signs a few autographs.

It used to surprise me how frequently fans show up, sometimes in the most random places, but I've since learned about the very active online network of Freddie fans, fans who are constantly discussing and posting updates about Freddie's whereabouts. The radio station was more of a given, since the interview was live. Of course people would assume he'd be leaving the building eventually. But it happens everywhere. More in bigger cities.

The last time we were in Charleston, Freddie wanted to try this hole-in-the-wall seafood place he'd read about online. Not a soul outside of his team knew we were making a stop, but by the time we finished ordering and picking up our food, a crowd of at least thirty people had gathered outside. I have no idea how they mobilized so quickly, but I've stopped being surprised by it.

His fans are nothing short of completely devoted.

"How's your mom?" Freddie asks once we're both safe inside the car, Wayne in the front seat next to the driver.

"Good," I say. "But Carina has disappeared again."

"That feels very on-brand," Freddie says. "Any clue where she is?"

"Not one," I say. "Mom said it felt different this time. Like there was something off about her before she left." As much as I reassured Mom, I can't keep myself from clicking over to my text messages to make sure I haven't missed Carina's reply.

Freddie frowns. "Yeah?"

"I don't know," I say. "She's twenty-one. That's old enough to go where she wants, right?"

"I mean, probably *someone* should know where she is," Freddie says. "She isn't answering her phone?"

"Mom says her messages are going through, but Carina hasn't responded yet." I shake away the worry gnawing at my gut. "I'm sure she'll turn up. She always does."

Freddie nods. "Let me know if there's anything I can do to help."

"Like what?" I ask, and he shrugs.

"I don't know. Hire a PI? Whatever you want."

"I don't need to hire a PI," I say. "It's just Carina. That feels a little like overkill."

He shakes his head dismissively. "She's your sister. You take care of me, so I take care of you. That means I take care of her too."

We pull into a private garage at the back of the hotel, stopping outside of an elevator that will take Freddie directly to his suite, bypassing all the public areas of the hotel.

Freddie reaches over and squeezes my knee. He leans close enough for me to catch his scent, and for a split second, I'm back in my bunk on the bus, hand pressed against his bare chest. "Just know I'm good for whatever you need," he says. "I have to go nap. See you before the show?"

I nod. "Yeah. See you in a bit."

The elevator doors open, and Jason, another member of Freddie's security team, appears. He holds the door open while Freddie leaves the car and crosses the short distance to the elevator.

"Are you ready to head to the stadium?" Wayne asks, looking over his shoulder. Before tonight, he'll meet with the facility's security team and make sure everything is in place to keep Freddie safe.

There's a dull ache pulsing behind my eyes, probably

because I had just as little sleep last night as Freddie, but I should head to the stadium too. The crew will be finished with assembly by now, and I like to personally walk through Freddie's checklist, just to make sure everything is in place before he takes the stage. Not to mention the million other things I usually check on before he arrives. He'll need wardrobe updates before he goes on, and the catering team will definitely have questions I'll be able to answer better than Seth.

"Yeah, I'm good to go now," I say to Wayne, and he nods to the driver, who shifts into drive and circles out of the garage.

I lean my head against the seatback and close my eyes. If not for the worries running circles in my brain, I could almost sleep just like this, sitting up in the back of an SUV. I'm tired enough, that's for sure.

But I can't stop thinking about Carina.

And Freddie. And the album he isn't ready to record.

And the job I didn't apply for and the very complicated reasons why.

But it's fine, I think, as I stifle a yawn. Everything is fine.

Maybe I'll sleep when I'm thirty.

CHAPTER FOUR

Freddie

IVY APPEARS IN THE DOORWAY OF THE ROOM SET UP FOR THE pre-concert meet-and-greet and meets my eye. The tension collecting in my shoulders eases at the sight of her. I don't mind interacting with fans—most of the time, I really enjoy it. But it's always easier when Ivy is around. She keeps me grounded, but she also has a way of sensing possible problems before they happen.

The number of times she's stepped in, gentle but firm, and steered fans away—it's too many to count. She always says the right thing, emphasizes precisely what people need to hear to remember who they are and what they *aren't* entitled to. Information about my personal life. My signature on *any* of their body parts. Kisses, even on cheeks. Any of my bodily fluids. Yes—people have asked. And no. You don't want to know why.

Ivy lifts her eyebrows in question, and I give her a nod, then square my shoulders and take a few deep breaths. She disappears back down the hall, then reappears thirty seconds later with a line of fans directly behind her. Last tour, meet-and-greets were for VIP guests—the ones who paid ridiculous amounts of money to attend and have access to a private signing.

I appreciate those fans, but this tour, we wanted to do something different. So the only people who get a meet-and-greet are random people Ivy picks out of the crowd. People in the nosebleed seats. People who saved up to come to their first show and have no expectation of ever meeting me. There's something about the surprise of it all that makes it more fun.

I need the VIP guests—the ones who have the time and money to attend multiple shows and pay for front-row seats. But the nosebleed fans are just as valuable.

Ivy tells me a whole lore has developed online around the odds of getting picked for the secret meet-and-greet. People know it happens, and they've developed all kinds of theories about how people are chosen.

They're all making it too complicated because it's completely random. Ivy used to wander the crowds and pick people herself. But after a few shows, fans started to recognize her. So then she started working with event staff—not my staff, but people working the venues—instructing them on how to search the crowds.

Wayne moves into position behind me, arms folded across his midsection in a way that is both impressive and intimidating. Hopefully, he'll only have to stand there. I'm never so happy as I am when I'm paying my security team for nothing.

We make eye contact, and he lifts an eyebrow. "You good?"

I roll my neck a few times and nod, but my head isn't quite in the game, and I wonder if that's why he's asking. If he somehow senses that I've got too much on my mind to feel any enthusiasm about meeting fans.

Fans need me to be happy. To be *on*.

It doesn't matter if I've got it in me or not.

I watch as Ivy leads everyone through the ropes that will keep the line organized while people wait for their turn. The setup is pretty simple. I stand at the front of the room next to a banner that shows the concert logo, Ivy stands with me so she's available to take photos, and there's a table to the left of us where people pick up their signed merch.

Once everyone is in and event staff have taken control of the line, Ivy steps up beside me.

"Smile, Freddie," she whispers, clearly sensing the same thing Wayne did. "You're having fun, remember?"

Right. Fun. I give my head a quick shake and force a smile as the first person in line steps up.

This used to be fun. It *should* be fun. But it suddenly occurs to me I can't quite remember the last time it was.

"How are you?" I say to the woman in front of me. I hold out my hand, and she takes it, but then she squeezes her eyes closed, her whole body shaking as she takes several deep breaths.

"I can't believe this is happening," she says, her voice barely above a whisper.

The sincerity in her voice turns something over in my heart, and my bad mood vanishes.

What's wrong with me?

I get to make music for a living, and that's no small thing.

And it's because of people like her that it's possible.

"There you are," Ivy whispers. "You've got this."

I shoot her a grateful glance, then wrap my free hand around the back of the woman's fingers so her hand is cupped in both of mine. "It's happening," I say gently. "Can you tell me your name?"

"Darcy," she whispers, eyes still closed.

"Hi, Darcy," I say. "Can you open your eyes for me?"

"I don't think so," she says, and I let out a chuckle.

"I bet you can."

She presses her lips together, then slowly cracks one eye open.

I grin. "Nice to see you."

She breathes out a stuttering breath and finally smiles, tears brimming in her eyes.

"Should we take a photo?"

She nods, and Ivy steps up, holding out her hand for Darcy's phone. Ivy moves Darcy into place in front of the backdrop, and I step up beside her, pushing my hands into my back pockets as I lean in just enough to look friendly without actually touching her.

Ivy holds up the phone, then pauses. "Actually, wait," she says, stepping toward Darcy. She fixes something with her clothes—I can't see what—then steps back again. "Maybe prop your hand on your hip?" Ivy says, and Darcy must do it because Ivy nods. "Right. Perfect. That looks better."

I'm used to this part of Ivy's involvement. I asked her once why she couldn't just take the picture, and she explained that a once-in-a-lifetime meet-and-greet with someone's favorite artist should not be ruined by bad angles or inept photography. If she can spend four seconds to help someone look cute standing beside me, she's going to do it.

I've always appreciated that Ivy cares like this. That she wants these moments to feel special for people.

As the meet-and-greet progresses, I smile my way through a lot of photos and happy tears and giggling teenagers, but the last woman in line gives me pause.

She can't be older than twenty, wearing a black tank top and jeans, her arms covered in tattoos. It only takes me a second to realize they're *my* tattoos.

The lightness that's carried me through the meet-and-greet so far evaporates, replaced by a heaviness that settles into my gut. I force myself to smile anyway.

"Hey," I say, holding out my hand. "I'm Freddie."

She gives me a confident smile. "Obviously," she says. "I'm Leah."

"Hi, Leah. Thanks for being here."

She leans a little closer. "I have eleven tattoos," she says, a quiet intensity in her tone. "They all match. Or they almost match. I'm trying to get them as close as I possibly can. I'm saving money for the rest—all seventeen—though I've read there's a secret number eighteen that no one knows about. Want to fill me in? Then I could match all of them."

I push my hands into my pockets and take a deep breath. It's pretty frequent that I see someone who has a tattoo inspired by my music. I like it most when people do song titles or lyrics because it means I wrote something that resonated.

But I'm less comfortable when people try to match a tattoo that I have.

This is the first time I've met someone who's trying to match *all* of them.

Ivy steps closer. "We're running out of time, Freddie. Maybe just a quick picture?"

I give my head a small shake, a silent communication to Ivy that I've got this. I appreciate what she's trying to do, but if there's any chance I can stop this woman from getting ink I'm guessing she'll regret in a few years, I have to try.

"Leah, how old are you?" I gently ask.

She swallows, a new uneasiness flitting across her expression. "Nineteen."

I nod as I reach behind me to pick up a tour poster so I can sign it for her. "Have you ever been in love?"

She frowns at this question. "Um, I don't know. I don't think so."

"Do you want to be? Not with me," I quickly add. "This is not a proposition. Just generally."

She still looks confused, but she answers the question anyway. "I mean, sure. Don't most people?"

I hold her gaze, hoping I'm not making a mistake when I say, "Do me a favor, okay? Don't get any more tattoos. At least not ones that look like mine."

A blush climbs her cheeks, and she chokes out an embarrassed laugh. "Why not?"

"Because one day, you're going to meet someone. You'll fall in love. Maybe you'll get married. Get a dog. Have a couple of kids. You'll have a whole life. And I will not be that important to you." I take a step forward, crouching down the slightest bit to catch her downward gaze, to implore her to look at me. "I'm just a guy, Leah. I love that you love my music. That means the world to me. And your artwork—it's amazing. But if you get more ink, get something that speaks to *you*. Something that maps *your* history. Not mine."

She takes a deep breath. "I've never thought of it like that." Her expression is earnest when she asks, "Is that what yours do? Your tattoos map your history?"

I nod. "Moments. People. They all remind me of something that matters to me."

"Freddie, the time," Ivy repeats. "Mellow Mood just took the stage."

I nod, then look back at Leah. "Want to get that picture?"

"Yes! Definitely," Leah says. She pulls out her phone and hands it to Ivy, then steps up next to me. "Thanks for the advice," she says after Ivy snaps a few photos. "I appreciate it."

As soon as Leah is gone, Ivy hands me a water bottle and motions toward a back door that will keep us away from any fans. "Sorry for rushing you," she says. "We're fifteen minutes over schedule, and Seth is seconds away from completely losing his mind."

"He always thinks I need more downtime than I do," I say as I follow her out the door. "I'll be fine." I fall into step beside her as we head down the hall toward my dressing room.

"Maybe," she says. "But it's also nice to let your fans see the opening act. Maybe they aren't just here to see you."

I shoot her a cheeky grin, and she rolls her eyes.

"Fine. They're *mostly* just here to see you, but on principle, it's still the courteous thing to do." We walk in silence for a beat before she adds, "You gave her good advice, by the way. The woman with all the tattoos."

I look over to meet her eyes, serious this time. "Yeah?" Fame can be trippy in both good and bad ways. But to see someone so young put permanent ink on her body just to match me—it was pretty unnerving.

Ivy nods. "It has to feel weird to see that. Like a responsibility you didn't ask for." We reach my dressing room door, and she spins around to face me, leaning her back against it.

"Yeah," I say, suddenly noticing how close we're standing. "That's a good way to say it."

Light catches in her brown eyes as she holds my gaze. There's a dark ring outlining her irises that's almost black, then the color lightens as it shifts toward a ring of warm honey gold around her pupils.

Ivy's nose twitches, and she lifts a hand, brushing it across her face. "What? Do I have something on my face?"

I give my head a little shake. Was I staring? I must have been staring, or she wouldn't be asking. "No, I was just looking at your eyes."

I push past her into my dressing room, and she follows, heading straight for the mirror on the far wall. She leans close like she's inspecting her face. "Is there something wrong with them?"

"Why is that the first thing you assume?"

She spins around. "So there isn't?"

"Of course not."

"Then why were you looking at them?"

I huff out an awkward laugh even as heat climbs my cheeks. I've looked at Ivy thousands of times and never been struck by her eyes, but for whatever reason, tonight, I saw them differently. I *noticed* them. And I'm not sure what that means.

Maybe nothing. But if it's nothing, why does this conversation suddenly feel so significant?

"Because they're on your face, and I was looking at you," I answer.

"You were *staring*," she says. "I've always had this face. You've never stared like that before." She spins back around and smiles into the mirror like she's checking her teeth.

"Ivy," I say through a chuckle. "Relax. There's nothing in your teeth, and there's nothing wrong with your face."

She turns back around and props her hands on her hips, giving me an expectant look.

I swallow and my heart rate spikes, a burst of nervous adrenaline flooding my system. I'm about to perform in front of a hundred thousand people, and I'm not nervous about that. But the thought of telling Ivy I think her eyes are pretty makes me want to crawl out of my own skin.

I can't make it make sense.

"There's a ring of gold around your pupils that I've never noticed before," I finally say. Because with the way she's looking at me, I have to say something. "It's pretty."

Ivy's hands fall from her hips. "Oh," she says simply. "Well, thanks, then."

"You're welcome."

The air shifts between us, a new energy buzzing that I've never experienced before. Does she sense it too? Should I acknowledge it? Am I making it up?

I'm still debating when the dressing room door opens and Wren, my wardrobe manager, steps inside.

She freezes as soon as the door clicks shut behind her as her eyes move from me, to Ivy, then back to me again. "Am I interrupting something?" she asks.

"Nope," Ivy says a little too quickly. "Nothing at all. We were just—" She pulls her phone out. "Oh, look. A text from Seth. I should..." Her words trail off as her thumbs start flying over the screen.

Wren gives me a questioning look, but I ignore it as I shrug out of my jacket and toss it onto the couch. There's nothing to explain.

Ivy has pretty eyes, but lots of people have pretty eyes. This doesn't have to be anything more than that. A casual observation. Like seeing that someone has blond hair or freckles.

I look at Wren, willing myself to notice something—*anything*—about her appearance. She's young-ish. Definitely in her twenties. Her hair is short, shaved on one side, then it lifts over her crown like a wave. I actually really like her style. She's big into repurposing used clothes, and she's made some really cool pieces in the couple of years we've been working together—both for herself and for me. She also has a killer glasses collection. The pair she's wearing today are red with white stripes down the side.

There. See? Noticing Ivy's eyes isn't any different than noticing Wren's glasses.

Wren holds out a white button-down with an oversized collar and some sort of shimmery sparkle woven into the fabric. "See what you think of this," she says. "The fabric is a lighter blend, so it should be more breathable for you."

I pull my t-shirt over my head, leaving it with my discarded jacket, and reach for the shirt. The fabric is soft and stretchy, definitely an improvement from what I wore last show.

"Yeah, it feels great," I say as I stick one arm through the sleeve, pausing when a button lands on the floor at my feet with a tiny plink.

Ivy ducks down to pick it up. "Here. I've got it," she says, handing the button over to Wren.

"For real?" Wren asks. "I *just* checked them all." She motions for me to hand the shirt back, so I dutifully strip down again, then she moves over to the vanity and pulls a sewing kit out of her bag.

"It'll only take me a second," she says. "How are we on time?"

"We're running out of it," Ivy says at the same time I say, "We're fine."

Ivy meets my eye, and I grin. "We *are* fine," I repeat, and she shrugs, her expression playful.

"Tell that to Seth."

"The fans won't mind waiting," I say.

She folds her arms across her chest. "So cocky."

I push my hands into my back pockets, suddenly very aware that I'm shirtless. Which is ridiculous. Ivy has been in the room when I've stripped down to my boxer briefs for wardrobe changes more times than I can count. This shouldn't matter at all.

"Confident," I say. "Not cocky."

My skin prickles with awareness as Ivy's eyes move over my torso. Then she bites her lip, eyebrows furrowing before she asks, "Is it true what you said about your tattoos? They all mean something?"

I nod, my eyes drawn to that same gold circle at the center of her irises. It'll be the first thing I see every time I look at her now. I swallow. "Have I never explained them to you?"

"I mean, I know *some* of them," she says. She points at the flower on my left pectoral muscle. "This one is for your grandmother, right? A Lily—like her name."

I nod. "Right."

She steps closer. "And then your grandfather's initials are here." Her fingers skim over to my bicep, to the small CR inked into my skin, and I draw in a breath at the contact. "And your parents and your brother's initials are here, here, and here," she says as she moves toward my wrist.

Her touch feels good, sending a skitter of goosebumps up my arm and across my shoulders. The same energy that hummed between us before Wren interrupted sparks again now, and my mind drifts back to the conversation we had in her bunk, to the tug I felt to be close to her. Then I think of the hug I gave her in the middle of CVS, how good it felt to hold her in my arms. As good as it feels right now to stand here and stare at those eyes while she skates her fingers over my skin.

For a split second, I stop fighting and let myself consider what it would mean if I let this stirring turn into an actual *feeling.*

Could I have feelings for Ivy?

As quickly as the thought takes root, fear—or maybe just logic—wells up and yanks it back out again.

Ivy is my assistant.

Just my assistant.

A woman I hired partly because she promised she would never be in danger of falling for me.

As far as my work life goes—and let's face it, my work life is basically my *only* life—Ivy is the best thing that's ever happened to me. I can't lose her, so I have to think about this rationally. Noticing Ivy's eyes, enjoying her touch—those are complications neither of us needs. I remind myself for a second time that one of her reasons for wanting to move out is to *date* more.

That's the most important thing to remember. There's no reason to want something Ivy clearly doesn't want herself.

Then again, she's the one touching me right now, standing close enough that if I wanted to lean down and kiss her, I could.

"This one, I don't know." Ivy brushes her pointer finger over the tiny pawprints moving up the inside of my arm.

"But based on the theme, I'm guessing they reference a childhood pet?"

"Her name was Panda," I say. "A border collie."

"And the leaves here," Ivy says, jumping her fingers over to my ribs. "An apple tree?"

I wince the slightest bit—she's close to the only spot I'm ticklish—and I grin. "For Washington state."

"Right. And your guitar—that one is obvious."

"My grandfather's guitar," I correct. "The one he gave me."

She doesn't comment on the fact that I have three tattoos that are tributes to my grandparents while I only have tiny initials referencing my parents and brother. But I doubt she's surprised.

Ivy's met my family. She probably only needed one interaction to fully understand the dynamic of our relationship.

"And these stars here…" Ivy says. Her hand skims over to my other side. "These are for Midnight Rush, right?"

I nod. "And the letters here," I say. I turn my arm to show her the back of my wrist.

Ivy touches each letter as she says, "J for Jace, L for Leo, D for Deke. I love that." Her eyes move over my body one last time then finally lift to meet mine. "Okay. That's all I got."

I look down at my chest and tap right in the center, just over my sternum. "This one is a symbol of mindfulness. It reminds me that whatever I do, I do it with intention. And this one," I say, turning and pointing to the one that wraps over the top of my right shoulder, "is a longevity knot. I got it when I decided not to drink anymore. Sort of a live long and prosper kind of thing."

"Right. I did know about that one," she says. She taps on

the treble clef on the right side of my heart. "And I guess this one is pretty obvious."

"Look closer," I say, and she leans in.

I catch the scent of her, and for the second time in less than twenty-four hours, I resist the urge to tug her against me, press her body flush against mine. All my thoughts about her working for me, about why this *isn't* a good idea, seem a lot less important when she's close enough for me to breathe her in.

What is happening to me?

Better question. What am I supposed to do about it?

"Oh, there are hearts," Ivy says. "All the swirly parts around the clef, they make hearts."

"Because I don't want to make music that doesn't have heart." Maybe I should have shown this tattoo to Sloane. It might have made her more forgiving about my lack of progress on the songs I can't seem to write for the album I may never record.

Ivy presses her lips together, like she's fighting a grin. "That one is kind of cheesy, Freddie."

"You say to a man who started his career in a *boyband*."

Behind us, the dressing room door bursts open, and Seth strides in. I jump back from Ivy, though I don't really have a reason to. We weren't doing anything wrong, but somehow, it still feels like we were caught.

Seth's eyes move around the room, finally settling on Wren, who is still sitting at the vanity, glasses perched on her nose as she sews on a button.

I forgot she was even in the room.

Because I forgot everything.

Everything but Ivy and the way she looked as she studied my body, used her fingertips to trace my skin.

"I lost a button," I say to Seth, because that's easier than admitting what's really going through my mind right now.

"Should I go out there and tell that to your fans?" Seth asks dryly. "There won't be a concert tonight because of a missing button?"

"There will definitely be a concert," Wren says, holding up the shirt. "Button is fixed. He'll be fully dressed in less than two minutes." She motions Seth toward the door with a shooing motion. "Now go and let me work my magic."

"Two minutes," Seth repeats, then he disappears out the door, motioning for Ivy to follow him.

I make quick work of getting out of my street clothes and into the rest of my wardrobe. Pale blue suit pants with a high waist and a wide hem, boots, bracelets, necklace, and a matching suit jacket I will absolutely lose after two, possibly three songs.

"Good?" I ask Wren as she adjusts my jacket collar. She reaches up and unbuttons two more buttons so a little more of my chest tattoos are visible.

"Perfect," she says.

"You're the best, Wren," I say, meaning every word. I generally keep my concert wardrobe pretty simple, but Wren is constantly working to improve and perfect what I wear, and I never want her efforts to be underappreciated.

Seth reappears in the dressing room doorway, and now Charlie, my stage manager, is with him, clipboard in hand and eyes glued to his watch.

Ivy appears on the other side of Seth and hands me a water bottle, but there's something off about her body language, and she won't make eye contact.

I hesitate, wanting to make sure she's okay, but Charlie isn't going to tolerate any delays.

"No, he's coming now," he says into his headset. "Bring the mic. We'll put it on him while he walks."

I glance at Ivy one more time, trying and failing to make eye contact.

It's probably nothing. Or maybe she's feeling the same weird vibe I am?

Whatever it is, I'll have to sort it out later.

Because right now, it's go time.

CHAPTER FIVE

Ivy

"Um, is there something you want to tell me?" Wren asks as she picks up Freddie's discarded clothes.

"Like what?" I say, knowing as soon as the words are out of my mouth that my attempt at nonchalance probably sounds a lot more like guilt.

"Ivy," Wren says, clearly seeing right through me. "What was that? Is there something happening between you and Freddie?"

I roll my eyes. At least I can be honest about this part. "Absolutely not."

"Then why are you acting so weird?"

I look down at my hands. I've been mindlessly shifting around a collection of water bottles on top of the mini fridge in Freddie's dressing room, reorganizing them from five to a row to three to a row, then back to five again.

I force my hands to still and look up at Wren, who is

studying me with pursed lips, her arms folded across her chest. "I'm not acting weird," I say.

It's her turn to roll her eyes. Wren is only a year or two older than I am, but she has a strong big sister vibe, and she often treats me and Freddie like we're younger siblings she has to keep in line. Having lost Daphne, it's nice to feel like someone is looking out for me. Especially when we're touring. But I don't like the way she's looking at me right now, like she knows exactly what I'm thinking. Like she can tell that for the five minutes I spent cataloging Freddie's tattoos, I completely forgot she was even in the room. My vision narrowed to him and only him.

"Don't even try to pretend like you inspecting Freddie's body wasn't significant. I could feel the tension buzzing between you two, and I was on the other side of the room."

"It wasn't tension," I say with a dismissive wave. "It was just a conversation, and it had everything to do with this fan we met at the meet-and-greet who's trying to copy all of Freddie's tattoos. I swear that's all it was."

She shrugs. "Okay. I'll take your word for it," she says, but I don't miss her smirk when I finally leave the dressing room and head backstage.

It's concerning that Wren picked up on something. I'm usually so careful, but I've been soft the last few days, first pretending to kiss Freddie in the drugstore, then letting him crawl into my bunk like it wasn't monumentally significant to be so close to him.

I can justify my actions. Say the drugstore thing was necessary to protect Freddie, and the bunk—it's not like he gave me a choice in the matter. But I won't lie to myself and say I didn't love every second of being so close to him.

The first year I worked for Freddie, I was in so far over my head, I didn't have time to form a crush. I was learning everything I possibly could about the industry, and he was right in the middle of an international tour. My to-do list far outpaced my abilities and know-how, so I was too focused on my survival to notice Freddie's charm or his good looks.

But then I learned. I figured stuff out. Got better at my job. And I started to recognize things about my boss that made him different.

Despite having to grow up in the midst of his fame—he was only fifteen when Midnight Rush made it big—Freddie is surprisingly decent. He's loyal and generous. He doesn't drink or party. He has an insatiable curiosity, and he generally starts every day believing that he's going to be surprised or impressed by something. It gives him this unfailing optimism that I can't help but admire.

At the end of his last tour, he gave every single person on his payroll—from caterers to truck drivers to stagehands—an enormous bonus check and wrote handwritten thank you cards, delivering each one in person. It took him days, but he was unflagging in his determination to shake hands with everyone who'd made even the smallest contribution to his success.

That might have been when things started to shift for me. I was the one who coordinated his efforts, made each individual connection possible.

How could I not develop feelings, helping with something like that? It started as admiration and respect, but we just spent so much time together. And let's be honest. Freddie Ridgefield has a very handsome face.

I tried to fight it. I *had* to fight it. And I mostly did. I mostly *have*. What Freddie has in optimism, I have in determination. I made a promise to myself that my feelings would never keep me from doing my job. And they haven't.

But I must be slacking because this is the first time anyone has ever picked up on them. Even Seth, who spends more time with me and Freddie than anyone else, has never picked up on anything.

All the more reason for me to find a new place to live as soon as possible.

Despite what my mother might think, I really don't want to be an assistant forever. Except—if I'm honest with myself, that isn't what this is really about. Freddie would give me a different job title if I asked for it, one more reflective of everything I do.

But moving out is a logical first step in the gradual unweaving of myself from Freddie's life.

That's what this is really about—preparing myself to move on.

I can't love Freddie forever. Not if I want to find someone who will love me in return.

But as long as I work for him, I'm not sure I'll be able to stop.

I find Seth and Charlie standing side by side backstage, their postures similar as they watch Freddie performing "Give Me More." It's one of the few Midnight Rush songs he includes in his setlist because it's such a fan favorite. Most of the chorus, the fans will do the singing for him.

I have no idea how Freddie shifts into performance mode so fast, but after so many shows with the same set list, he could probably perform this concert in his sleep. He sounds great—his tone rich and clear, perfectly on pitch. Sure enough, when he reaches the chorus, he points at the fans, and they sing the next few lines of the song.

Freddie presses a hand over his heart, a gesture of gratitude that makes his fans cheer even louder, then he launches into the next verse of the song.

"He's really on tonight," Seth says, "Better than he has been." He looks down at me. "Did you say something to him?"

"Me? What would *I* say?" I shrug, hoping it's dark enough for Seth not to notice the heat climbing my cheeks. "Probably just good crowd energy."

I turn and walk toward the staging area at the back of the stadium, hidden by enormous black drapes hanging down from the ceiling, mostly so Seth and Charlie won't ask me any more questions. Usually, this area is full of stagehands waiting for the wash, rinse, repeat of taking down what they *just* set up this morning. But since tonight is the first of two shows in Chicago, they won't have anything to take down tonight. They're probably all out, enjoying a much-deserved night off.

I make my way over to one of the huge storage crates that houses Freddie's set when it's disassembled and climb on top, resting my back against the bigger crate directly behind me. I pull out my phone and spend a few minutes scrolling through apartment listings, but I don't see anything new. I have three places bookmarked, but for all I know, by the time I'm in town to check the places out in person, they won't be available anymore, and I'll have to start all over again.

I close out the listings and pull up the text thread with my sister, sending yet another message checking in. She still hasn't responded to the one I sent earlier, but it can't hurt to try again.

I don't expect a reply, so I'm not surprised when one doesn't come through. I send a few more texts to a couple of Carina's friends—the ones who are enough of my friends that I also have their numbers—but no one responds with anything helpful.

I make my way back to her Instagram feed, but this time, I click over to the posts she's tagged in and not just the ones she's posted herself.

The most recent image makes my stomach fall into my shoes.

Carina is smiling, and she looks great. Gorgeous and healthy, her eyes wide and bright. It's the other person in the photo who concerns me.

I zoom in, pulling the woman's face into focus just to make sure I'm not seeing things. But there's no mistaking it. Carina's arm is draped over Margot Valemont's shoulders. And Margot Valemont has never been anything but bad news.

At least when it comes to Freddie.

I sigh and drop my phone into my lap, lifting my fingers to my temples.

Margot is an influencer—the daughter of a very wealthy fashion designer—and has an enormous presence on social media. Carina met her briefly, outside of Freddie's release party for his last album, but I had no idea they knew each other well enough for Carina to show up in Margot's Instagram photos. And I can't shake the certainty that however this happened, the fact that I work for Freddie and Carina is *my* sister has something to do with it.

Freddie's history with Margot is pretty straightforward. They went out a couple of times when he was still part of Midnight Rush. They were both teenagers and it didn't go anywhere. But Margot had a harder time with that than Freddie did, and since then, she's developed a habit of dropping his name whenever it suits her purposes. Every time they happen to be in the same place, she latches onto him like they're long-lost friends. She tags him in photos of parties he hasn't attended. She mentions him in interviews, hinting just enough to keep rumors going that they've been in an on-again, off-again relationship for years.

I can easily imagine Margot reaching out to Carina on purpose—a way to narrow the degrees of separation between her and Freddie just a little bit more.

Which, rumors are just rumors. And most of the time, they don't matter.

But Margot has...shall we say...a *complicated* reputation. She's known for throwing days-long parties wilder than anything any normal person could imagine. She's been arrested multiple times on a variety of charges—shoplifting, driving under the influence, malicious destruction of personal property. The list is long, but not as long as the line of zeroes at the end of her father's bank account balance, so she's never been held accountable. At least not publicly.

The point is, with Freddie's newly rehabbed reputation, the last thing he needs is for his name to appear in a headline anywhere near Margot's. Which means Carina needs to get away from Margot—the sooner the better.

I switch back to my text thread and send another message.

IVY

Hey. Are you with Margot? Carina, it's not a good idea. Can you call me? Wherever you are, I can help you leave. Send a car. Buy you a plane ticket. Whatever you need.

Back on Instagram, I click over to Margot's account. I can't find anything else that suggests she and Carina are still together, but Carina's lack of response is still concerning. The photo of the two of them was posted just yesterday. It looks like they're at a beach, but the background is generic enough that it could be *any* beach. East Coast, West Coast, or anywhere else.

I could always just call Margot and ask where they are. I doubt Freddie still has her number, but he could get it if he wanted it.

But if word got back to Margot that Freddie was looking for her, he'd never hear the end of it. And neither would the paparazzi. I've never known any celebrity—if you can even call Margot a celebrity—who leans into tabloid attention more than she does.

Which means—maybe I just leave this alone?

Carina's an adult. She's got enough sense in her head to take care of herself.

But she's usually pretty good at responding to text messages, so her lack of response is more concerning than not.

I turn off my phone and lean my head back against the

crate, closing my eyes. The bass from Freddie's show reverberates through my body, making my ribs rattle, but I'm so used to it at this point, I hardly notice the noise.

"Thank you," Freddie says to the crowd when a particularly loud eruption of cheers comes to a stop. "I'm liking the energy here tonight, but we're going to slow things down for a minute. Do we have any couples in the crowd?"

Another cheer fills the stadium.

"A few, then," Freddie jokes. "What about right here in the front row? The two of you? You're together?"

I can't hear the other side of Freddie's conversation, but it's easy enough to follow along. It helps that he does this every show—finds a couple in the crowd before singing his first single from his first solo album. As far as love songs go, it's pretty perfect. Freddie is tagged in wedding videos multiple times a day by couples who use it for their first dance, even years after its release. It's still trending on TikTok, and rightly so. Even though Freddie's music is strongly pop, "Only Always" has a more timeless vibe to it, and the lyrics are smart enough that they don't really get stale.

I tend to get tired of music really fast, cycling stuff through my playlist regularly, but even *I* still like this song. Which is saying a lot.

"How many years have you been together?" I hear Freddie ask. "Ten?" he says, after another pause. "And tonight is your anniversary?"

I stretch and climb off the box, knowing that the next time Freddie is backstage, he'll ask me to get a gift basket to the couple in the front row. It's become somewhat of a game for me to anticipate when and if Freddie will request one, mostly so I can give him a smug look when he asks and I get to tell him it's already done.

I always have a few ready just in case, but I'll need to personalize the card and coordinate with security to make sure it's delivered to the couples' seats before the end of the concert.

"Happy Anniversary," Freddie says. "And thanks for celebrating with me and one hundred thousand of my friends." The crowd laughs, then Freddie adds, "Melanie and Jared, this one's for you."

"HOW DID you know I was going to ask for a gift basket?" Freddie asks. He's lying on the couch in his hotel suite, and when he lifts his arms to stretch, a tiny band of skin appears at the hem of his t-shirt. His pants are sitting low enough that I catch a glimpse of a swirl of ink just beside his hip bone, and I wonder if I've just discovered secret tattoo number eighteen. But then he shifts and rolls over, tugging his t-shirt back down.

I clear my throat. "How could I *not* know?" I say. "You're very predictable."

"I'm not predictable." He adjusts the throw pillow under his head. "Can you toss me one of the pillows from the bed in there?"

"Absolutely not," I say. "Because then you'll fall asleep on the couch, which is criminal when you have an entire hotel suite at your disposal. Also, you need to eat."

"I didn't eat?" he asks, and I let out a chuckle.

"Not yet." I walk over and nudge the bottom of his foot. Freddie is lean and lanky and over six feet tall, built more like Tom Hiddleston's Loki than Chris Hemsworth's Thor, but he's still making the couch look tiny, his long limbs hanging off the end like it belongs in a Hobbit house. "Come on. Sit up. Your food will be here any second."

Right on time, a knock sounds on the hotel suite door.

I cross to open it, knowing it'll be Wayne with the Door-Dash I ordered.

"Thanks, Wayne," I say as he hands over the food.

He nods. "No problem. He's in for the night?"

"Pretty sure."

"I'm going to do the rounds and check in with the security team, then I'll be up." He holds up a finger and points it at me. "Are *you* in for the night? Because if you try to pull another—"

"It happened *once*, Wayne. *Once.* You're worse than my dad."

"It only takes once," he says dryly.

I roll my eyes, even though I know he's right. The *once* he's thinking of, I snuck out of a hotel in Kansas to satisfy a craving for Krispy Kreme and wound up running into a fan who actually recognized me. That almost never happens. I'm pretty good at staying out of the limelight. But I'm always traveling with Freddie, so his most serious fans know who I am.

Inside the Krispy Kreme, the fan cornered me and pestered me with question after question. I was afraid to leave because I'd walked three blocks from the hotel, and I was pretty sure she would follow me back if I did. I managed to text Wayne an SOS, and he came to my rescue, but he hasn't let me forget how important it is that when I'm traveling with Freddie, I can't go anywhere without a member of the security team.

Going into the CVS the other night stretched my leash about as far as Wayne will allow.

"It's my job to be worse than your dad," he says.

"Yeah, yeah, I get it. I promise. When I leave here, I'll walk straight to my room and nowhere else."

Since Freddie has a second show in Chicago the day after tomorrow, his entire crew is spread across a few different hotels—a blissful break from the tour bus and a little more downtime than we normally get.

"Good," Wayne says. "Be right back."

When I make it back to the suite's living room, Freddie is sitting up, elbows propped onto his knees and his fingers pressed into his eye sockets. I drop the bag onto the coffee table.

"Your dinner."

His eyes pop open. "Mushroom and Swiss?"

"With fries *and* cheese curds," I say.

"Did you get the—"

"It's in the bag."

He lets out a groan as he pulls out a Culver's burger, followed by a container of cheese sauce because he's a total weirdo and likes to dip his cheese curds in *more cheese*.

"I didn't even have to tell you, and you still knew what I wanted."

"I did," I say. Because I always do.

He unwraps his burger and takes a huge bite, then lets out a low groan. "Ivy, I love you with my whole entire soul."

I stumble at his words, catching myself on the back of the chair sitting opposite the sofa.

He looks up. "You okay?"

"Yep!" I say, my voice a little too high. "Just...tripped on the rug." I walk to the mini fridge at the wet bar against the wall and pull out a water bottle, twisting the cap off as I walk it back to him.

"Marry me?" Freddie says as he takes the water, and I force myself to roll my eyes, even as a tiny pinch registers somewhere in the back of my heart.

I don't know why I thought things might be different after what happened in his dressing room earlier, but this is a joke he's made a thousand times. The fact he'll still make it has to mean the interaction didn't register for him the same way it did for me.

Which sucks because the deeper my *real* feelings become, the harder it is to hear him joke about having fake ones.

I sit down across from him, forcing myself to act normal. To pretend like there isn't anything about this interaction that hurts. "I'm too good for you, Freddie," I say, and he grins.

"Truest words you've ever spoken."

"Have you heard back from your parents?" I ask. We have a Seattle show coming up, and Freddie asked me to keep a private box open for them just in case, but I'll eat my favorite Converse if they actually show up. This won't be the first time he's played Seattle, and they never come.

He frowns before taking another enormous bite of his burger. "Yeah. Mom texted back. They've got something going on that night."

"Of course they do," I say dryly. "One of Harold's tournaments?"

"Some sort of faculty something. I don't know. She didn't give me much detail. It's fine. It would probably stress me out to have them there. I'd worry about them, and then I'd get all up in my head, and the show would suck, and for what? It's honestly easier this way."

I cross my arms, letting out a frustrated huff. I hate the way his parents treat him. Like he's barely an afterthought.

He looks up and chuckles. "Tell me how you really feel."

"I just hate it for you," I say. "It's not fair that they're so entirely indifferent."

"I'll take indifference over disdain," he says. "Trust me. It could be so much worse." He pulls his fries out of the food bag and shoves a few in his mouth. After a show, he tends to eat like he's starving, but then, even a meal like this probably doesn't come close to making up for the calories he burned while performing.

"You sure you're okay?" he asks around another bite of food. "You seem like something else is bothering you."

"Yeah," I say, but Freddie doesn't look convinced. "Just thinking about my sister."

"You're worried about her." He says this like a statement, not a question, and I lean back into my chair, breathing out a sigh.

"Let's talk about something else," I say.

"We can talk about whatever you want." He offers me a cheese curd. "But you'll feel better if you tell me what's on your mind."

I look at Freddie, his green eyes wide and sincere, and for a split second I imagine telling him the truth. Five words.

I'm in love with you.

I hold my breath until my logical mind squashes the impulse, the words dissolving on my tongue before I can say them out loud. As liberating as it would be to own that particular truth, there's too much at stake. And I'm too certain the feeling isn't mutual.

So I settle on a different truth—one that's been occupying almost as much of my bandwidth as my unrequited feelings.

"When I was little, we used to go to Dollywood every summer." I tug a throw pillow out from behind me and pull it to my chest, wrapping my arms around it like it's some sort of shield. "One year, I was maybe eleven or twelve—I'm not sure exactly how old—but I remember that year because Carina was finally tall enough to ride this one specific roller coaster. She was so excited, and she kept bouncing back and forth between me and Daphne, talking nonstop about who would sit next to her and how long the wait would be and if it would be scary when the ride went upside down."

"Was it?" Freddie asks. He takes a long drink of his water. "Did you like roller coasters?"

"Loved them," I say. "Daphne only tolerated them, but she put on a brave face for Carina, because she knew if she wasn't excited, Carina might lose her nerve, and then she'd be mad at herself for chickening out."

"Sounds like a good big sister," Freddie says.

A dull pain stretches across my ribs. "The very best."

Freddie holds my gaze for a long moment. "So how was it? Did Carina end up liking it?"

"That's the thing," I say. "We waited in line for almost an hour, but then a thunderstorm popped up and they shut it down right before we reached the front of the line."

"No," Freddie says.

"Carina was furious—way more upset than she should have been—but I think she'd been psyching herself up the whole time, so the disappointment just hit differently. Anyway, she totally lost it and took off running across the park."

"By herself?"

I nod. "Dad tried to catch her, but then Daphne stopped him and was like, 'Dad, I've got this,' and she took off after her. Fifteen minutes later, the two of them came back, walking hand in hand. Carina had a frozen lemonade some park employee had given them for free, and she was totally fine. Happy. Chill. Like nothing had ever happened."

Freddie chuckles. "What did Daphne say to her?"

I shrug. "I didn't even think to ask. Because stuff like that happened all the time. That's the point. Daphne always knew the right thing to say. She always knew exactly how to solve every problem." I tilt my head to meet Freddie's gaze. "I wish I could ask her what to do about Carina now."

Freddie nods, his green eyes full of understanding. "It really sucks that you can't."

My heart squeezes as warmth spreads across my chest.

It was the exact right thing to say. I have grieved and processed and mourned the loss of my older sister over and over again, struggled and wrestled my way to a place where I can remember her with gratitude instead of sadness, feel joy for having known her instead of just the crippling weight of her loss. But that doesn't mean it doesn't suck that I have to do life without her.

And it feels really good to hear someone say that out loud.

"It does suck," I agree. "So, so much."

Freddie is quiet for a beat before he says, "The thing is though, maybe the whole problem-solving thing is something you and Daphne had in common because I don't know anyone who solves problems like you do."

"Maybe," I say. "But not when it comes to Carina."

"No? Come on." He leans forward and nudges my knee

with the side of his hand. "Don't sell yourself short. You're a great sister."

"I appreciate the vote of confidence," I say. "But things are more complicated this time." I pull out my phone and find the picture I screenshotted from Carina's Instagram account. "I'm not sure where Carina is, but I did figure out who she's with." I hand him the phone. "And you aren't going to like it."

CHAPTER SIX

Freddie

I STARE AT IVY'S PHONE, MY DINNER SUDDENLY FEELING LIKE lead in my stomach.

Margot Valemont's plastic face smiles up at me, and I can't help but feel responsible. I'm the reason Carina met Margot. The reason Ivy's admittedly impulsive and sometimes stupid sister was pulled into her toxic orbit.

"Where are they?" I offer Ivy the rest of my cheese curds, and she takes them, sinking back into her chair with a sigh.

"No clue," she says. "Carina still hasn't responded to any of my text messages. There's no location attached to any of the pictures on Instagram, and Mom says the tracking app she uses says Carina is offline. Margot has posted a few other photos, and it looks like they're at the beach, but that's all I know. I can't even tell if it's east or west coast."

"Or Hawaii," I add. "Or Jamaica or Costa Rica or anywhere else in the world. Margot loves to travel with a party."

Ivy frowns, and I realize too late that probably isn't a worry she needs right now. Worrying about her sister is one thing. Worrying about her sister in a foreign country with only Margot Valemont as a chaperone is something else altogether.

"Kevin probably has her number," I say, but Ivy only groans.

"Oh, gross," she says. "I'm definitely not calling Kevin."

I grin. There is no love lost between my former agent and my assistant. And rightly so.

"I can text him," I say. "Or I can ask Sloane. She probably knows someone who could track down Margot."

"Don't." Ivy sits up a little taller. "I don't trust Kevin not to leak that you're looking for her, and that's not news your reputation can handle right now. And Sloane shouldn't have to deal with my family drama. That's not her job."

"*I'm* her job," I say. "And I don't mind asking. This is my fault. You should let me help."

"It's not your fault. It's Carina's fault. And I'm not letting you get anywhere near Margot Valemont just because my sister is making questionable choices. It's not worth it." She breathes out a frustrated sigh. "I just wish Carina would answer my freaking messages. She's never ignored me for this long before."

"Have you tried calling her?"

"Multiple times," Ivy says. "She's not answering those either."

I drain the last of my water bottle and gather up the trash from my dinner. "Could something be up with her phone?"

"I don't think so. If it were dead or broken or lost or whatever, it would just go straight to voicemail. But it's still ringing when I call, and my messages are marked as delivered." She stands and takes the trash out of my hands, carrying it across the hotel room to throw it away. "I might worry less if I didn't know she was with Margot. But I've just got this feeling in my gut, you know? She's never ignored me like this."

Ivy is always telling me I'm too trusting, but if I had a sister, I wouldn't want her hanging out with Margot Valemont either. And it *is* suspicious that Carina is ignoring all of Ivy's attempts to reach out.

"You have to trust that feeling," I say. "I don't like that she's ignoring you either."

"So what do I do?" she asks.

"Let me ask around," I say. "I'll talk to Sloane. Or even ask Wayne. He knows a lot of people. Someone will know someone who knows where they are and could help us get a message to Carina."

"I'm *already* getting messages to Carina, and she's ignoring me," Ivy says.

"Then we'll find out where she is and go confront her."

Ivy quickly shakes her head. "Absolutely not. *We* won't do anything. You cannot afford contact with Margot. Besides, this is probably just Carina being Carina."

I lean forward, propping my elbows on my knees. "Maybe. But with the way Margot parties, I'd still be worried about Carina spending so much time with her. Just let me make a few phone calls. I could at least find out if she's okay. Safe."

She bites her lip, narrowing her gaze the slightest bit. "Why are you so worried about this?"

I shrug. "Carina only knows Margot because of me."

"That's a false equivalency," Ivy says, shaking her head. "Margot showed up to your release party uninvited. The fact that she ran into Carina outside was terrible luck, but it wasn't your fault. There's no reason for you to play the hero here." She reaches for her phone. "I'll just message Carina again. If I threaten to go searching for her, she might respond just to keep me from doing it."

Ivy's probably right, but I'd still feel better if we had a way to make sure. I don't want any contact with Margot, but I'm pretty sure Wayne knows someone working on her security staff. It can't hurt to at least ask.

Ivy stands and lifts her arms over her head, arching her back as she stretches. My eyes drop to the subtle curve of her hips before I force them upward again. The woman knows how to wear a pair of jeans, but somehow, I've never really noticed until now.

How have I not noticed?

And how am I going to *stop* noticing?

"Oh, hey," she says. "I forgot to mention I got a text from Mira Stapleton this morning."

I lift my eyebrows. "You did?"

"Are you ignoring her, Freddie? It's the only reason she would text me. She asked if your number changed."

I breathe out a sigh. "She wants to see me when we're in LA next week."

Ivy folds her arms across her chest. "How do you feel about that?"

"Like if I wanted to see her, I probably would have texted her back by now."

"Then tell her that," Ivy says. "Put the poor woman out of her misery."

"She isn't miserable," I argue. "She wants a photo op. That's not the same thing."

Ivy frowns. "Is that really what you think?"

I shift on the couch, suddenly uncomfortable with the level of Ivy's scrutiny.

"Freddie." Ivy moves closer and sits down beside me, turning sideways and tucking one leg under her so she's facing me. "I know you've been burned before, but there are women capable of liking you for *you*. It isn't always about your fame."

I turn to face her. There are faint circles under her dark brown eyes, and I'm suddenly aware of how late it is. She got up as early as I did this morning, and she's been working ever since. *Without* the three-hour nap I took before the show.

"I'll believe it when I see it," I say, and Ivy rolls her eyes.

"Is that the only reason you aren't calling Mira? Because of the fame thing? If you just randomly met her on the street somewhere, would she interest you? If neither one of you was famous, would she catch your eye?"

"That's a stupid question," I say. "We *are* both famous. You can't separate that out of the equation."

"Sure you can," Ivy says. "Your fame won't always matter as much as it does now." She nudges my leg with her foot. "Just think about it. Think about Mira in a vacuum. Just her. Her personality. Her vibe. Does she interest you?"

"I still don't think—"

"Humor me," Ivy says, cutting me off.

I frown and grab a pillow from the opposite end of the couch, tucking it against my chest. "Why are you being so mean to me?"

Ivy rolls her eyes. "Asking you to be honest is mean? Come on. Think."

I've gotten very good at following Ivy's instructions over the years, so I force myself to think about the last interaction

I had with Mira. But it only takes a moment to come to the same conclusion I did when her last text came in. Mira's fame *is* overwhelming, but it's not the only problem. We don't have the sparks I want.

"She's not the one for me," I finally say. "And not just because of the fame thing."

Ivy nods. "Okay, good," she says. "Was that so hard?"

For a split second, it sounds like there's relief in her tone, but I can't be sure it isn't wishful thinking. That I only want Ivy to be relieved because I've suddenly, inexplicably started noticing her in ways I never have before.

"Is it good?" I ask.

"It's decisive," Ivy says, "which is always good. But you have to tell her, Freddie. Tell her you aren't feeling it, and you don't want to lead her on."

I groan out a protest, but I know Ivy's right. Mira deserves the truth. "Fine," I say. "I'll respond to her text."

"Good," Ivy says. "You should."

Silence stretches for a beat before I ask, "Do you really think I can have a relationship with someone who doesn't care about my fame?"

It's a pointed question, and I realize, as soon as it's out of my mouth, that I'm baiting her. Luring her into a conversation about my love life to see how she'll respond. To see if I can guess whether she's picked up on any of the shifting vibes between us or if it's all inside my head.

"Of course you can," Ivy says. "You're more than your fame, Freddie. You always have been."

Warmth spreads across my chest. Ivy is too real a person to blow smoke, which means I can only take her words at face value. "Maybe," I say. "But I don't remember the last time I met a woman who didn't already know who I was. That's a weird feeling."

Ivy bites her lip. "I barely knew who you were when we met." Her eyes widen. "Not that I'm saying—I mean, I know I don't count. I'm just saying generally. I exist. There have to be more women out there like me." She closes her eyes, visibly wincing as her face scrunches up. "Not that you need a woman like me. I just mean like me in the sense that she wouldn't be a fan."

I can't decide if Ivy's obvious discomfort with this subject is a good sign or not. There's a blush climbing up her cheeks bright enough to hide her freckles, and that's saying something, because Ivy has a lot of freckles.

"I get what you mean," I say, but I'm not all that sure I agree with her. I'm beginning to think someone like Ivy is exactly who I need.

"Good," she says as she hops off the couch. "Definitely text Mira then."

Ivy won't look at me as she gathers up her stuff, slinging her bag over her shoulder, then retrieving her lanyard and crew badge from the coffee table where she left them. She mumbles something about getting some sleep, then she heads for the door without looking back.

"Good night!" I call to her retreating form, but I'm smiling as I sink back onto the couch. Ivy only squirms like that when she doesn't want to talk about her feelings. And if she doesn't want to talk about *these* feelings, it could mean she actually has some.

It could also mean she *doesn't,* and she wants to avoid an awkward conversation in which she lets me down gently.

I think back to the first conversation I ever had with Ivy.

She was a senior at Belmont and an intern at New

Groove Records, my previous label, when I ran into her in a women's bathroom just down the hall from the conference room where I'd been reviewing the terms of my recording contract.

I needed a minute to breathe without my agent hovering over me, and I was banking on the fact that Kevin was exactly the kind of guy who wouldn't follow me into the ladies room.

"Sorry," I said, glancing over my shoulder to where Ivy was washing her hands. "Just need to hide from my agent for a minute."

She lifted an eyebrow, her entire demeanor cool and comfortable. "You must really like the guy."

I grinned before nudging the door open to peek into the hallway. "His intentions are mostly good."

"But they aren't good right now?" she asked.

I let the door fall closed, then turned to face her, truly taking her in for the first time. Young, beautiful, wild curly hair that hung halfway down her back. Her glasses were bright red, the same color as her sneakers, but the thing I noticed most was that she really didn't seem to care who I was.

"Not at the moment, no," I finally answered.

She finished drying her hands and threw away her paper towel. "Well, good luck with that," she said, before crossing to where I stood with my back against the door. She pushed her hands into her pockets. "Is it necessary that I hide from your agent too?"

"Oh! Absolutely not," I said, stepping to the side. "Sorry."

She took a step forward, but then I called her back, chasing a sudden impulse to not let her go.

"Hey, wait."

She turned around.

"What's your name?"

"Ivy Conway."

"Nice to meet you, Ivy. I'm Freddie."

A question passed over her expression before she finally said, "I know. I know who you are."

"Ah," I said. "I wondered, but I didn't want to assume. You didn't seem to."

She lifted an eyebrow. "I'm an intern for your record label. I think I'd be a pretty terrible one if I didn't."

I rubbed a hand over my jaw even as an idea popped into my head. "Fair enough. Okay, how about this? If you had to, could you name the four members of Midnight Rush?"

"Midnight—wait, is that the boyband you were in? When you first started in music?"

I nodded. "That's the one."

She offered me an apologetic smile. "Sorry. I remember the band, and I'd probably recognize a few songs, but I was never the kind of fan to learn names."

"So you don't know my middle name."

"Definitely not."

"Or where I grew up."

"No—I'm sorry, are these things I'm supposed to know? Am I being tested somehow?"

"No and yes," I said. "Okay, last question." I propped my hands on my hips and looked at her for a long moment, already hoping she would forgive me for how truly ridiculous our entire conversation had been so far. "Can you promise you are *not* in danger of falling in love with me?"

She scoffed. "What?"

"Take a minute," I said. "Am I your type?"

"You're a musician," she said, "which means, by default, you aren't my type."

I liked her answer, even if it wasn't one I expected. "You don't date musicians?"

"I mean, I've never had the opportunity, but I'd like to be taken seriously in the industry, so no. I don't."

"Okay. Good. That's great," I said.

And then I offered her a job.

I'd been looking for an assistant for weeks, and she was perfect. Unaffected by my fame. Smart. Career-driven. And *not* a fan.

She told me she didn't graduate for another six weeks.

I told her I wasn't in a hurry.

She told me her goal was to work for a record label as an artist relations manager.

I suggested what better way to learn about the life of an artist than by working with one directly?

Then I mentioned the salary I was willing to pay her, and she ran out of arguments.

That was five years ago—when she said without hesitation that I wasn't her type. But she didn't really know me then. She only said it because I'm a musician and she wanted to be taken seriously in the industry. But does that truly matter if she's working for me?

I don't have a lot of experience with love, despite how much I sing about it. But it still feels like something is shifting between us.

Ivy must pass Wayne at the door, because he walks in seconds later, and I don't hear the latch click more than once.

"What's up with you?" he says, eyebrows pulled together.

I sit up a little taller. "What? Nothing. Why?"

He motions to his face. "Because you've got this weird goofy grin on your face."

I reach a hand up and wipe it over my mouth. "It's nothing. Ivy was—never mind. It's not important. How's everything out there?"

His jaw tenses, but then he nods. "Good. Everything is good."

Wayne isn't exactly emotive, but I can still tell he's lying. "What happened? What aren't you telling me?"

"Nothing," he says. "There was a minor issue with some hotel staff, but we figured it out before anything could happen. Everything is good."

"Wayne," I say. "Just tell me what it was."

He sits down in the armchair perpendicular to me and breathes out a sigh. "A guy who works the front desk loaned his employee badge to a friend. Or at least someone he *claims* is a friend. I'm more inclined to think it was someone willing to pay him a lot of cash to get her inside the hotel. We caught her in a maids' uniform with a load of sheets in her arms, on her way up to *refresh your linens*." He adds air quotes to the last part of his sentence, and I frown.

"He gave her my room number?"

Wayne nods. "And he was fired for it." He leans back and runs a palm over his shaved head, the light catching in his pale blue eyes. "They both swore they didn't have any malicious intent. She just wanted to meet you."

I choke out a laugh. "It's never malicious, is it? All in good fun."

When I'm traveling on my own, I can usually stay in hotels under a pseudonym, and most hotel staff don't even know it's me. But that's harder to do with an entire tour. Even when we use fake names, concert schedules are public. And tour buses are pretty conspicuous. If you're looking, it isn't hard to figure out where we are.

Wayne leans forward and props his elbows on his knees. "I'll be extra vigilant through our last tour stops. You know it's why I'm here. I won't let anything happen."

"Grateful for you, man," I say. "Thank you."

I mean the words, but on the heels of my conversation with Ivy, it's hard not to wonder if I'm inching toward a place where this kind of attention isn't worth it.

It's not so much that I want to stop performing. Stop making music. I just don't want to do it at the expense of having any *other* kind of life. And when stuff like this happens, it's hard to imagine having a real relationship when so much of my life is so completely *unreal*. Or at least unrelatable.

I think of Adam, my former bandmate who left Midnight Rush after his mom died. He often comes to mind when I'm feeling reflective, mostly because he had the same life I do, then he walked away, and now, everything is different for him.

When I crashed with him in North Carolina, I was fascinated by the simplicity of his life. With his freedom to just live and do what he wants.

When he first met his girlfriend, Laney, she didn't even know who he was. She fell for a simple guy running a dog rescue. Maybe that's the thing I'm most envious of. His ability to control when and how much his past with Midnight Rush plays into his current relationships.

Wayne stands, pushing himself up off his thighs. "You need anything else before I go to bed? Jason is posted outside your room. Just as an extra precaution after what happened."

"Tell him to get some sleep. I'm sure everything will be fine."

Wayne doesn't answer, just looks at me, his expression patient. He will not, under any circumstances, tell Jason to get some sleep just because I tell him to. No matter how much I hate the idea of him staying up all night for me.

"Actually, there is one thing you can help me with," I say.

Wayne nods. "Okay."

"Any chance you can get Margot Valemont's cell number for me? You know one of the guys on her security team, right?"

Wayne frowns. "No."

"No, you don't know the guy?"

"No, I won't get you her number."

"Not for me, Wayne. Chill. Ivy's sister is hanging out with her, and she's not answering her phone. I'm just trying to help Ivy track her down."

"You don't need Margot's number for that," he says. "She's always telling the internet where she is."

"Not anymore. She's on a beach somewhere, but she isn't tagging her locations like she used to."

"Hmm," Wayne grumbles. "Maybe she's finally getting smart."

"I don't want to see Margot," I say. "Or even talk to her. I just want to reach out so I can connect with Carina. Maybe find out where they are."

Wayne rubs a hand across his jaw, eyes cast skyward like he's considering his options. "I won't get you her number," he finally says. "But I will find out where she is."

His confidence takes me by surprise. "How? Is there some underground security guard network I don't know about?"

Wayne doesn't respond, his face perfectly impassive.

"Seriously?" I ask. "For real? Do you compare stories? What's the weirdest one? Who is it? Musician? Actor? I've always thought musicians have to be weirder. Am I right? Tell me I'm right."

Wayne blows out a patient breath. "Do you want my help or not?"

"Yeah, of course I do."

"Then stop asking questions."

I hold my hands up. "Fine. I'll leave it to you."

He turns and takes a few steps toward his bedroom on the other side of the suite. I'd rather have the place all to myself, but it's incidents like the one that happened tonight that make it easier to have someone inside the suite with me.

"What about Flint Hawthorne?" I call after him. "Is it true what they say about him only drinking water bottled in North Carolina?"

Wayne turns around. "Aren't you friends with Flint Hawthorne? Ask him yourself."

I grin. "Just testing your secret network."

"Go to bed, Freddie."

Ten minutes later, I climb into my bed and reach for my phone one last time before turning off the light. I key out a quick message to Ivy and hit send.

FREDDIE

Honestly, I'd be lucky to wind up with someone like you. And not just because you don't care about my fame.

CHAPTER SEVEN

Ivy

THE THING IS, FREDDIE'S TEXT REALLY COULD HAVE JUST BEEN friendly. Spoken out of friendship. Something he would say to *any* assistant he cares about and admires.

Which, those things have never been in question. I know Freddie cares about me. I know he admires me. I'd even go so far as to say he legitimately thinks I'm amazing.

As his assistant.

But that text. There was a thread of...I don't know. *Something* that felt like more.

I would be lucky to wind up with someone like you.

I don't want to believe it means something. But I still haven't been able to get it out of my head. For the past week, show after show, it's been hovering around the edges of my brain, coloring every single interaction I have with Freddie.

It's gotten so bad that I've started to avoid him just to keep myself from dissecting his every move.

Did that touch mean something? Were his words

charged with just a little something extra? Did he glance backstage before singing that one particular love song because he was thinking of me while he sang it?

It's bad.

So bad.

I need our approaching vacation more than anyone, if only so I can spend a few days *away* from Freddie and break this new, very annoying habit.

Three more shows.

Then we'll be back in Nashville.

In Seattle, fifteen minutes before he's scheduled to go on, he tugs me into his dressing room and closes the door behind us. His movements are so quick, so completely unexpected, that I'm breathless when I lean against the door, Freddie hovering over me with light dancing in his green eyes.

Maybe it's my aforementioned newly discovered propensity to read into *everything* Freddie does, but for a split second, I could swear he looks like he wants to kiss me.

"Hey," he says, his voice low and smooth.

I curl my hands into fists, fighting the urge to tilt my chin up and angle my lips toward his, to lean just a little bit closer.

"Hi," I say instead, my voice a little too breathy. "What's up?"

"Have you been avoiding me?" He presses one hand against the door behind me and leans forward, piercing me with his gaze.

I choke out a nervous laugh. "What? Of course not."

His eyes narrow. "Are you sure?"

"Freddie, we're together all the time." It's a stupid point to make. Even if it's technically true, I've done an exceptional job of making sure that while we're frequently in the same space, I'm almost always engaged in something else. Talking on the phone. Sending emails. Fielding texts.

On the upside, I've never been so on top of my work responsibilities.

But I didn't think Freddie had noticed.

I shouldn't like it so much that he has.

"Okay," he concedes. "I just wanted to make sure you're okay. That *we're* okay."

I swallow against the sudden dryness in my throat. "Perfect," I manage to say. "Same as always."

He holds my gaze for a beat longer, long enough for my heart to start pounding a little faster. If he had any idea what he does to me when he looks at me like that, he wouldn't do it.

"In that case, I have something else to tell you," he says.

"Okay."

He lifts his hands to my shoulders and gives them a gentle squeeze. "I found Carina."

It's not quite as exciting as a kiss, but after so many days without word from my sister, it's a close second.

Well, technically, I've gotten a few words. A text came in almost a week ago that read: *Dom Worby. I fide.*

Pretty sure it's supposed to read *Don't worry. I'm fine.* But the spelling errors didn't do much to make me trust the words were true.

They did the opposite, really. Carina doesn't drink or party. Maybe her jumbled words were just typos—that's happened to everyone.

Or maybe she was texting under the influence.

I asked her that exact question when I responded, and

I've texted half a dozen more times since then and called every single day.

She hasn't texted again, and she hasn't answered a single phone call.

She has, however, shown up in several more of Margot's photos, which was evidence enough for the police to think there was nothing to worry about.

Yes. I called the police. But only to explore my options. Turns out I don't have any. She isn't really missing if she's showing up on Instagram and responding—albeit badly—to text messages.

"You found her?" I ask Freddie. "How? Where?"

"She's in Malibu," he says. "Still with Margot, unfortunately. They're in a beach house, probably one Margot is renting, but"—Freddie glances at his watch—"as of an hour ago when Wayne filled me in, Carina seems to be safe and well."

I breathe out a sigh. Those words loosen a knot of tension I've been carrying around for days. She's safe. Still with Margot, and still not responding to my messages, but at least I know she's okay. "You asked Wayne to help?"

Freddie nods. "He's friends with a guy who's on Margot's security team. It took some back and forth, but Wayne just got confirmation. He's asked for the address, so as soon as we have that, we'll know where to go to find her."

"You think I should?" I ask. "Even though Wayne said she's fine?"

He lifts one shoulder. "If it were me, I'd be worried about the text she sent. If she's drinking, and she doesn't have a lot of experience with that whole scene, she could easily be in over her head."

I nod, biting my lip as I sink back into the door.

It's been nine years, ten months, and seventeen days since my brilliant, beautiful, amazing older sister was killed in a car accident the night of her senior prom. Her boyfriend didn't think he'd had too much to drink—but it was still enough that two blocks after leaving the dance, he missed a stop sign and pulled through an intersection, where an enormous diesel pick-up t-boned him, hitting the passenger side first and killing Daphne instantly.

I was seventeen, one year behind Daphne in school and following behind her with my own date, on our way to the same afterparty she'd invited me to. It was a party just for seniors, but I had special privileges because Daphne was the prom queen, the one everyone loved, and I was her little sister.

I've since stopped asking all the what-if questions that plagued me for years.

What if I'd told Daphne I caught a whiff of alcohol on her boyfriend's breath?

What if I'd followed her to the parking lot and insisted she take his keys and drive instead?

What if I'd begged her to ride with me?

None of those questions will ever have answers, and even if they did, they wouldn't bring Daphne back.

But two things have been true since that warm spring night.

One: I hate getting dressed up. My junior prom dress was the last formal dress I've ever worn, and I have zero plans to change that anytime soon.

Tricky, seeing as how Freddie has attended the Grammys every year I've worked for him, and he's been to the Oscars twice. It's typical for PAs, even multiple PAs to attend with their employers, but I've gotten pretty good at weaseling out of formal events.

I'm pretty sure Freddie thinks I just don't want to give up my Converse. Which, he's not entirely wrong about that.

And two: I do not drink alcohol. Not ever.

That's something Carina and I have in common—a promise we made to each other.

It's hard to process what it means if she broke that promise.

"Yeah, I probably should make sure she's okay," I say.

Freddie nods. "I think that's a good call. And we'll be in LA on Sunday."

"Which is very close to Malibu."

He smiles. "Yep."

"So I can go get her."

"You can send *Wayne* to go get her," Freddie says. "You aren't going anywhere near Margot."

I don't roll my eyes, and I don't argue with him. Partly because he has to be on stage in a matter of minutes. My eyes drop to the maroon suit he's currently wearing. On anyone else it might look silly, but Freddie pulls off looks like this one with ease. With several inches of skin visible at his collar, his tattoos peeking out in multiple places, he looks anything *but* silly. Fit. Confident. Sexy. Like a rockstar.

A rockstar who *can't* actually keep me from going after Carina myself. I know my sister well enough to guess how much she'd hate having a security guard sent to retrieve her like she's a wayward, troublesome child. Even if that's exactly how I'm thinking about her right now.

But that's a conversation I can have with Freddie another time.

Freddie squeezes my shoulders. "You okay?" he asks. "I thought you'd be happy."

I look up and meet his sharp, green gaze. "Better than okay," I say. "Thank you for finding her. I'll thank Wayne too."

"Anything for you," Freddie says, and my breath catches. Why does he have to look at me like this? Why does he have to be so good? To care so much? It makes it impossible to read any potential signals.

Anything for me. But *why* me? Because I'm an employee? His friend? This is the man who hand-delivered thank you cards to every single person who worked on his tour. He is exactly the kind of man who would do anything to help anyone. His words, the gestures, the touches, they really could have nothing to do with romance.

It could—and I've reminded myself of this no less than a thousand times—be all in my head.

I shrug out of his grip and take a step backward.

Freddie's hands fall to his sides, and for a brief second, something flashes across his expression—something like hurt, or maybe confusion? It disappears so quickly, I have to think I imagined it, but the weird tension hovering between us stays.

"Your suit is ridiculous," I finally say, because I have to say something, and teasing each other is something Freddie and I have always done well.

Freddie smirks and turns toward the mirror, then flips his lapels up. "Liar. This suit is amazing and you know it."

"Nope," I say. "1987 called, and they want it back."

He grins. "Don't let Wren hear you. She loves this suit."

I roll my eyes. "Yeah, yeah. Break a leg out there."

"See you after?" he asks, holding my gaze.

I nod, but as soon as he disappears out the door, I sink onto the couch behind me and sigh. "Where else am I going to be?"

CHAPTER EIGHT

Ivy

"Freddie, you can't come with me," I say, hands gripping the steering wheel.

"Too late." He tugs the Appies Hockey cap he stole from Adam a little lower on his forehead. "I'm already buckled in."

"Then *unbuckle*," I say, voice rising. "Does Wayne know you're out here?"

"Relax," Freddie says. "Wayne *basically* knows. Or he will as soon as he realizes I'm not getting the massage you booked for me."

"Freddie."

"Just drive, all right?" he says. "It'll be fine."

I shift the rental car from reverse into park. I had one delivered to the hotel in Los Angeles this morning and cleared my travel with Wayne. He wasn't thrilled with the idea of me going by myself, but since his connection within

Margot's security detail knows I'm coming, he begrudgingly agreed. Not that I gave him any choice in the matter.

I'm not his responsibility like Freddie is his responsibility. If I want to go somewhere on my own, I still have that luxury.

But Freddie doesn't.

"I'm not driving anywhere with you in the car," I say. "This is not like going to CVS where you only *might* get into trouble. This is going to see Margot where you will *absolutely* get into trouble."

"What kind of car even is this?" Freddie asks, tugging at the strap of his seatbelt.

"It's a Honda. The kind of car *normal* people drive."

"You're saying I'm not normal?"

I let out a little laugh. "Yes, Freddie. I'm saying it's *not* normal that you aren't familiar with the interior of a Honda."

"I wasn't judging," he says. "It's fine. Nice, even. How long will it take us to get to Malibu?"

I groan. "Freddie, please don't do this. I covered for you when you went to North Carolina on your own, but there's more at stake here. Carina is *my* sister. Just let me handle this."

His jaw tightens. "No," he says simply.

"Why are you being so stubborn about this? If you don't get out of the car, I'm not going. It's really that black and white."

"Why are *you* being so stubborn?" Freddie shoots back, eyes flashing. "It's my fault you're even having to deal with this in the first place. Do you know what it feels like to always have *other* people fix your problems? Clean up your messes? To just sit, idle, because going anywhere or doing anything is too risky? I care about this. I care about you. And I'm going with you. Now drive."

My heart rate spikes at the vehemence in his voice. Freddie is always so good-natured, so chronically optimistic, it's not very often I see this side of him.

"Margot's security detail knows I'm coming," I say, my tone gentler now. "If Wayne trusts that I can do this on my own, you should too. I appreciate you wanting to come, but there's a lot more at stake for you than there is for me."

Before he has the chance to respond, the back door of the Honda opens, and Wayne climbs inside. It takes him a minute—he is a very large man, and the backseat of the Civic I rented is not particularly accommodating. But after a few seconds of struggle, he pulls the door closed with a grunt and buckles his seatbelt.

"Seriously?" I say, glancing at him through the rearview mirror. He looks ridiculous squeezed into such a tiny space, his knees almost up to his ears.

He shrugs and motions toward Freddie. "If he goes, I go."

"Wayne," I say, turning so I can make direct eye contact. "Are you sure?"

"I texted Cole," he says. "That's Margot's security guard. He says things there are very low key and it isn't going to be a problem." He looks over at Freddie. "But you're staying in the car, man. You agree to that right now, or we aren't going anywhere."

"Done. Agreed," Freddie says. "My butt won't move from this seat."

I look over and meet Freddie's gaze, and he grins, looking annoyingly smug. "I get to control the music, right?" he says. "Do we have time to stop for snacks?"

The drive to Malibu is beautiful. Traffic-filled, but still beautiful, with a view of the ocean on one side of the highway and steep hillsides on the other. By the time we arrive, I'm convinced Freddie mostly wanted to come for the drive. I sometimes forget how infrequently he gets to do "normal person" things. But seeing him relax, windows down, music blaring, I can't really blame him for wanting to come. We've been on tour for months, moving from the bus to concert venues to hotels then back to the tour bus. Always, Freddie is hiding from fans, ducking out of sight as quickly as possible.

But the truth is, if he wasn't famous, he'd be exactly the kind of friend who would want to tag along on a trip like this. He's always up for an adventure, and that's definitely part of it. But he's also just a really good friend.

And despite how much I protested his coming at first, when I pull up to the gate at the palatial beach house Margot Valemont currently occupies, nerves making me grip the steering wheel a little too tightly, I'm glad he's beside me.

"I'll call Cole and see if we can get the gates open," Wayne says, pulling out his phone.

Freddie reaches over and wraps his larger hand around mine, giving it a quick squeeze. "Relax," he says. "It's just Carina. Things will be fine."

Carina, who hasn't texted or answered any of my calls. Who must, by virtue of her behavior, have very little desire to see me or else she would have responded to one of my many, *many* messages.

I've always had a solid relationship with my sister even if I don't always understand her. We've never been close enough that we tell each other everything. But we've never ignored each other. We've never kept secrets about the stuff that matters most.

"What if she won't come with me?" I ask.

"She might not," Freddie says.

"What if she really is Margot's new best friend, and I've lost her to the dark side?"

"Then I'll knock Margot out with the closest frying pan, and we'll have Wayne toss Carina over his shoulder and force her into the car."

I let out a chuckle as the wide gates slowly swing open. "That sounds a lot like kidnapping."

"All jokes aside," Freddie says, "you probably should prepare yourself for the possibility. You really just want to know she's safe, right? She might be fine. And if she is, you might have to leave her here."

I think of Carina's jumbled text message.

Maybe it's just sisterly intuition, but I don't think Carina *is* fine.

"I hope she's okay," I say. "But I'm not leaving her here either way." I turn off the car and unbuckle my seatbelt. "You'll stay here, right?" I say, even though Wayne made it very clear those were the terms of our trip.

Freddie rolls his eyes. "I'm not an idiot. I don't want to see Margot any more than either of you. But if you aren't back out here in thirty minutes, you can't stop me from coming in after you."

I look at Wayne. "Please don't let him do that."

"Thirty minutes," Freddie repeats, even as Wayne gives me a reassuring nod that seems to say he'll keep Freddie under control. As I walk across the seashell gravel to the front of the house, I set a timer on my watch for thirty minutes. Just in case.

An older man dressed in black slacks and a black polo opens the door.

"Cole?" I ask, and he nods.

He looks over my shoulder, lifting his chin in Wayne's direction—he's outside the car now, leaning against it with his arms folded over his chest—then cuts his gaze back to me.

"You're looking for Carina."

I nod. "Is she around?"

His jaw twitches. "In a manner of speaking. Everyone is out back."

I follow him through a vast entryway into a living room decorated in classy beach decor. The room is littered with discarded wine glasses and empty bottles and there is a person curled up on each of two sofas. Both look to be asleep, despite the afternoon hour. It's obvious neither person is Carina, but worry still pools in my gut. This is not the kind of atmosphere I'd wish for *anyone's* baby sister. Especially not mine.

At the back of the room, a set of French doors are open onto the patio, where a dozen or so people are stretched out in similar fashion. The air is thick with the smell of booze and weed, but based on the paraphernalia covering the tabletops, those aren't the only drugs in play.

My eyes scan the patio, but I don't see Carina anywhere.

I don't see Margot either, and I can't decide if that makes me more or less comfortable.

But then laughter sounds from across the yard, and my heart rate spikes. I'd recognize my sister's laugh anywhere.

I look across the sparkling pool to a gazebo nestled next to a row of orange trees and hurry in that direction.

It's good that she's laughing, right? Laughing is so much

better than passed out on a couch next to a bong or a discarded needle.

I see Margot before I see Carina. She's in a black bikini, her blond hair piled on top of her head, a gauzy cover up draped over her shoulders. She looks flawless. And *entirely* sober. Her eyes move up and down my person, her gaze calculating, but before she has time to say anything, a gasp sounds from the other side of the gazebo.

"Ivy?" Carina stands and runs toward me, throwing her arms around my neck. She reeks of alcohol, something that makes my heart pinch with pain, but she's at least whole and alive. "What are you doing here?" she asks.

"I could ask you the same thing," I say. "I've been worried about you."

Her head lolls forward and drops onto my shoulder. "Oop. I don't feel so good," she slurs.

I tighten my grip around Carina's waist, and sweat breaks out across my forehead. She was a lot younger than I was when Daphne died. But she wasn't too young to understand what killed her. To get that if not for Daphne's idiot boyfriend having too much to drink, our sister would still be alive.

We've had the conversation a thousand times. Mom whispered her pleas like prayers before we went to bed every night. That we would be safe. Leave alcohol alone. Make smart choices because we were still alive to make them when Daphne wasn't.

I've never been able to touch the stuff. Mom's words are etched into my heart as deeply as the image of the ambulance pulling away with my sister inside.

I thought Carina felt the same way.

But I guess I was wrong.

"I've been trying to call you," I say, repositioning us both so I can hold her up without toppling over.

"I know!" Carina says. "My phone is broken. But I texted from my watch. I told you not to worry." She holds up a wobbly finger and points it at Margot. "It's all good. Margot's getting me a new phone. Isn't that nice? She's so nice."

I look at Margot, eyebrows raised, but she only shrugs.

Something in her expression makes me think she has exactly zero intention of getting Carina a new phone. She has the money—she could probably make one phone call and have a dozen iPhones on the doorstep in a matter of hours—so if she hasn't already, she probably won't.

"That's nice of her," I say to Carina, not breaking eye contact with Margot. "But I'm happy to get you a new phone. We can go get one right now, actually. Then you can spend a couple of days with me in LA."

Carina's head pops up, her eyes wide and glassy. "Really? You're in LA?"

I nod. "I'd love to see you and hang out for a bit."

"But you're on tour with Freddie," Carina says.

My eyes dart to Margot, who is still watching us, her gaze cool.

"Not right now," I say, trusting Carina will forgive the lie as soon as she understands what's at stake. "I just came here hoping to spend a little time with you."

Luckily, Carina sighs and smiles. "You're such a good sister."

"You should just stay here," Margot says from behind us. "The house is huge. Plenty of bedrooms are still empty."

"You should!" Carina says, giving me a little shake. "The beach is right there! We would have so much fun." She spins and points toward the ocean, just visible through a line of palm trees at the edge of the property, but the gesture throws off her balance just enough that I have to reach out to keep her from falling over.

"I don't think that's a good idea," I say. "I already have a nice place. And I think a little sister time would be good for us." I tug her toward the house. "Want to help me get your stuff?"

It takes a *long* time to gather Carina's stuff. Mostly because she's only half-present, her mind focused one minute, then completely vacant the next. She's clearly been drinking, but I'm not sure that's the only thing in her system. She seems too agitated, too manic. Not that I would know. I've never been around Carina when she's drinking. Maybe this is just how she is.

Either way, I have no idea how to process what this means. It isn't about me—but it *feels* like it is. Like it's about our whole family.

Losing Daphne almost killed me.

I can't lose Carina too.

For her to be so careless, to make such stupid, reckless choices, it feels like someone has pulled the rug out from under me.

How am I supposed to deal with this? To help her? How am I supposed to keep her safe?

By the time we make it downstairs, Carina seems worse off than she was before. Maybe all the exertion is finally getting to her? Fortunately, the entryway is empty, so there's nothing stopping us from making a clean escape.

I hoist Carina's bag a little higher on my shoulder and half drag, half carry my sister to the door.

Cole appears and opens it for us, and we make our way onto the porch. "Tell Wayne I said hello," he says, then he glances over his shoulder back into the house. "But I'd hurry, if I were you."

I follow his gaze and see a shadow that can only be Margot moving toward the open front door.

"Okay," I say to Carina. "Time to run."

CHAPTER NINE

Freddie

I SEE IVY BEFORE WAYNE DOES, RUNNING FROM THE FRONT door, her arm hooked through Carina's as she drags her sister forward. Carina slips, falling to her knees and nearly pulling Ivy down with her.

I'm out of the car before Wayne can stop me, running across the seashell driveway to help.

I try to catch Ivy's gaze, but she's focused on the car, looking past me—maybe *through* me?—with singular focus.

"Let's get you into the car," I say, stepping under Carina's free arm and shifting her into my arms. Wayne is out of the car now too, and he's got the back door open and ready for us.

"Margot's coming," Ivy says as soon as Carina is in the backseat. She shoves Carina's bag onto the floorboard behind the driver's seat. "We need to go *now*."

I nod but we haven't made it two steps before Margot appears on the porch. She's motioning to someone inside the house, then a man appears beside her, wearing a backward baseball cap and holding a camera in his hand.

I don't always love that I've never known adulthood without fame. But it's taught me a lot, and right now, everything I've picked up from Wayne's constant vigilance is helping me recognize all kinds of red flags. It only takes me a matter of seconds to read my current situation and intuitively sense exactly what's going to happen next.

Margot is walking toward me, *in a bikini,* with a purpose that immediately makes my skin crawl, while the man on the porch has his camera lifted, one hand adjusting the lens.

I have no idea why there's a photographer camped out at Margot's party in the first place—though I shouldn't be surprised. It feels like a very Margot move to invite the paparazzi into her personal space. She's always loved being *seen.*

Regardless of why he's here, with the backdrop of Margot's Malibu beach house, one photo of the two of us together would be tabloid fodder for weeks.

We don't even need to be side by side. We only need to be in the same *frame* for Margot to use it to her advantage.

Rumors about the two of us vacationing together or having some sort of secret rendezvous. A hidden relationship, a one-night stand, however she spins it—and she will —it won't be good for me.

So much of my audience is *young.* Teenagers. Even middle-schoolers. I'm a role model for them whether I want to be or not, and Margot is constantly mixed up in things that make that harder. Plus, I'm just so tired of her lying about me. And that's all she seems to do these days.

My frustration grows at the futility of my situation, but

then Ivy reaches out and grips my arm. "Do you remember that moment in CVS?"

I shake my head, struggling to understand why she's asking me this *now*. "What?"

"When we pretended to make out," she says. "This is just like that moment. Except, this time, you need to kiss me for real."

I blink, still not fully processing what Ivy is telling me.

She reaches for me, wrapping her arms around my waist. "Trust me," she quickly whispers. "This will work. We just have to give the photographer a bigger story than you and Margot together at a Malibu beach house."

Understanding finally clicks in my brain. If I'm kissing someone else, a photo of Margot and me in the same frame won't matter nearly as much.

I look back at Margot, who is closing in quickly. She lifts her hands to her bikini top, adjusting the straps as she walks.

Ivy's right. This is the only move I've got.

So I lift my hands to my assistant's face and press my lips to hers.

It's a quick kiss—it has to be, because the gesture needs to seem like something we've done a million times before. Like we're *together*. Like I'm kissing her because I was worried she was taking so long, and now I'm happy to see her. Like the only reason I came to Margot's beach house was to pick up my very serious girlfriend's sister.

But I don't miss the zing of electricity that passes through me when my lips touch hers. All this talk of shifting feelings, all the moments of questioning—they crystalize into tangible certainty in a matter of seconds.

I like kissing Ivy Conway.

I lean forward, pressing another quick kiss to Ivy's jaw

just beside her ear. "We've got to stop meeting like this," I joke. "Also thank you for saving me."

I kiss Ivy one more time, two quick pecks, then we turn to face Margot. Ivy slips an arm around my waist, tucking herself into my side like a real girlfriend might.

"Hey, Margot," I say as I turn to face her. "Thanks for hosting Carina. I'm sure she had a great time."

Margot presses her lips together, not even trying to hide her frustration. "No problem," she says dryly.

Ivy lifts her chin and looks at me. "I'm ready to go, babe."

We really *do* need to get out of here. The quicker the better.

"I'm driving," Wayne says, and Ivy doesn't argue. She just climbs into the backseat next to her sister without another word.

Seconds later, we're pulling down the driveway toward the security gate, Margot a disappearing figure in the rearview mirror.

I finally breathe out a sigh as I turn in my seat so I can look at Ivy. "That was amazing thinking on your part," I say, but something feels off about her body language. She looks dazed, maybe a little frustrated? It's hard to tell.

As happy as I was to kiss Ivy and thwart Margot's attempts to co-op the moment for a photo, the reality is, I wouldn't have thought to do it had Ivy not suggested it. Once she did, agreeing seemed like a clear and obvious choice. Having the world think I'm in a relationship with Ivy is worlds better than having them think I'm in a relationship with Margot.

But now I'm beginning to question my judgment.

Does Ivy have regrets? Was it so bad of a kiss that she wishes she'd never suggested it?

Carina lets out a low moan, and Ivy reaches for her, shifting her sister so her head is resting in Ivy's lap. Ivy runs a hand over Carina's hair, but the movement is mechanical, her gaze locked on the window as the California landscape slides by.

Several moments pass before Ivy says, "You should probably reach out to Sloane. She'll want to call Kat so she can come up with a plan before the photos of us are released."

"*If* they're released," I say. "Margot might persuade the guy not to sell them. He was there for her, after all. It doesn't really serve her purposes for the world to know we're together."

"We *aren't* together," Ivy says, her words clipped.

"No, I know," I quickly correct. "Just—if the photos are released, the world will *believe* we are. I know it's not the same thing."

"Freddie, no paparazzi is going to ignore an opportunity to sell photos of *you* kissing someone. Not for Margot. Her influence doesn't come close to competing with yours."

I sigh and sink into my seat, knowing that Ivy is right.

"The reality is," she continues, "we don't know what Margot is going to do or what the photographer will do. But you need to brace yourself for any possibility, and that means your team needs to know what happened."

It's not lost on me that even with her drunk sister asleep in her lap, Ivy is still calm. Still collected. Still thinking about what's best for *me*. That's why she asked me to kiss her in the first place. She was looking out for *my* image. *My* reputation.

I'm not sure I deserve that kind of loyalty.

And I can't quite shake the feeling that I've knocked over the first domino in a cascade of consequences I can't yet see.

Carina is awake but still woozy by the time we make it back to the hotel. Wayne swipes his key card to get us into the private garage, then we wordlessly make our way to the elevator. There's no show tonight—I don't perform until tomorrow—so for once, I don't have anywhere to be or anything to do. My plan was to spend the time writing, figuring out what I'm going to put on the next album, but now, all I want to do is talk to Ivy.

Make sure she's okay.

Make sure what happened didn't somehow ruin everything between us.

Outside of our working relationship, I also don't want to lose my *friendship* with Ivy. She means a lot to me. Too much for me to have something like this screw things up.

I think of the way it felt to press my lips against hers.

In any other circumstance, a feeling like that might compel me to try for something more. To explore the possibility of a real relationship.

But it feels wrong to pursue something now when it feels like the relationship we already have is suddenly on the line. I don't want to doubt what I felt when I kissed her, but emotions were high. I was thinking fast and acting faster. Who's to say my judgment wasn't clouded?

Even if my feelings *are* legit and Ivy happens to feel the same way, if a photo of us kissing is released, we will have lost the opportunity to explore something more in private. To see how we feel about each other before we find a way to make it fit with my very public life.

Our situation would have made dating complicated before, but I just took complicated and threw it into a blender with a side of stressful, a full cup of uncertainty, and two helpings of *very, very public*.

Ivy doesn't even look at me before she peels off from the group and heads to her own hotel room, her arm wrapped protectively around Carina's waist.

I follow Wayne to my suite, the ache in my chest shifting into frustration. I'm self-aware enough to realize that my frustration shouldn't be directed at Ivy. But I'm frustrated with the situation, I'm anxious to talk to her, and I'm completely incapable of fixing any of it.

Wayne follows me into my suite, but something about his body language feels off, and it makes my skin prickle with annoyance. "What's wrong with you?"

He shoots me a look. "Nothing."

"Don't lie to me, man."

"What's done is done," he says. "There's nothing to say. No reason to fight about it."

I scoff. "What are you talking about?"

He gives his head a little shake. "Freddie, you *kissed* her," Wayne says. "Did you think for two seconds about how that might impact her life?"

"I kissed her because she *told* me to," I shoot back. "I guess I didn't have to agree. But we're talking about Margot here. She was trying to get close to me, and Ivy saw a way to prevent that from happening."

"You're right," Wayne says. "You didn't have to agree. Also, you could have stayed in the car."

"Ivy needed help," I insist. "Carina fell. I wasn't going to just sit and watch her struggle."

"*I* could have helped," Wayne says. "Better yet, you should have stayed at the hotel, man. We both told you that."

"Right. Because that's what my life is now. Stay out of

sight. Don't go places. Hide from fans. Do you realize how exhausting that is? How isolating it is? Ivy is my friend, and her sister was in trouble because of me. Why does everyone keep wanting me to do nothing? That's not living. That's not caring for the people in my life."

Wayne sighs, his arms folded across his chest. "I get that. I do."

He lifts a shoulder. "But she was looking out for you, and she put herself on the line to do that. And now, in a matter of hours, the whole world will probably know that you kissed her. Her parents. Her friends. The guy she's been talking to."

I frown, a hot flash of jealousy burning through my limbs. "She's talking to a guy?"

"She could be," Wayne says. "She has a life outside of you, Freddie. Sometimes I think you forget that."

I drop onto the edge of the couch, elbows propped on my knees, and let my shoulders drop.

"I just want to make sure someone is looking out for *her* too," Wayne says.

I run a hand through my hair, thinking through what this will mean for Ivy if the photos drop. Ivy's right that I need to talk to Sloane and Kat. We'll need to be ahead of the story so we can control the narrative.

Because there *will* be a narrative. People will look into Ivy's family. They'll dig into Carina's past. They'll pull up old articles about Daphne's accident and splash them all over the internet. They will dig and poke and prod and speculate because that's what people do.

And Ivy knows all of that.

And she was still willing to help me.

I reach for my phone, itching to talk to her. To thank her, but also to apologize.

Wayne is right. The kiss might have been Ivy's idea, but she was acting to protect me. And I'm the one who put us in a position where I needed protecting in the first place.

I also can't deny that when it comes to stuff like this, Ivy has the better brain. She's smart and logical and practical. She can always see the clearest path forward, the one that will minimize drama and have the least amount of collateral damage. It's one of the things I appreciate about her the most—she has good vision. And she's great at reading emotion, at guessing how people will react and steering focus to the things that matter the most.

But is that even fair? Can I truly expect her to advise me, assist me, when I've pulled her right into the middle of the drama?

I pull up our text thread, fingers hovering over my screen as I debate what to say.

FREDDIE

Hey. I owe you an apology. Once Carina is settled, can we talk?

She reads the message almost immediately, but she doesn't reply. Little dots appear letting me know she's typing a message, but then the dots disappear, and no message comes through.

I breathe out a sigh, then I switch over to Sloane's profile and hit *call.*

Maybe I'll get lucky.

Maybe the photographer won't sell the photos. Maybe his camera was broken or the lighting was bad or Margot was standing in the way and he didn't get any shots of me and Ivy kissing.

"What have you done?" Sloane asks as she answers the call, which can only mean one thing.

I didn't get lucky, and the photos are already live.

CHAPTER TEN

Ivy

It's late when I finally make my way to Freddie's hotel room. Carina sobered up enough to take a shower and climb into pajamas, but she fell asleep as soon as her head hit the pillow.

I already called my parents to let them know Carina is safe, and I've been making a list of questions I intend to ask her as soon as she's well enough to hear them. But for now, I have bigger problems to worry about.

My phone has been blowing up all afternoon—texts and emails from all the important people who manage Freddie's career. His agent, his record label's publicist, his personal publicist—that conversation was the longest and the most overwhelming, by far. I also heard from my best friends from college, three friends from high school I haven't talked to in years, and my mother's Pilates instructor. Which, I need to talk to Mom about why her Pilates instructor has my number.

Then there are the texts from Leo, Jace, Adam, and Adam's girlfriend, Laney, who all messaged me separately to offer some form of congratulations. It was Adam's message that stung the most.

ADAM

It shouldn't have taken him so long to realize how great you are. I'm glad he finally did.

They're going to be so disappointed when they realize it's all pretend.

Not that my mother's Pilates instructor will hear the truth.

But Freddie will tell his former bandmates. Of course he will. Since the four of them reunited last year, they've only gotten closer. He basically tells them everything.

I pace outside Freddie's room for five full minutes before Wayne opens the door and finds me. He pauses as soon as we make eye contact, then glances back into the room before tugging the door closed behind him and leaning against it.

"You okay?" he asks.

"A guy I haven't talked to since the tenth grade just texted me a link to his demo on YouTube," I say. "He asked if I could pass it along."

Wayne grimaces. "Guess that comes with the territory, huh?"

"Something like that."

"Do you want to go inside?"

I love the patience in Wayne's voice as he asks this. He's not judging me for pacing outside—he's acting more like he's not at all surprised to have found me here and he'll understand if I turn around and go back to my own room instead.

"I think I have to," I say. "But I'm not sure I *want* to."

"He's pretty beat up about everything," Wayne says. "If that matters."

"I'm the one who asked him to kiss me," I say. "This isn't his fault."

"He was only there in the first place because he insisted on coming along," Wayne says. "That *is* his fault."

"Does he think I'm mad about that?" I ask.

Wayne shrugs. "You aren't? You seemed pretty upset in the car."

Upset isn't *quite* the right word for what I was in the car.

I was mostly just stunned.

When Freddie's lips touched mine, fire exploded through my veins, my heart practically climbing into my throat. The feel of his hand on my cheek, the concern in his bright green eyes. For a split second, I forgot it wasn't real. That he wasn't kissing me just because he wanted to.

Once we left and got away from Margot, my stupid, traitorous heart wondered if he felt the same thing I did. If the kiss awakened something, prompted him to see me as something *more* than just his assistant. But then he turned around in the car and talked about my "brilliant idea," and my hope fizzled and died.

The kiss was a well-executed strategy. But that's all it was.

My brain gets it, but after kissing him, it's going to take a measure of Herculean strength to convince my heart of the same thing—strength I'm not sure I have.

Especially now—when the whole world thinks Freddie Ridgefield is in love with me.

That's why I was distant in the car. Why I seemed upset.

I was just trying to reorder my heart.

It's stupid, honestly.

What did I think?

That somehow, one tiny kiss, initiated under duress, was going to trigger an epiphany and show Freddie he's actually in love with me? That doesn't make even a little bit of sense.

But during that kiss, my heart didn't care about what made sense. It only cared about how right it felt to be close to him, to have his hands cradling my face.

I shove my hands deep into the pockets of my hoodie. "I'm not mad at him," I say. "Just a little overwhelmed."

Something passes over Wayne's expression, and I catch a glimpse of how much he respects his boss.

"He's probably been on the phone all day," I say.

Wayne nods. "Nonstop." He pulls out his keycard and opens Freddie's hotel room door. "You ready?"

I nod. "Yeah. Thanks, Wayne."

I find Freddie leaning against the headboard in his bedroom, legs stretched out in front of him, his guitar perched on his lap. He's picking out a melody I don't recognize, but he stops the second he sees me, immediately setting his guitar to the side.

"Any luck?" I say. Because it's easier to talk about music than to start the conversation I actually came here to have.

"Nah. Nothing much. A few bars of a melody maybe, but nothing that feels promising."

"Let me hear it," I say, and his eyebrows lift. I don't know what he was expecting when I appeared in his doorway, but after the day we've had, I'm sure it wasn't this.

"For real?"

I nod as I climb onto the foot of his bed, and he reaches for his guitar.

"Okay, well...I was thinking something that starts like this..." He plays a chord. "Then shifts into something softer like this." He plays through a few more measures.

I must be too tired to filter my emotions, because Freddie frowns as soon as he finishes.

"That bad?"

"Not at all," I say. "It's pretty. It just..."

"Sounds like my dog died?"

I grimace. "Definitely. But maybe that's the sound you're going for? Not all of your music needs to be happy."

He sighs. "But it does need to feel real, and that..." His words trail off. "I don't know. I'll figure it out eventually. Probably."

I pull my feet up and sit cross-legged on the bed. "It wasn't this much of a struggle last time, was it?" I ask. "The writing?"

In the five years I've worked for Freddie, he's released two albums. The first was complete when he hired me, but the second I witnessed from beginning to end—when the songs started as ideas, little snatches of melody played late at night on the tour bus, lyrics scribbled onto random sheets of paper and left like a trail of confetti in Freddie's wake. He was practically feverish, possessed by his own creativity, energy buzzing under his skin for weeks and weeks until he finally landed on a track list that he loved and that still made his label happy.

People are sometimes dismissive of Freddie because of his boyband start. But watching him take three chords and six measures and turn them into a song that hit number one on the Billboard charts was as impressive as it was captivating.

But this time around, it's been nothing like that.

Now, he's not writing at all. He *talks* about writing all the time. Hides himself away, certain that this time, inspiration will strike. But from the outside looking in, it mostly seems like he's spinning his wheels. I know he has at least a dozen tracks that *could* go on the album, so the situation isn't truly dire. But he isn't happy with them. He thinks the track list lacks cohesion, and it definitely doesn't have the *one song* everyone will remember most.

He runs a hand through his hair and licks his lips, reminding me of the kiss, of the conversation we *aren't* having. Honestly, I've been so tense all afternoon, it's a nice reprieve to just be here with him, to remember the parts of our friendship that I love.

"It's never been this hard," Freddie says.

I'm not sure I've ever heard this level of defeat in his voice. "Maybe it'll be better once you're with Leo. Maybe you just need time with him—or Adam, even. Did you decide whether to include the song he sent over?"

Freddie huffs out a laugh. "I'd be stupid not to. It's the only one that's any good."

I pull my knees up to my chest and wrap my arms around them. "I'm sure you'll get there."

"Will I?" He's quiet for a long beat before he says, "Sometimes I think about Adam living out on his farm, spending time with Laney, his dogs. Of course he can write songs, you know? He's *living.* What if I can't write because..."

He doesn't finish his sentence, but I can fill in the end easily enough. Is that really how he feels? Like he isn't living?

When he's on stage in an arena full of people all cheering his name or meeting women who have his tattoos inked all over their bodies—that doesn't feel like a life?

Maybe not. Those connections are all superficial. Freddie

has spent the last six months on the road, sleeping in a different city every night. He has me and Seth and the rest of his staff, but we all work for him. It's not exactly the same, is it?

"I don't know," he says, finally setting his guitar to the side. "I'll write something eventually. One more made-up love song." His tone shifts from discouraged to downright derisive, and a new thought pops into my brain.

Is Freddie lonely? Is that what this is about? He wants to be in love?

Despite my frustration, a very silly part of me wants to throw my arm into the air and volunteer as tribute. I'm right here, perfectly available, and mostly in love with him already. I know everything there is to know about the man—good and bad—and I still like him. That should count for something.

Except it can't, and every cell of my stupid body knows it.

Because if Freddie had even a smidgen of real feelings for me, would he have agreed to kiss me like it was no big deal? He was that sure of my romantic indifference. So sure that he didn't even hesitate before using me as a prop—a publicity stunt.

But more than that, it can't count because when Freddie hired me, I promised him it never would. I've honored every single term of our agreement except one. And I'll swallow that one until the day I die.

"What do you mean by one more made-up love song?" I say. "You've written a lot of love songs. They all feel real enough."

He runs a hand over his face, and for once, I can't tell what Freddie is feeling. I've gotten good at reading his emotions, but now, he's wearing a mask of indifference I can't interpret.

"You didn't come here to talk about my music," Freddie says. He breathes out a sigh, then sits up a little taller, sliding his legs toward his chest so he can rest his arms on top of his knees.

Silence settles between us, not quite awkward, just heavy with all the things we aren't saying. I'm normally one to jump right in, fill the silence, say the hard thing when no one else will. But for once, I hope Freddie will steer our conversation.

Finally, he says, "Ivy, I'm really sorry about what happened." He winces, tilting his head to the side, then says, "Not what happened. What I *did* by insisting to go with you today. I put you in an impossible situation."

Heat rushes to my cheeks, and I drop my gaze to the bed. I shouldn't feel embarrassed for asking him to kiss me. I really *was* just thinking about his career. And he already admitted it was a smart move. But I can't help feeling like he can see my emotions through my skin. Read the color flushing my cheeks and intuitively know how much I loved the feel of his lips against mine.

"I also really appreciate what you did—and your willingness to help," Freddie says. "The kiss was a perfect way to thwart whatever Margot might have done. But I hate that I've pulled you into the spotlight. I think you were acting with my best interest in mind, but I'm not sure I was doing the same for you. And I'm sorry for that."

I quickly shake my head. "I wouldn't have suggested it if I hadn't known what I was getting into," I say. "I've worked for you a long time. I know how these things work."

He stands and picks up his guitar, carrying it across the

room to the dresser where the case is lying open. He sets it inside, then turns to face me, pushing his hands into his pockets. "I gotta be honest. After this afternoon, I've been worried you might not be working for me anymore. That this might finally push you into quitting."

"I *asked* you to kiss me, Freddie. I'm not blaming you for anything here."

"Maybe you should," he says. "You do too much for me, Ivy. And I'm not sure I've been as aware or as appreciative as I should be."

"It's really not a big—"

"It is a big deal," he says, cutting me off. "So I'm just saying. Anything I can do for you in return, please tell me. Anything."

I hate that we're talking about this like it's a business transaction instead of something that involves actual feelings, but if I turn on the practical side of my brain, maybe I can play this to my advantage.

"How about a better job title?" I ask.

Freddie's eyebrows lift. "Really?"

"I'm more than your assistant, Freddie. And if I'm ever going to get a job at a record label, it would be nice to have a better title on my resume."

He frowns. "You're going to work for a record label?"

I bite my lip. "You've always known that was my goal."

"Right. I know. I just—" He runs a hand through his hair. "Are you not happy working for me?"

"Of course I'm happy. But I can't do this forever."

He swallows. "Right. I guess not. Whatever you want, then. You are definitely more than an assistant, and I'm sorry I haven't acknowledged that before now. Let's just call you my manager from now on."

"Thank you," I say, buoyed both by the acknowledgement and by how well he seemed to read what I needed to hear. I know Freddie feels this way about me. The man is generous with his praise and very self-aware when it comes to how little he can accomplish without me. But it still feels good to have him say it—and not just when he's trying to convince me to shop for his favorite candy at two in the morning.

"Is Carina okay?" Freddie asks.

"I assume so," I say. "She's sleeping and wasn't really sober enough to have a conversation before she crashed."

"I'm sure she'll be better in the morning," he says.

I swallow against the sudden tightness in my throat. "Yeah, I'm sure she will."

We're quiet for another beat before Freddie asks, "I assume you've talked to Kat? Gotten her take on the situation?"

I huff out a little laugh. "Yeah. She was very thorough."

Kat Michaels has been Freddie's publicist for years, and since she helped him weather his last PR crisis, it's easy to trust her. Though it feels a little different this time, since my name is on the line now too.

As far as Kat sees it, kissing me was the smartest thing Freddie could have done. He both distanced himself from Margot and gave the internet something to be excited about. It's only been a few hours, but Freddie is already trending in ways that are making his record label *very* happy.

"Just think of what would have happened otherwise," she said. "Honestly, Ivy, this is the kind of love story the public eats up. Famous rock star falls in love with a normal girl from Kansas. It's the plot of every romance novel."

"I'm not from Kansas," I argued, which, in retrospect,

seems like a stupid thing to say. I should have led with, "But we aren't in love."

"That's not the point," Kat said. "The point is, you *aren't* famous, and you still captured Freddie's heart. Or everyone thinks you did, and that's what matters most."

It took everything in me to swallow how much I wished her words were true.

Kat proceeded to walk me through her three-point plan.

Number one: Acknowledge the relationship but ask for privacy and respect.

Number two: orchestrate two or more public sightings as the release date of Freddie's new album approaches.

Number three: leak anonymous rumors that one or more songs on the new album are about me.

A few months after the album releases, we can hint at trouble in paradise, then issue a press release about our amicable breakup.

She made it seem simple. And I know the industry well enough to understand that things like this happen all the time. Actors in leading roles will hold hands on the red carpet just long enough to fuel rumors and create the kind of speculation that keeps people talking. Music artists collaborating on a song will stare into each other's eyes like they were only ever meant to sing to each other because listeners *want* to believe in love.

So much of entertainment is about telling stories. What's this but one more story? What does it truly hurt?

When I asked Freddie to kiss me, I didn't think it *would* hurt anything. I saw a problem, and I figured out a way to solve it.

But I couldn't have guessed how that kiss would feel. And if we do this, if I agree to go through with Kat's plan, I'll be leaning into feelings I'm supposed to be fighting. The effort might kill me. At the very least, it will utterly wreck my heart.

"Ivy," Freddie says, pulling me back to the present, "I know Kat thinks we should ride this, but I don't expect that of you. It's important to me that you know that."

"Does it matter?" I ask. "We kissed, Freddie. Even if we deny it, people will still talk."

He's quiet for a beat before he says, "You only have to ask, and I'll release a statement owning everything. Explaining why we were there, admitting that I acted in haste to protect my reputation and we are not, and never have been, in a relationship."

"It wasn't your idea though," I say.

"But nobody else knows that," he says. "Not even Sloane or Kat. As far as they know, I made the decision to kiss you. It was my idea. My plan. And I'll own all of it if that's what you want me to do."

I'm shaking my head before he's even finished his sentence. "You can't do that."

"I *can* do that. Or we can do nothing. Let the speculation die. Tell Kat we aren't going to deny anything, but we also don't want to push the narrative."

I breathe out a sigh. "Kat's plan is good. If it's going to keep you trending, it can only help your relationship with your label. You need them to be patient with you right now, and positive press that keeps your name in headlines will give them more incentive to extend your deadline."

He shrugs. "Maybe. But that's not really your problem to solve. If you don't want to fake a relationship with me, then we don't do it. I can figure out things with my label."

I appreciate his willingness to prioritize my needs first,

but at this point, we might be too far in for anything we do to make a difference. The kiss already happened, so people aren't going to stop speculating. Even if Freddie denied any romantic connection between us, people would still talk. Are we together and just trying to hide it? Trying to throw them off our trail so we can have a little privacy? And what would people say about Margot? How would *she* respond to the news? Would she start spinning new lies about why we were at her beach house?

As long as we're together and very publicly in love, whatever Margot claims about Freddie won't hold any water.

As terrible as she's been to Freddie over the years, she doesn't deserve a single headline that includes his name.

I'm not thrilled about what it will do to my reputation as a "very serious" businesswoman in the music industry, but I'm not sure one look is better than the other. Do I want to be the woman Freddie Ridgefield used in a cover-up to fend off Margot Valemont's claws, or the woman who dated Freddie Ridgefield for a few months before parting ways with no bad feelings?

Honestly, maybe I'm overthinking, and it doesn't matter either way. I *do* have connections. If I truly wanted to get a job somewhere else, Freddie would only have to make one phone call, and I'd probably have three different offers on the table. That's the kind of sway he has in this industry.

And he'd definitely do that for me.

Even if he didn't want to let me go. If I asked him, he'd call any music executive I wanted him to.

It's more a question of whether I'll have the courage to actually leave him. I'm so completely enmeshed in Freddie's life, I'm not even sure what mine would look like without him.

But how long can I keep that up?

How long *should* I keep it up?

Telling him I want to move out as soon as we're back in Nashville was a minor miracle. And asking for a new job title was another step in the right direction.

But getting myself fully and completely out of his grasp? I might need to gamify things—give myself a guaranteed exit strategy.

"I'll do it," I blurt out, startling us both. I take a steadying breath. "I'll do whatever Kat thinks is best. Fake a relationship. Make public appearances. All of it." It suddenly occurs to me that might mean kissing him again, and my skin flushes with the thought. I lick my lips. "But only on one condition."

Freddie nods. "Okay. Lay it on me."

I swallow against the anxiety clawing its way up my throat. "As soon as your album releases, you call your record label and get them to hire me. I want to work for Voltage Records."

CHAPTER ELEVEN

Ivy

After my conversation with Freddie, it takes me a very long time to fall asleep. Mostly because I can't stop cataloging all the reasons why faking a relationship with Freddie Ridgefield is a terrible idea.

A small part of my brain wonders if I agreed because of how much I wish we could be in a relationship for real.

If we can't be, maybe faking is the next best thing?

It's a ridiculous thought. But as I toss and turn, readjusting my hotel pillow for the millionth time, my brain keeps circling back to the feel of his lips on mine, and I find myself hoping that at some point, I'll have a reason to kiss him again.

I manage to grab a few hours of sleep, but I wake up just after six a.m. and make the mistake of reaching for my phone. As soon as I see the screen, lit up with dozens of notifications, any hope of going *back* to sleep quickly vanishes.

I glance over at Carina, still snoring softly on the other

side of our king-size bed. As early as she crashed yesterday, she can't sleep much longer, but I try to be quiet anyway. We need to have a serious conversation as soon as she's awake, and I'd rather have my wits about me—read: coffee in my bloodstream—before we do.

After a shower and a latte I have delivered from the coffee shop a block away from the hotel, I sneak into the bathroom with my cell phone and laptop and start wading through my many notifications. They've doubled since I first woke up, and they include a text from my mom that, based on the first few words visible in the notification, I'm nervous to read in full.

Bracing myself, I open the message and squint at my phone, reading it through one eye.

MOM

IVY CLARE CONWAY, why did you not tell me your boss kissed you? THIS IS SO EXCITING! Assuming you're excited. You are, right? This is a good thing? I always suspected there was something going on between the two of you. I want all the details as soon as you have time!

Well. Okay, then. I thought her all-caps use of my name might take the message in a different direction, but this isn't that bad.

Except, it *is* bad. Because now I have to decide if I tell my parents that it's all a publicity stunt. Mom would understand, but my salt-of-the-earth father would find the whole situation utterly ridiculous. He hates pretense. He's honest and straightforward and thinks the truth should *always* be most important.

I don't disagree with him—most of the time. But the situation is so much more complicated. Too complicated. Which is why I settle on a benign response to my mom that feels true, even if it isn't the *entire* truth.

IVY

Definitely exciting. I'm swamped with work —kind of a lot of PR stuff happening right now—but I'll call soon and fill you in!

MOM

Sounds good. How's Carina?

I exhale slowly, happy she bought my excuse. At least for now.

IVY

Still sleeping.

MOM

I'm so glad she's safe. Will she stay with you until you're back in Tennessee?

IVY

We only have one more show before the break, and it's tonight, so she can travel back with me. Freddie won't mind.

MOM

Not now, he won't. ;)

The winking emoji makes me smile, even as it triggers a tiny twinge of guilt I choose to ignore.

IVY

I'll call you once Carina is up and we've had the chance to talk.

MOM
Thanks. I'm glad you're there for her. So grateful for you and your steadying presence.

I read her last text two times before I set the phone face down on the counter and reach for my laptop. That's always been my role when it comes to Carina. Keep her safe. Help her make good choices. Set a good example.

I don't mind it. Not really. But sometimes I hardly feel capable of making good choices for *myself*, much less someone else, my present circumstances notwithstanding.

After reading—and ignoring—a few more Freddie-related messages from old friends, approving a stack of invoices from the tour's catering team, and reading through the first draft of Kat's press release, I order Carina a new cell phone and make arrangements for it to be delivered to the hotel before we leave in the morning.

"Ivy?"

I jump off the closed toilet seat where I set up office and fling open the door. "Hey! You're awake!"

Carina's face is flushed, but her eyes are clear, and a wave of relief washes over me.

She yawns. "What time is it? Did I sleep all night?"

"It's almost eight." I move to the dresser where I left a latte for her. I pick it up and carry it over. "It's still warm," I say, handing her the cup. "I don't know how they insulate these so well. Magic, probably."

She takes it with one hand while she rubs her eyes with the other, smudging a little mascara onto her cheek. "Where's Freddie?"

"A few rooms over. Probably still asleep. He has a show tonight. How are you feeling?"

She takes a long sip of her latte before looking around the room like she can't quite figure out how she got here. "Foggy," she finally says.

"I bet." I move over to my bag and pull out some acetaminophen, then take them back to her. "You'll probably need these."

She nods gratefully and swallows them down.

There are a million questions coursing through my brain, the loudest one being, *What on earth were you thinking?!* But what's done is done. Asking that question isn't going to change anything that already happened.

I sit on the edge of the bed and tug my feet up, crossing them under me. "How much do you remember about yesterday?"

She frowns. "Bits and pieces. It was bad, wasn't it?"

"Yeah. You were pretty out of it." I hesitate a beat before asking, "Was it just alcohol?"

She quickly nods. "I didn't do any of the harder stuff. I mean, not really. I had some weed yesterday morning. I was probably a tiny bit high when you showed up."

"But have you been drinking every day? You were at the beach house, what, two weeks? Please tell me you weren't just partying the whole time."

She shrugs, her eyes darting away like that's *exactly* what she was doing.

I force myself to take a deep breath. "Carina—"

"I know," she says, cutting me off. "I know. Please don't lecture me. I was thinking about Daphne the whole time, and I was so careful because of that. But Margot was just being so nice to me and acting like I was her very favorite person. I was wearing her clothes, eating all this delicious food—caterers were constantly in and out. And so many famous people were there, Ivy." She sits up a little taller. "You would not believe the things I saw."

I *would* believe it, which is exactly why it makes my stomach churn to think of Carina in the middle of it.

"When did your phone break?"

"Like the second freaking day," Carina says. "It was so annoying. Then Margot kept saying she'd get me a new one, then that she *had* gotten me a new one and it would be there any minute. But I think she was probably lying to me the whole time. Seems like something she would do."

"I wouldn't put it past her," I say. "I ordered you a new phone. So we don't need one from her anyway. It should be delivered within the hour."

Carina blinks. "You just...ordered a whole new phone? Isn't that, like, at least a thousand bucks?"

I wave a dismissive hand. "Freddie can afford it as well as Margot can. And he insisted because he feels responsible. Since you met Margot at his release party."

On this, I didn't fight Freddie. He pays me well enough that I could have afforded to buy it myself, but I know Freddie, and I know how guilty he feels about everything that happened. For him, paying to replace Carina's phone is a small thing financially but a big thing emotionally.

I won't take that away from him just to make a point.

"Tell him thanks for me," Carina says.

"You can tell him yourself," I say. "I figured you'd just fly home with us tomorrow."

"You're going home?"

"Back to Nashville. We've got two months off. I can drive you the rest of the way to Knoxville once we're there."

"Or I could just stay with you in Nashville," she says, a little too eagerly.

"I'm not inviting you to crash at Freddie's place," I say. "We've had this conversation before."

She rolls her eyes. "It's not like his place isn't big enough."

"Not the point."

I almost tell her that as soon as I have my own place, she can come stay with me anytime she wants. But she'll want to know all my reasons for moving out of my very free living situation, and that's not a conversation I feel like having right now.

Besides, if she thought she had a chance, I can easily see her wanting to move in with me full time. She's never lived away from home—she lived with Mom and Dad while she attended UT—so she'd probably love to get out on her own. But I'm not sure living with *me* is the right answer.

It's hard enough not to worry about her all the time as it is. If I were constantly aware of what she's up to and where she's going, I might never sleep.

And Mom would probably call me twelve million times a day.

Carina flops back onto her pillows, propping herself up enough that she can reach for her latte and take a long sip. "So when you say *fly home with us,* are we talking on a commercial flight? Or...on Freddie's plane?" She looks much too excited about this possibility.

"Freddie does not have his own plane."

"So we *are* flying commercial," she says.

"It's a private plane that we chartered for the trip. But trust me when I say America's airports do not want to deal with Freddie Ridgefield on a commercial flight. This is definitely easiest on everyone."

"Chill," Carina says. "I'm not going to send you hate mail

about his carbon footprint. I'm just happy I get to see Freddie again." Carina says this with a breezy nonchalance, but I don't miss the excitement dancing in her eyes. She likes to act like she's no longer star-struck when she's around Freddie—she's met him multiple times—but she's clearly still impacted.

Honestly, if this is what it takes to keep her from fighting me, I'm happy to exploit Freddie's fame to suit my purposes. At least in this sense.

A knock sounds on the door, and I move to it, guessing correctly that it's a member of the hotel staff bringing up Carina's new phone. I carry the Apple bag back into the room and toss it onto the bed.

"How did this even work?" she asks, reaching for the phone. "Did the hotel staff just go buy one for you? They do crap like that?"

"People will do anything when there are enough dollar signs attached," I say. I sit down on the foot of the bed and face her. "So I was thinking, to repay me—"

"You mean Freddie," she says saucily.

"To repay Freddie," I say, amending my statement, "do you want to tell me how you wound up with Margot in the first place?"

She sighs and sets her latte on the nightstand before leaning back on her pillows, her unopened iPhone resting on her chest. "She texted me," she finally says. "Offered to buy my plane ticket. She even sent a driver to pick me up at the house and drive me to the airport."

I stare at her for a long moment before asking, "Honey, why didn't you tell me?" I put all my effort into keeping my tone gentle instead of judgmental. "This is Margot we're talking about."

"That's exactly why I didn't tell you," she says. "Because I knew that's what you'd say. She was offering me a summer in her Malibu beach house. Who says no to that?"

"Mom said she got the sense you were running from something. She thought maybe it was the fruitless job hunting."

Carina rolls her eyes. "Geez, it's only been two months. And it hasn't been entirely fruitless. I have an interview in a couple of weeks."

I lift my eyebrows. "That you still would have gone to had I left you in Malibu?"

She doesn't answer, but the shifty look that crosses over her expression tells me everything I need to know.

"You know you can be honest with me," I say, and she gives her head a tiny shake. Like she thinks maybe she *can't* be.

I reach forward and squeeze her ankle through the comforter covering the bed.

"I know it probably feels stressful just living with Mom and Dad, not knowing what you're going to do next. And I even get wanting to get away for a little while, though I *really* wish you hadn't chosen Margot. But..." I hesitate, because I don't know how to say what I want to say without it sounding like I'm judging my sister, and that isn't what I'm trying to do.

"But you wish I hadn't been drinking?" Carina says, finishing for me, and I breathe out a sigh, relieved that she said the words for me.

"It was hard to see you like that," I say.

She holds my gaze for a long moment, and something passes between us, some sisterly awareness that says far more than anything our words could cover. Carina's expression softens, and for a split second, it almost feels like Daphne is in the room with us—a whisper of air brushing against my cheek, an extra beat of blood pumping through my heart.

The logical side of me knows it's possible to drink responsibly. But the emotional side can't separate the smell of alcohol from the sound of the sirens responding to the scene of Daphne's accident.

"I know," Carina says, her voice small. "I knew you'd be disappointed. But..." She takes a deep breath. "Ivy, this wasn't the first time I've had a drink."

My heart squeezes tighter than I expect at her admission. I don't want it to matter. Carina is twenty-one. She's entitled to make her own decisions. I always knew she might drink, and I've told myself I wouldn't judge her if she did.

But then, it's never been about judgment. It's been about fear.

I already lost one sister.

I can't lose another.

And any choice she makes that increases her risk even a little bit is a choice I don't want her to make.

"Okay," I manage to say. "I guess that's..."

I press my palms into my thighs, wishing I knew how to finish my sentence. Maybe I'm just drained from everything that happened with Freddie, but I feel completely incapable of processing my emotions. I definitely can't turn them into words.

"I didn't make good choices with Margot," Carina says. "I'll own that. I let her celebrity and her money go to my head. But I might still have a cocktail with my friends every once in a while. And I feel like Daphne would be okay with that."

It takes me a long time to look up to meet my sister's eyes. When I do, they're wide and clear, her expression calm. Carina has always been my baby sister—someone I have to protect. Keep safe. But now, she looks all grown up. Like an adult.

Still, I can't keep my voice from cracking when I say, "But you promised."

"I know," she says. "And I'm glad I did. I didn't touch the stuff through all of high school, and trust me, I had so many opportunities. You did such a good job of making the world safe for me." She sits up a little bit and reaches for my hand, giving it a quick squeeze. "But sometimes, it feels like staying in that box, it's...keeping me from actually living."

"You don't have to drink alcohol to live," I say, my tone defensive.

Carina winces. "I know. Of course I know that. I'm saying this all wrong. It isn't even about the drinking, really. I just mean that—Ivy, you can't control everything. You aren't going to be able to *always* keep me safe."

"That's not what I'm trying to do."

"You drove all the way to Malibu to retrieve me from a beach house," Carina says. "It's exactly what you were doing."

"You weren't responding to my texts!" I say, finally getting defensive. "And you were with Margot Valemont, of all people. I couldn't just leave you there."

"I *did* text," she says. "I tried to tell you I was fine."

I roll my eyes. "Carina, your message was full of typos. You sounded drunk. Which, maybe you were. Since that seems to be your new thing now."

I regret the words as soon as they're out of my mouth.

Carina isn't a drunk just because she spent two weeks partying.

But is she for real right now? She was with Margot, and she wanted me to just sit by and let her do her thing? Assume the pictures on Instagram were proof enough that she was alive and well?

"I shouldn't have used my present circumstances as an example," Carina says, her voice remarkably calm for how elevated she just made me. "But generally, Ivy, you know you do it. You drew me twelve different maps my freshman year at UT, showing me all the safest routes from my dorm to every single one of my classes. And you weren't even a student there."

"Those maps were useful," I say, and Carina offers me a small smile before sitting up all the way and scooting toward me. She echoes my posture, sitting cross-legged on the bed, and reaches forward, taking both my hands in hers.

I begrudgingly comply, hating that Carina is somehow still charming me, even though I haven't decided if I should forgive her for landing Freddie—and me—in the middle of a massive PR crisis she doesn't even know about yet.

"They *were* useful," she says. "And I will always believe that I have the best big sister on the whole planet. But I'm not a dummy. You have to let me grow up. You have to trust me to decide for myself what kinds of risks I want to take." She squeezes my hands. "And maybe you ought to take a few risks of your own."

I roll my eyes. "Seriously? You're gonna say I'm the one who never takes any risks? Have you forgotten what I do for a living?"

"Shut up. Your life is planned down to the minute. You never take any risks."

"I took a job from a complete stranger whom I met in a bathroom."

"Okay, that's fair. But he wasn't *actually* a stranger."

"Definitely still a stranger," I say. "Just because I knew his name didn't mean I knew *him*."

"Fine," Carina says. "Five points for the *one time* you were brave five years ago."

I purse my lips, happy to have won the point, but I can't keep my brain from imagining all the risks she thinks I'm *not* taking.

Except, she has to be wrong. Just because I'm not *impulsive* doesn't mean I don't take risks. I cross my arms over my chest. "I need an example."

"An example of you not taking risks?" she says, and I nod. She smirks. "You've never told Freddie how you feel."

I narrow my eyes. I've never told Carina how I feel about Freddie. Which means...what? She thinks she knows something about my feelings based on her own observations?

That has to be it, because as far as I know, she was already in the car when Freddie kissed me yesterday, and since she hasn't said anything about it, I feel safe assuming she didn't see it happen. And since she doesn't have a phone, at least one not still wrapped in cellophane, and she's been dead asleep for the past fourteen hours, she hasn't seen any of the online buzz.

"I do not have feelings for Freddie," I say, but the words sound completely hollow. If Mom figured me out, I guess it shouldn't surprise me that Carina did too.

"Yes, you do. It doesn't matter how many times you deny it. You aren't going to make it any less true."

"What makes you so sure?" I ask, clinging to the last tattered shreds of my denial.

Carina grins. "Mom was the one who first suggested it, but once she did, I started looking for clues, and they were so easy to spot."

"Clues? Like what?"

She holds up her hands, ticking things off on her fingers. "The way you look at him, the way your voice changes when you talk about him, the way you have literally dated no one since you started working for him."

"I have definitely dated," I say.

She gives me a pointed look.

"A few times," I amend.

"Just admit it," she says, her tone gentle. "At least admit it to me."

I fold my arms across my chest, holding her gaze for a long moment before finally caving. "Fine," I say. "I have feelings. Happy now?"

Her shoulders bunch around her ears as she smiles wide, clapping her hands like I've just given her the best news. "This is so exciting!" she practically yells.

I lift my palms to my face and groan. "It is not exciting. It's a giant colossal mess, thanks to you. This whole situation is so incredibly stupid."

"Wait. What situation?" Carina asks. "You working for him?"

"Yes. But no. More than that. This whole—" I push myself to my feet and motion to her even as I start pacing around the room. "Honestly, I should be mad at you for this. It wouldn't have happened if we hadn't had to come pick you up."

She frowns. "Wait, what do I have to do with anything? What are you talking about?"

I sigh and prop my hands on my hips. "Freddie kissed me."

"What?"

"Yesterday outside the beach house. You were already inside the car, but Margot was coming, and there was a photographer, so I asked him to kiss me."

Her eyebrows bunch up, like she's puzzling out my words. "You *asked* him to kiss you."

I shrug. "We had to give the photographer a bigger story."

It takes her a few more questions, but finally, Carina seems to grasp what happened.

"So it was your idea," she says. "To have your boss—who you happen to be in love with—kiss you in front of a photographer? What happened? Were the photos released?"

I breathe out a sigh. "They were."

"So the whole world thinks you're dating Freddie Ridgefield."

"It was the only practical choice," I argue, but Carina hardly seems to care about practicalities.

"Oh my gosh!" she practically screams as she jumps up in the center of the bed. She pauses, wobbling as one hand moves to her head. "Whoa. Maybe too soon for that kind of excitement."

I roll my eyes and step close enough to offer her a hand. She braces against me as she steps off the bed and finds her balance. "You good?"

She nods, moving her hands to my shoulders. "Ivy, this is perfect."

"It's nothing of the sort."

"It is! Because now he will fall in love with you. I mean, if he hasn't already, which, it honestly wouldn't surprise me if he has."

"Don't say stuff like that," I say, shrugging out of her grip and moving around the bed to pick up her discarded coffee. "You should drink this. And eat something."

"Stop momming me for five seconds," she says with a heavy dose of Carina-style drama, "and tell me why I shouldn't say that."

I sigh and take a long swig of her coffee, which is finally starting to feel cold. I turn and put the cup down, keeping my back to Carina for a long moment before I finally say, "Because I don't want to get my hopes up."

She steps closer and wraps her arms around my shoulders from behind. "Okay. I feel you. So what are you going to do?"

I tilt my head to the side, resting my head on her arm as I relax into her embrace. "Survive, I guess. Endure until his album is out and then make a clean break and start fresh."

"Um, that sounds like a terrible idea," Carina says. "What will you be enduring, and what do you mean *start fresh*? You're going to stop working for Freddie?"

I breathe out a sigh. "Let's get food," I say. "Then I'll explain everything."

CHAPTER TWELVE

Freddie

Six months.

That's how long I have left with Ivy. Long enough for the album to come out and for her to train her replacement.

I won't lie and pretend like our conversation last night wasn't a complete and total gut punch. It was bad enough knowing she wants to move out as soon as we get back to Nashville. But when she said she wanted to work for my label instead of me, a hollowness settled into my chest, and I'm not sure anything is going to fill it.

It doesn't even matter that I know she'd be great working for Voltage, helping an entire roster of artists rather than giving all her attention to me. That logic only gets me so far. I still feel like I'm losing her—like she's slipping out of my grasp for good.

But maybe she won't find her own place after all. At least for the time being. Not sure how we'd spin that to the press if she's seen moving out when we're supposed to be in a happy relationship.

"What do you think?" Kat says. "All sound agreeable?"

I've been so preoccupied thinking about Ivy, I actually have no idea what my publicist has been saying for the past five minutes, but I'm not about to tell her that, so I just nod. "Good," I say. "Great."

She purses her lips, leaning forward so her face fills up the entirety of my phone screen. Kat Michaels lives in New York, but she's surprisingly effective at working over Face-Time and Zoom, and our current phone call is no exception. I've only met her in person a handful of times, but her work speaks for itself. She's as relentless as Sloane, with the same sense of uncompromising integrity that makes me like working with her. She's not above faking a relationship for a little bit of PR—that's just spin, her words, not mine—but she made it clear she will not move forward with the plan if Ivy isn't on board.

"And you're sure Ivy isn't going to change her mind?"

"I can't promise that," I say. "We're asking a lot of her, Kat. If she wants to end things at any moment, I won't stop her or try to convince her not to."

Kat smiles tightly. "Generous of you," she says. "But please don't stop thinking about how much harder you'll make my job if this gets messy."

"It's already messy, isn't it?" I say. "The relationship isn't real, and we're pretending it is."

"We aren't going to say anything that isn't true," she argues. "Ivy means a lot to you. You'd consider her a close friend, wouldn't you? All we're doing is presenting a relation-ship to the public and letting them decide what to think.

That relationship could be something romantic, but it could also be something more like friendship."

"I thought you said we're doing a press release acknowledging the relationship," I say.

"We are, but it will be artfully vague. No lies, just the very intentional power of suggestion. As long as you and Ivy know where you both stand, I think you'll come through all right in the end."

A valid point, except Ivy and I *don't* know where we stand. I haven't told Ivy that when I kissed her, I felt a glimmer of something real. More than a glimmer—if I'm being honest. Or that when I think about her moving on, working for someone else, I'm overwhelmed with a sort of desperate, preemptive loneliness.

So Ivy and I are pretending, letting the world think we're in love, but I'm pretending with Ivy too. And I guess I'm also pretending with Kat, since I'm not being honest with her either. But I can't be honest with *anyone* if I have no idea how to make sense of my own feelings, and so far, the only thing I know for sure is how confused I am.

"Artfully vague, huh?"

"It's my specialty," Kat says. "Just trust me to handle this."

Across the room, Wayne stands and motions toward the door. "Time to go," he mouths.

I sigh and stand so I can follow Wayne to the open hotel room door. "Fine. I get it. Just let us read the press release first, all right?"

"I already sent it to Ivy," she says. "Review it together, then let me know when you're ready to launch."

"I gotta go," I say. "We're headed to the arena."

"Break a leg," Kat says. "Oh, and Freddie, if you wanted

to hold your assistant's hand on your way into the concert, I wouldn't be mad about it."

I wouldn't be mad about holding Ivy's hand, but a part of me still bristles at the thought of doing it just because Kat suggested it.

Ivy is already in the car when Wayne and I reach the black SUV that will drive us two blocks to the concert venue. I climb into the seat beside her, and a sudden yearning fills my chest, a desire to be close to her that takes me by surprise. It takes all my willpower to resist the impulse to shift across the bench seat so we're side by side.

Ivy's phone is up to her ear, but she pulls it away long enough to turn it to face me. Her Mom's picture fills the screen, and I nod my understanding as she returns her attention to the call.

Wayne climbs into the front seat of the SUV and looks at me over his shoulder. "Good to go?"

I nod, even as Ivy starts talking into the phone. "I promise she's good," she says. "A little hungover. But she's young. She'll bounce back quick. I really think you should call her." She's quiet for a beat before she adds, "I *do* think she'll answer. She told me she would." Another pause. "Same phone number. You won't be interrupting anything. I left her in the hotel room with a pizza and the five-hour version of *Pride and Prejudice*. But she can pause that long enough to talk." After another beat of silence, Ivy rolls her eyes. "Seriously? Fine, fine. Hang on." She puts the phone on speaker and looks pointedly at me. "She wants to say hi."

I grin. "Hi, Mrs. Conway."

"Hi, Freddie. I hope you're taking good care of my daughter."

I meet Ivy's gaze and lift my eyebrows.

She gives her head a quick shake, a silent answer to my question. She has *not* told her mom the truth.

Interesting.

I clear my throat. "I'm doing my best," I say.

"You'll have to come out to the farm when you're back in Tennessee. Stay a few days. We'd love to see you. We'll have a new baby in a couple weeks. That'd be a great time to come."

"Donkey," Ivy silently mouths. "Baby donkey."

"I'd love that," I say. "Will I be able to meet Pirate? He's the donkey with one eye, right?" I've heard a lot about the tree farm where Ivy grew up, and she's shown me dozens of pictures. But I've never been there in person.

Honestly, it feels weird I *haven't* been there in person, and I have a sudden desire to see Ivy's childhood home.

"Pirate and all the others," Mom says. "I might even have a few baby goats, though that rescue is still up in the air. Not sure they'll need me. But there's always something to see, with or without the goats."

"Sounds amazing," I say. "Thanks for the invitation."

"Of course! You have a great show tonight. And y'all be good to each other."

Ivy's gaze shifts to mine, and we stare for a long moment, her mother's words hanging between us. But then Ivy gives her head a little shake, and she looks back at the phone.

"Bye, Mom," she says.

"Bye," she calls back. "Love you lots."

"Um, I definitely want to meet the new baby donkey," I say as Ivy drops her phone in her lap.

"You'll never escape," Ivy says. "Mom will want to keep you. She'll also tell you you're too skinny and you need to eat more of her fried chicken, which, honestly, that's not a mistake. It's the best I've ever had."

That same yearning from before fills my chest. I do not have the kind of family who fosters much sense of belonging. The idea of Ivy's mom wanting to *keep me* sounds nice.

Silence settles between us as the SUV turns at the next intersection and the arena comes into view. Fans are already lined up outside the building, filling the sidewalk and clustering around the merch tents set up outside. One woman in a Midnight Rush t-shirt points at the SUV, then nudges her friend.

The windows are too dark for them to see who's inside, but it still makes my skin prickle with awareness that all those people out there are here to see me.

"So, you didn't tell your mom, then," I say, turning my attention back to Ivy.

"I will eventually. But—I didn't want to complicate things. My dad won't really understand the PR side of this."

I nod, wondering if I should have a conversation with *my* parents. They don't exactly follow me online—they find the fame side of what I do utterly baffling. But telling them still feels like the courteous thing to do.

"I should—"

"Call your parents?" Ivy finishes for me. "I thought you might want to. You'll have about fifteen minutes after soundcheck. Maybe you could call them then?"

"Perfect."

"After that, I thought we could review the press release Kat sent over. While you're eating. Does that work?"

Ivy has shifted into work mode, which...of course she has. The hours immediately before a concert are busy for us both. But it still feels odd for her to be focusing on her regular job while I'm sitting here wondering if I should hold her hand when we get out of the SUV.

"Yep. Sounds good," I agree, swallowing all my other concerns.

She shifts in her seat, making a note on her phone, and I catch the scent of her—something floral and a little fruity. Whatever it is, I really like it.

"You smell good," I say without really thinking about it. "Is it something new?"

Her cheeks turn the palest shade of pink. "Oh, uh—no. Just not something I wear all that often. It isn't too much?"

"It's amazing," I say, and she bites her lip. Usually, Ivy's approach to her wardrobe, at least when it comes to shows, is entirely practical. She wears a lot of sneakers and hoodies. Band t-shirts. Jeans. She probably logs a million miles every concert taking care of everything that needs to be done. She dresses for comfort, and I wouldn't expect anything different.

She's still in jeans today, but she's wearing a tank top that hugs her curves and a black leather jacket I've never seen before. She's also wearing earrings, just visible through the dark curls framing her face. And does she have on more makeup than usual?

She looks really good. Like, turn-my-head-on-the-street good.

"What?" she says, lifting her hands to cover her face. "Is it too much? You're staring at me like it's too much."

"No!" I quickly say. "You look amazing. Just different."

She peeks through her fingers. "Really? You aren't just saying that?"

"I wouldn't say it if it wasn't true."

"Yes, you would," she says. "You're nice enough that you'd absolutely lie to me to spare my feelings."

"Okay, probably," I say, "but I promise that's not what I'm doing now. You really do look nice." I reach over and wrap my hands around her wrists, tugging them from her face. "Now stop or you might mess it all up."

She lets me tug her hands down, but then she huffs out a sigh, dislodging one of her curls and tossing it askew.

I shift her hands so I'm holding them both with one of mine, then lift the other to her face, sliding the curl away from her cheek.

She holds my gaze for a long moment, and something turns over behind my ribs.

"I think I just thought," she finally says, but then she hesitates, her tongue darting out to slide along her bottom lip. I squeeze her hand, urging her to continue in the only way I know how. She takes a deep breath. "If people are speculating about us being together, I guess I just...wanted to make sure I look the part."

It hadn't even occurred to me that our fake relationship might have something to do with Ivy's extra effort, but now that she's said it out loud, it makes perfect sense. Not that she *needed* to make an extra effort. She always looks amazing, something I still feel stupid for never truly noticing until now. But I get it. She's never had the spotlight on her before —not really. And she definitely will now.

"You look amazing," I say, rubbing my thumb across the back of her hand. "Truly."

If Wayne turned around and told us we were stuck in traffic and it was going to be another four hours before we arrived at the concert venue, I wouldn't mind it. That's how much I'd like to sit right here, Ivy's hand in mine, and stare into her eyes. But then the SUV rolls to a stop, and Wayne unbuckles his seatbelt.

A lot of venues have underground parking garages so we can get inside without having to walk past any public areas, but here, we're in a narrow parking lot in an alleyway beside the arena. Maybe twenty yards away, a barrier blocks the alley from the sidewalk, and a security officer stands guard. Fans are lined up on the other side of the barrier, and I can already hear their screams. They can't know for sure I'm the one inside the SUV, but based on the volume of their cheers, they seem pretty confident in their guesswork.

When I first started touring, I might have walked the short distance to the barrier and spent some time signing autographs and taking photos, but these days, the security it requires to make that happen is more headache than it's worth. I can already hear Wayne listing off the reasons why it isn't a good idea.

But Kat's words are still fresh in my mind. Maybe I can't interact with the crowd, but they could at least see me and Ivy together.

"We should hold hands," she says before I can suggest it. She's staring out the window at the gathered fans, but as soon as the words are out of her mouth, she turns and looks back at me. "Maybe you could stop and wave?"

"Are you sure you wouldn't mind?"

She shrugs. "It's the plan, right? Also, you just told me I look *amazing,* Freddie. If fans are going to take pictures of us every chance they get, I'd rather it happen now when I don't look like a bridge troll."

I huff out a laugh. "You could never look like a bridge troll."

"Trust me. I can." She holds out her palm face up, and I thread my fingers through hers.

"You're sure about this?" I study the uncertainty in Ivy's

expression and tell myself this is a good thing. It's the thing we want. The thing we *need* so we can be in charge of the story.

But I suddenly wonder what would happen if I asked Ivy to be with me for real. What would she say?

A relationship with me surely seems like a gamble. The traveling, the lack of privacy, the demanding schedule. It wouldn't be easy.

Then again, she already knows that. She's been living this life with me for five years.

And...she just told me she wants to work for someone else, to move out of my house. She's clearly craving a normalcy I can't give her.

A fake relationship is probably the only thing I'm ever going to get.

"Absolutely not," Ivy says. "But we're doing it anyway, and I'm okay with that."

I look at Wayne, who is watching expectantly, waiting for my cue. "Okay," I say, squeezing Ivy's hand. "Let's do it."

He nods, then exits the car, circling around to the door closest to the arena. This means Ivy will get out first, but that's not what I want. I want to go first so I can turn and help her—make it look less like she's working for me and more like I'm paying attention, taking care of *her* for a change.

"Here, switch places with me," I say as Wayne opens the door.

"What?"

"Let me get out first," I say.

"Why? Does it really matter?"

"If you're my assistant, you get out first," I say. "But you aren't. Not anymore."

"Technically, I *am*," Ivy argues, but she still unbuckles her seatbelt and climbs over the front of me. The car suddenly seems very small for this kind of movement, but we're committed, so I lift my arms to give her as much room as possible.

Ivy only makes it halfway before the button on the sleeve of her jacket snags on the zipper on the front of my hoodie.

"Wait, wait," I say, shifting my hands to her hips to stop her movement. "You're caught."

She relaxes her weight, sitting down on my lap so she's fully straddling me. "Am I?" she asks, but then she seems to see and sets to work trying to free herself from my clothes. "Oh," she grumbles. "Well, this is annoying."

I should be annoyed, but I'm mostly just thinking about how good it feels to have her against me like this, my hands resting on the curve of her hips, her knees bracketing either side of my lap. That's a dangerous train of thought though, so I tilt my gaze upward and force myself to think about something else.

My favorite hockey team just made it to the Stanley Cup Playoffs. That's exciting. They're a relatively new franchise, and no one thought they stood a chance this year. I wonder if I could get tickets to a game. I bet Wayne would enjoy that—

"There," Ivy finally says as she shifts off my lap. "Free. Sorry about that."

I clear my throat. "No worries," I say. But the tightness pinching a spot right behind my ribs makes me think I *should* be worried.

"Whenever you're ready, Freddie," Wayne says from where he's standing by the open car door.

"Right. Got it," I say sliding toward the door. When I

meet Wayne's gaze, he gives me an amused look that seems to say *he* thinks I should be worried too.

I step out of the car, and the cheers of the onlooking fans grow even louder. I don't look at them—not yet. I stay focused on Ivy, holding out my hand, which she takes as she emerges from the car. As soon as she's upright, I tuck an arm around her shoulders, pulling her into my side, and guide us toward the arena.

If I thought the cheers were loud before, they're twice that as soon as everyone sees us together.

A strange sense of protectiveness surges inside me. I'm used to fans looking at me, screaming at *me,* but knowing they're watching Ivy now too—that's different.

I tug her even closer, my hand sliding under the hem of her jacket and settling into the curve of her waist. But it doesn't feel like enough. I don't know how to protect her from this. From everything that comes with *me.*

"We should wave at them," she says, slowing her steps.

I'm too lost in my thoughts to protest, so I follow Ivy's lead, turning and lifting an arm to wave at the watching crowd.

Kat's going to be thrilled, because we couldn't possibly look more like a couple.

Ivy leans in, her lips close to my ear. "You're tense. Is everything okay?"

I nod, but I still don't move my feet. Not until Ivy hooks her hand through mine and tugs us forward.

Seconds later, we're inside the arena, a heavy steel door cutting us off from the noise of the crowd outside.

"What happened?" Ivy says. "You okay? You completely froze out there."

"No, I...I'm good," I say as I take in her face, the concern in her deep brown eyes.

For years, it's only been me in the spotlight. I've dated, yes. But only people who are also famous. Who are used to the spotlight like I am.

Practically speaking, I knew this would happen when we decided to move forward with Kat's plan. But understanding it *will* happen and actually experiencing it are two different things.

Even though Ivy has been with me for years, she's never had to step into the spotlight. Not like this.

I feel a sudden *desperate* need to protect her from it. Like I would do anything—walk away from all of it—if that's what it took to keep her safe.

I've never felt anything like this before, and it over-whelms me. It feels like my brain is realigning, priorities clicking into a new and different order.

"I'm good," I repeat. "Sorry. I don't know what happened."

She studies me closely. "Are you sure?"

"Yeah. Yeah, I'm sure."

"Okay," she says. "Then I'm going to go find Seth." She glances at her watch. "You'll be ready for soundcheck in a few minutes?"

I nod. "Absolutely."

She turns and heads down the hallway, leaving me with Wayne and a member of the arena staff who just showed up, presumably to take me to my dressing room. I fully under-stand why Ivy has to be in work mode right now, but that doesn't mean I don't wish she was still standing beside me.

Wayne lets out a chuckle, and I frown. "What? Why are you laughing?"

"No reason."

"You have to have a reason."

We move down the hallway side by side, but my grouchy security guard doesn't say anything else, not until we reach my dressing room and the arena staff has left us alone.

"I'm just saying," he says when he's sure only I can hear him. "You're a great singer, man. But you've never been much of an actor."

"What's that supposed to mean?"

He shrugs like he's admitting something as casual as the forecast for tomorrow's weather. "There's no way you faked the way you just looked at her."

CHAPTER THIRTEEN

Ivy

Los Angeles crowds are always great, but last night's show had a magic to it that's been missing the last few stops of the tour. Freddie was on fire, filled with a kind of joy I didn't realize was missing until I watched him on stage. He's always amazing. A natural performer. But last night, he was having *fun* again. Like it wasn't just about hitting his marks and singing his songs. It was about engaging with the crowd. About letting their energy fill him up.

"Dang," Carina says as we ride the elevator down to the garage where Wayne and Freddie are already waiting for us. "Freddie really killed it last night. He's all over Instagram." She holds out her phone, showing me a video of Freddie singing "She's Got Me," a fan favorite that always gets the crowds riled up.

"It was a great show," I say. "His best in a while." The *LA Times* already published a review in today's edition of the paper that I read and immediately forwarded to Freddie. It was a glowing summary—exactly the kind of thing we want to see.

Carina pulls her phone back. "People are saying it's because he's in love," she says, nudging my shoulder with hers. I nudge her right back, making her bag drop onto the floor next to my suitcase.

"Stop it," I say. "You can't say stuff like that. He just had a good show. That's all it was."

She presses her lips together like she's suppressing a smile. "I didn't say *I* was saying it, I said *they* are saying it. His fans. The world at large."

"Good," I say as the elevator dings and the doors slide open. "That means they're buying it. Which means Kat's press release worked."

"The new meme of you and Freddie kissing is probably *also* helping," Carina says. This time, when she flips her phone around, I take it, pausing just outside of the elevator to watch the three-second clip of Freddie taking my face in his hands and kissing me squarely on the mouth.

It's the first time I've seen a video. For all I knew, the photographer only captured images of our kiss. Then again, I've made a point to avoid social media the past couple of days. Self-preservation and all that.

The clip repeats over and over, the text at the bottom reading "When your mood is 'I was just kissed by Freddie Ridgefield' good."

It's disconcerting to watch the clip, to see Freddie lift his hands to my face and lower his mouth to mine. Watching it like this, repeated in slow motion, triggers a flurry of emotions in my chest that make my skin flush and my heart race.

Freddie Ridgefield kissed *me*. And the whole world knows it.

I hand Carina her phone. "Please stop watching that."

"I'm just saying," she argues. "It feels believable that there's a correlation."

"Well, stop saying," I shoot back. "At least in front of Freddie."

In front of us, Wayne is waiting outside a black SUV with our driver, who jumps forward to take our bags as soon as we approach.

"Freddie's already inside?" I ask, and Wayne nods.

"It's rare he beats you," he says.

I tilt my head toward my sister. "I was waiting on *her*."

"Not a morning person," Carina says. "Sorry about that."

Wayne opens the door for us, and I climb in first, realizing as I do that with Carina joining us, I'm going to be sitting *very* close to Freddie. Most of the tour staff, including Seth, will be driving back to Nashville on the buses we've been traveling on for the past four months, but Freddie and I, along with Wayne and now Carina, are flying so he can get into the studio with Leo as quickly as possible.

At least, that's been the plan. I have no idea what he'll actually do once he's in the studio with Leo since, as far as I know, he doesn't have any new music to record. But that's a problem only Freddie can solve.

I settle into the middle seat, trying not to notice the warmth of Freddie's body or how good he smells.

"Morning," I say breezily. "Sorry you had to wait for us."

"That's my fault," Carina says from the seat beside me. She leans forward and smiles. "Hi, Freddie. Good to see you again. Thanks for..." She hesitates. "For helping with the whole Margot thing. And for the new phone."

"No problem," Freddie says. "And you're welcome. How are you feeling?"

"Good as new," Carina says. She settles back into her seat, and Freddie looks down at me. "How are you?"

My heart rate spikes at the warmth in his voice, at his lower, quieter tone that feels like it's just for me.

"Good," I say, voice breathier than I would like. "Great." I look up and meet his eye. "You're getting excellent reviews for last night. I already forwarded you one from the *LA Times*."

"I saw," he says. "Thanks for sending it." He clears his throat, shifting in his seat so that the entire span of his leg, from the top of his thigh all the way down to his knee is pressed up against mine. I don't think it was intentional—three grown adults sitting across the bench seat of an SUV makes *not* touching practically impossible—but I'm still keenly aware of every place we're touching. "Did you sleep okay?" Freddie asks.

I think back, trying to remember if Freddie has ever asked me about my sleep before. I don't think he has, but it could also be that he does all the time—it's just never felt significant until now.

Until my stupid brain started cataloging every little thing, adding meaning where it isn't intended.

"Good," I answer. "I only woke up once. But only to pee, which, you know. That's normal. So all in all, a really good night's sleep."

Freddie lifts an eyebrow as I silently die inside.

Did I just tell him about peeing? What am I doing? Have I forgotten how to talk to this man?

"Good to know," he says through a smirk. "I got up to pee

twice, but that's my own fault since I drank coffee before bed. How about you, Carina?"

He's teasing me—I know he's teasing me—but I don't care because this at least feels normal. Like the kind of stupid banter that has always been a part of our relationship.

"You don't have to answer that," I say to Carina. "Freddie's just making fun of me."

He grins. "You started it."

"You guys sound like an old married couple," Carina says. "But actually, I just heard Dad say the other day that peeing a lot in the middle of the night could be a sign of prostate trouble, so I'm just saying...you might should get that checked."

"Oh my gosh, can we please stop talking about pee?" I say.

"I second that request," Wayne says from the front seat.

Freddie chuckles, then leans his head back on the seat and closes his eyes.

I poke my sister in the ribs, hoping she knows it's for the *married couple* comment, then occupy myself by tackling the morning's long list of unanswered texts and emails. The first two messages are easy. One from Wren about her wardrobe budget for the second leg of the tour, and one from Freddie's stage manager, Charlie, about needing Freddie's approval on the stage setup for the Nashville show at the end of the break.

I look over the setup, then flag the message so I can show it to Freddie later. He'd be annoyed if I tried to make him work right now.

Before I can open a third, Freddie's voice sounds close to my ear. "You know, you don't *have* to be working all the time."

I tilt my head and look up at him. "Do you know how unmanageable my inbox would be if I didn't?"

"Unmanageable as in...people will get responses in forty-eight hours instead of one?"

"I do not answer emails in..." My words trail off because the time stamp on the email I just opened really *was* less than an hour ago.

I sigh and turn off my phone. "Fine. But there could be something urgent in there. And now I'm missing it."

"There isn't," Freddie says.

"There could be," I fire back.

"Not urgent enough that you can't enjoy a twenty-minute car ride without reading your emails."

"They're *your* emails," I grumble, and he smirks.

"Which only strengthens my point." He lifts his arm and drapes it over my shoulders, giving them a quick squeeze. "Just relax."

I lean into him, the action more reflexive than intentional, turning his quick shoulder squeeze into what feels more like a side hug. But then I don't pull away. He lifts his arm, but when I don't move, he drops it back down again, letting his hand rub up and down my back.

It all happens so suddenly, I don't quite realize what I'm doing, not until his hand brushes down my opposite side, hitting a ticklish spot between my ribs and clueing me in to the fact that I'm basically snuggling with Freddie.

With my sister less than six inches away from me.

I shift away, and Freddie immediately moves his arm, giving me space, and I slide over so I'm practically in Carina's lap.

"Sorry. I'm sorry," I say quickly. "I don't know what I was..."

"No worries," Freddie says casually. "I thought you might be practicing."

"Right," I say, grasping onto whatever thread he's willing to give me. "Exactly. That's exactly what I was doing."

"Oh my gosh," Carina mutters under her breath. "That is not—"

I elbow her—easy since I'm sitting so close to her now—and clear my throat loudly enough to cover however she was going to finish her sentence.

"Actually, practicing isn't a bad idea," Freddie says. "If we're going to sell this, it would probably help to have a conversation about how we're going to act around each other. How much touching is too much, that sort of thing." He looks at me and grins. "For the record, you leaning against me in the car is *not* too much touching for me."

I swallow, embarrassed enough to want to hide and hating that we're talking about this with Carina present. Freddie is far more immune to having private conversations with members of his team listening, but now that *I* am the subject of said private conversation, I would rather crawl through the desert naked than talk about how much touching is acceptable when my little sister is listening in.

"Right. We should for sure talk about it," I say. "Set some ground rules. Maybe we can discuss it on the plane?" I tilt my head toward Carina and shoot Freddie a pleading look.

"Just talk about it now," Carina says. "I promise I won't listen, if that would make it easier." She makes a show of pulling her headphones out of her bag and putting them on. I look toward the front of the car, but the driver has already raised the privacy screen. It isn't completely soundproof, but it at least gives us the illusion of a private conversation.

Freddie's expression sobers, losing the playful edge from

moments before. "It's important to me that you set the boundaries here. I'm the one who got you into this mess, and I'm grateful for your help. But I don't want to take advantage or ever make you feel uncomfortable."

"Freddie, I'm not worried about that," I say without thinking. Because it's true. I feel safe with Freddie in every single respect. "I trust you."

He nods. "Good. So how do we feel about occasional touching? Handholding? Small gestures? Can we assume those are always welcome?"

I nod. "Definitely."

"Good," Freddie says. "What about kissing?"

Carina leans forward and looks around me at Freddie. "I think you can't really sell it if you don't kiss."

"You aren't supposed to be listening!" I say.

"Sorry, sorry!" she says as she leans back again.

To Freddie's credit, his eyes don't leave my face. "What do you think?"

I lick my lips. "Kissing is..." I have no idea how to answer this question. I *want* to kiss Freddie. Of course I do. But I'd rather it be real. Kissing him for less than genuine reasons feels like a chocolate chip cookie without chocolate chips. It might still taste sweet, but it's not nearly as delicious.

Then again, I've never been able to say no to any kind of cookie. Chocolate chips or not.

"Kissing is fine," I say. "But maybe we can talk about it first? Or you can give me a signal or something. So I know to expect it."

"A signal," Freddie says. "I like that. What should it be?"

"You could scratch your nose," Carina says. "Or tug on your earlobe."

I roll my eyes and reach over to tug off her headphones.

If she isn't going to pretend to give us privacy, I'm not going to pretend either.

"Let's avoid our noses," Freddie says. "Too easy for that to look like something else."

I press my lips together, fighting a laugh. Two years ago, the internet blew up for weeks when a picture of Freddie went viral. He was absolutely just scratching his nose in the photo, but it *looked* like he was picking his nose, and gossip sites thought it was hilarious.

Freddie was a good sport about it, but the whole thing made me *eternally* grateful that I've never been subject to so much scrutiny. The thought sends a wave of discomfort washing over me as I remember that I no longer have that luxury. I'll never garner the attention Freddie does. But I'll never be able to blend into the background of his life like I did before.

"The earlobe, then?" I ask.

"Works for me," Freddie says. "No kissing unless we warn each other with a tug on the earlobe first."

"And only if we feel like it's absolutely necessary," I add, my self-preservation instincts finally kicking in. "If we need to kiss to sell the relationship, then we can. But no kissing just for fun."

Something like disappointment flickers across Freddie's expression, but I'm not entirely sure I didn't imagine it before he wipes a hand across his face and nods, his face neutral again.

"Good. I agree," he says. "What about moving out? Should you hold off on that for the time being?"

"You're moving out?" Carina asks, and I wince. "You didn't tell me that!"

"Oops," Freddie says, catching my gaze. "Sorry."

"I'm thinking about it," I say, looking over at my sister. "I didn't tell you because I don't have any actual concrete plans. Either way, you're right," I say, turning back to Freddie. "I shouldn't until this whole thing is behind us."

"What about your origin story?" Carina asks.

"Like, how we met?" I ask. "That seems pretty obvious."

"Yeah, but like...when did your relationship turn from boss/assistant to something more? Because probably someone's going to ask."

My brain snags on Carina's words. *Boss/assistant.* Honestly, we're good enough friends that I don't always think of Freddie as my boss. It helps that when it comes to most things, I'm more in charge of his life than he is. He might sign the paychecks, but I keep everything running smoothly. It's never really *felt* like there's a power dynamic between us. But that doesn't change the reality. He *is* my boss. There *is* a power dynamic whether we give it much heed or not.

And that's something we both ought to keep in mind.

Freddie nods. "She's right, but I think the answer is easy enough. We just tell everyone it happened on tour. We spent so much time together, we couldn't help it." He looks at me, green eyes bright in the morning sun streaming through the window of the SUV. "We fell in love."

My heart stills, and I'm momentarily transfixed by the sound of those words delivered by those lips. If he only knew how much I wished the statement were true.

"Aww," Carina says. "If you say it just like that, everyone will absolutely believe you."

Minutes later, we pull through a private access gate at the Burbank airport and head toward the chartered jet parked in the distance. Carina's eyes are wide as she stares out the window.

"This is so much better than waiting in line at TSA," she says, and Freddie chuckles.

The SUV pulls to a stop, and Wayne and the driver both jump out. A few other members of Freddie's security team have already arrived, and they move up to the SUV, pulling double duty as they unload our bags and move them over to the flight team, who will screen our bags before loading them onto the plane.

While Carina gets out on her side of the car, Freddie climbs out too, then turns and reaches in, offering me his hand.

I pause, looking at him, taking in his open, earnest expression, and a sense of trepidation washes over me. Somehow, it feels like taking his hand is the beginning of something I'll never be able to undo. Like a snowball rolling down a hill.

"You coming?" Freddie asks.

The warmth in his voice gives me the courage I can't seem to find on my own, and I slide my hand into his.

Here goes freaking nothing.

CHAPTER FOURTEEN

Freddie

I'M STILL HOLDING IVY'S HAND, HALFWAY ACROSS THE TARMAC, when Sloane appears in the open doorway of the jet.

I slow my steps, tugging Ivy to a stop beside me. "Uh, did you know Sloane was going to be flying with us today?"

Before Ivy can answer, Kat appears beside Sloane, lifting a hand to wave like her presence should be wholly expected.

"Or Kat?" I add.

It's a very Sloane move to just show up, but Kat being here is a little more surprising. Then again, I have no idea how the public has responded to the press release she put out, so maybe it *is* good she's here.

"Nope," Ivy says, "though it might have been mentioned in the emails you didn't let me read earlier." She tugs on my hand. "Come on. There's nothing we can do about it now."

Once we're all settled on the plane and Carina has been introduced to everyone, Sloane and Kat sit down across from

Ivy and me, an iPad on the table between us with what looks like a long list of bullet points.

"Sorry for the surprise ambush," Sloane says. "I was up in San Francisco when I heard that Kat was in LA for a meeting, so I suggested we meet here so we could see you in person."

"Just to go over the finer points of your schedule for the next few weeks," Kat says.

My stomach sinks at the sight of Kat's list. I get that we have things to discuss. But I was looking forward to relaxing on the flight home. Normally, Ivy would just update me on stuff like this, but I clearly can't expect that of her now. Not when she's in the middle of everything too. Still, I can't keep myself from looking over at her. "I think I've got a pretty solid handle on my schedule. Is it changing?"

"Only in the sense that now, you won't be attending anything alone," Kat answers. She reaches over and offers her hand to Ivy. "It's good to see you again, Ivy. We met in New York, didn't we?"

Ivy nods as she shakes Kat's hand. "We did."

When she tries to pull away, Kat keeps her hand, her gaze moving over Ivy like she's assessing her. I instantly feel defensive, but then Kat says, "I forgot how adorable you are in person. The fans are going to eat you up."

Ivy tugs her hand back and presses it into her lap. "Um, I'm not sure what that means."

Kat shrugs. "Some women are beautiful in a way that makes other women hate them. Others are beautiful in a way that makes everyone want to be their best friend. You're the second one." She reaches for the iPad. "Should we get down to business?"

I don't fully understand Kat's logic about beauty, but I do

understand what she means about everyone wanting to be Ivy's best friend.

She just has that effect on people. She is incredibly competent, which could be an intimidating quality in some people, but Ivy is so good at taking care of everything, of *everyone,* she seems to have the opposite effect. She puts people at ease because they know if she's around, everything is probably going to be okay.

At least that's what being around her is like for me.

I do my best to focus on what Kat is saying. But everything she's telling me is stuff I already know.

Voltage Records is throwing a party in a few days, and I'm expected to make an appearance. That was already on the schedule. But now, Ivy will attend with me.

A few days after that, I have to attend a movie premiere, since one of the Midnight Rush songs we released in conjunction with our reunion concert last year is being used in the movie. Luckily, the premiere is *also* in Nashville. The movie is about a burned-out country music star and his son, so I guess the marketing team thought Nashville made more sense than New York or LA. Better for me, since I'm determined to travel as little as possible over the next two months.

Since the rest of the band will be in attendance at the premiere, I assumed I'd walk the red carpet with them.

Now, I'll walk it with Ivy instead.

"Wait," she says from beside me. "The movie premiere. Will that be black tie?"

Sloane lifts her eyebrows. "They usually are. Will that be a problem?"

Ivy doesn't immediately answer, and I look over at her, my gaze narrowing as I take her in.

Her eyes are cast down, her hands gripping her armrests

like they're anchoring her to the earth. Or, at least to the bottom of the plane since we're thirty thousand feet in the air.

"Ivy doesn't really do fancy dresses," I answer for her, but based on her current body language, I'm wondering if there's more going on right now.

Ivy's had multiple opportunities to attend red carpet events with me—not as my date, but as my assistant. But even assistants dress up for the big events, enjoying the atmosphere even if they aren't actually in the limelight. But Ivy has always found a reason *not* to attend, claiming she's never been one for black-tie events.

I've never pushed her on it, but I'm wondering if I should have because right now, there's clearly something wrong, and I don't like not knowing what it is.

"What do you mean she doesn't *do* them?" Kat asks. "You wouldn't have to pick anything out, if that matters. I'm sure we can hire a stylist who would help you look amazing."

Ivy licks her lips. "It's not that I..." Her words falter, then drop off completely, and we all wait, but she doesn't pick them up again. She just sits there.

I nudge her knee with mine. "Hey. You know you don't have to do any of this. If you don't want to go to the movie premiere, you don't have to go."

She gives her head a little shake. "But I *do* want to go. I just don't know if I *can* go."

"I don't understand," Sloane says to Kat, her voice low, but not low enough that the rest of us can't hear.

I stand from my seat and offer a hand to Ivy. "Come here for a minute."

She slips her hand into mine and lets me tug her to her feet and toward the back of the plane.

Carina looks up as we walk past, eyes fixed on Ivy's face, and she makes a move to stand, but I motion her down, giving my head a quick shake.

Maybe I should let Carina handle this. But for whatever reason, I want to be the one who makes Ivy feel better right now.

We pass the bathroom and reach a second lounge area with a few recliners that are great for sleeping on longer flights. I turn and pull a curtain closed behind us, separating us from everyone else.

"Hey," I say, finally turning to face Ivy. I put my hands on her shoulders, letting them slide down to her arms where I give her a quick squeeze. "Talk to me. What are you feeling right now?"

She lifts a hand to her forehead, using it to shield her face. "It's stupid," she finally says.

"Nothing is stupid," I say. "Just tell me."

She folds her arms across her chest. Standing like this, she looks small, fragile, and I have a sudden impulse to pull her into an embrace.

Finally, she lets out a shaky breath. "The last formal dress I put on was for my junior prom," she says. "It was the night Daphne died."

Understanding floods my brain. Honestly, I'm surprised I didn't piece things together before now.

I swear softly, shaking my head. "I'm sorry, Ivy. I should have realized."

"It's not your fault," she says. "I realize it's a weird hang-up. That at some point, I will have to get over myself and figure this out. But I think I convinced myself that dressing up, going somewhere fancy, it wouldn't be fair, you know? Because Daphne can never get dressed up again."

"I don't think that's weird at all," I say gently. "But I also don't think it's true. I think your sister would want you to go wherever you want, wearing whatever you want."

She drops onto the armrest of the closest recliner and lifts her hands to her cheeks. "I've tried to tell myself as much. That if Daphne were here, she would scold me for being ridiculous, remind me to make sure my curls are fabulous, then send me on my way. My brain gets it. But whenever I think about actually doing it, I feel like my heart is breaking all over again." She lifts her hands to her hair, pulling it up and off her neck for a moment before letting it fall back into place again. "But at some point, I'm not going to have a choice, right? I'm going to have to get over this. Carina will get married eventually, and she will not let me wear denim to her wedding."

"What if you get married *before* Carina?" I ask. "Will you wear denim to your own wedding?" The image of Ivy in a wedding dress floats through my mind, her big brown eyes bright as she smiles up at...*someone*. Not me, necessarily. The groom in my hazy imaginings is faceless. But there is nothing hazy about the discomfort that pricks the back of my heart when I think of some faceless man standing across from Ivy on her wedding day.

It's jealousy, sharp and cutting.

I haven't made a lot of sense out of what's happening inside my heart right now. But I at least know this much. I don't want to lose her to someone else.

Ivy breathes out a sigh. "I really need to figure this out, don't I?"

I sit down opposite her and push my hands into my knees. "Probably. But that doesn't mean you have to do it *now*, at a movie premiere where you're also pretending to date me. Kat's press release, the social media, the public relations stuff, it's just noise. It's not more important than you. It's not more important than how you feel."

"I know," she says. "But honestly, it might actually be better this way. If I have something else to focus on, maybe the dress won't feel like a big deal."

"Okay," I say. "Then we do this together."

She still doesn't look convinced. "I wouldn't even know where to start," she says. "How to pick out a dress. How to fix my hair. Any of it."

"I'll help with that part. Natasha is always talking about how she'd love to get her hands on you. I'll have her come to the house. Bring over a thousand dresses for you to try. Then we'll pick one out together. Honestly, you'll make my stylist's year if you let her help."

She rolls her eyes the slightest bit. "You'd help me pick out a dress? That feels..."

"Like something I would love to do," I say. "Unless you don't want me to."

Tears fill her eyes. "You're being very sweet about this. Especially when it feels like such a stupid thing."

"It's not a stupid thing. You lost your sister. It's okay that this feels like a big deal."

She's quiet for a long moment before she asks, "If I freak out, can we leave?"

"Absolutely," I say. "I'll fake an illness. Claim I've got crippling diarrhea. Whatever it takes."

She huffs out a laugh as she wipes her eyes. "Please don't fake diarrhea."

I grin. "Why not? It works better than anything else. Nobody wants to get in the way of exploding bowels."

"Freddie, stop it," she says, but she's still laughing, so I don't care. "I don't think it'll come to faking diarrhea. But knowing we can sneak out early would be helpful."

"Done. We'll come up with another sign. One tug on your earlobe, and you're getting a kiss. Two, and we're making a run for the bathroom."

She shakes her head. "You're ridiculous."

"You're smiling, so...mission accomplished."

She stands and holds out her hands, and I let her pull me to my feet. "A tug on the earlobe means we should kiss," she says. "And if I squeeze your elbow like this—" She reaches up and grips my elbow, right below my bicep. "Then you know I'd like to go."

"Earlobe, kiss, elbow, leave. Got it."

She grins. "If our system gets any more complicated, we're going to need a cheat sheet."

If she gets any more adorable, I'm going to be tugging on my earlobes all the damn time. But I don't say that part out loud. I just smile and squeeze her hands before dropping them so I can shove my hands into my pockets. It's getting harder and harder to touch her because of how much I want to *keep* touching her.

If I start, I might not ever let her go.

I hold her gaze for one more moment. "I'm really sorry about Daphne," I say. "That we have to have this conversation at all."

There's a sadness in her eyes that makes my heart squeeze painfully in my chest, and I find myself wishing there was something—*anything*—I could do to make that sadness disappear.

The intensity of my response surprises me, and for a split second, I fight the impulse to flee, to pull myself back from what feels like teetering on the edge of a very high cliff.

But then Ivy reaches up and cups a hand around my cheek, her thumb brushing across the stubble lining my jaw. In a different circumstance, the gesture might pull my eyes to Ivy's lips, make me think of pulling her into my arms, finding more ways to touch her. But right now, the touch feels like something else entirely.

It feels like connection. Like her soul talking to mine.

The sense of overwhelm building inside me stills, then dissipates, and it's replaced with a sense of peace, of *rightness* that I've never experienced before.

"Thanks," Ivy says softly, then she lets her hand fall from my face.

I tilt my head toward the front of the plane. "Ready to head back in there?"

"Should we be scared of what else Kat has planned for us?" she asks.

"Nah. I read ahead. That's pretty much it as far as events go. The last few points are about social media posts. Dropping your name at the Nashville concert, maybe hinting somewhere that a song or two on the new album are about you."

She pushes the curtain aside, looking at me over her shoulder as she moves back to where Kat and Sloane are waiting for us. "I get to inspire an entire song?" she teases. "Lucky me."

Funny she mentions it, but I *have* had lyrics floating through my head the past couple of days. Nothing concrete yet, but I feel it—a shimmering, simmering something in the back of my mind just waiting for me to pull it out, to mold it into shape.

It doesn't always happen like this, but I've learned to trust the process when it does. To let the song come to me when it's ready. I don't want to get ahead of myself, but the fact that I'm feeling anything at all—I'm pretty sure it has something to do with Ivy and whatever feelings she's triggering inside me.

"Everything okay?" Sloane asks, her eyes moving from me to Ivy then back again.

"We're good," Ivy answers. "I can do the movie premiere. What else is on the list?"

I look past Sloane and Kat and meet Carina's eyes. She looks surprised by Ivy's declaration, her eyebrows lifted, and I offer her a tiny shrug and a nod, hoping she understands that I've got this. That I know why this is such a big deal for Ivy, and I won't make her do anything she isn't ready to do.

Carina smiles, gratitude clear in her expression, then I shift my focus back to Ivy as she talks through the last few bullet points with Kat. For all her vulnerability a few moments ago, there's no trace of it now. Now, she seems more like the assistant I'm used to. Efficient. Practical. Wicked smart.

"I'll make sure the paparazzi are aware you won't be attending alone," Kat says, referencing the movie premiere. "This is one instance when we need them to take as many photos as possible."

"Do we need to be more strategic?" Ivy says. "All of Midnight Rush will be at the premiere."

"Hmm," Kat says. "So you're worried the photographers will be more focused on the four of them together than on the two of you?"

"Freddie Ridgefield having a girlfriend is more exciting than the four of them together," Sloane says.

"Debatable," Ivy says. "Midnight Rush fans are intense. Either way, if we want *good* photos of the two of us, it can't hurt to relay our wishes to a specific photographer. I can reach out to Jeff Burns. He's honest, and he's been good to Freddie in the past."

Kat nods, like she's impressed with Ivy's insight. "Good thought," she says, "but let me reach out to him. You're not just the assistant now, Ivy."

"Manager," I correct. "She's not my assistant. She's my manager."

Sloane lifts her eyebrows, then nods. "Noted. Either way, Kat's right. Considering the circumstances, she should make the call instead of your girlfriend."

Ivy's eyes cut over to me, and my stomach swoops into my shoes. *Girlfriend.* Here lately, I've been liking the sound of that word more and more.

"I know Jeff," Kat says. "I can definitely let him know what we need." She looks over her list one more time. "Okay. The rest is pretty straightforward. We can coordinate on some social media posts that drop a few more hints, but after your appearances together, those will feel like gravy."

"Are we concerned about Margot at all?" I ask. "I know we've got the edge here, but she might still talk. She always does."

"Margot is a nonissue," Sloane says. "I've been in communication with her people. Our story is airtight. You were at her house to pick up your girlfriend's sister. Everything online corroborates that story."

"This might have *started* because of Margot," Kat says, "but we're keeping it up because it's generating a lot of really positive press. You're all over the news. Streaming is up. Downloads are up. Radio play is up. Those are all good things."

"I talked to Voltage this morning," Sloane adds, "and

they had nothing but positive things to say. They didn't mention your missed album deadline once."

Ivy reaches over and puts a hand on my arm. "Maybe the lack of pressure will make it easier to write."

"Let's hope," Kat says. "All right, then. So we're all in agreement?"

"Sounds good," I say, and Ivy nods.

"Yep. I think so."

"Excellent. Then just leave things in my very capable hands."

I don't doubt Kat's competence.

Or Sloane's.

But this isn't just about my career anymore.

It's about me and Ivy. And every minute I spend with her makes it more and more clear: that's what I'm worried about the most.

Not my career.

Not public opinion.

Just her. *Us.* And the possibility of there being an *us* long after all of this is behind us.

CHAPTER FIFTEEN

Ivy

When we pull into Freddie's driveway after we land at the airport in Nashville, I expect it to be dark and quiet, as it's been almost entirely unoccupied during our months-long absence. A housekeeper has stopped by every day to check the mail and water Freddie's plants and keep an eye on things, and the lawn service Freddie uses has continued its maintenance of the outside, but that's it.

I'm *sure* that's it, because I'm the one who made all the arrangements.

But Freddie's house is lit up like there's a party going on, with several cars parked in the driveway.

"Should I know who's at your house?" I say to Freddie, who is sitting in the front seat next to Wayne.

"Just the guys," Freddie says. "I gave Adam the code to the front door."

My shoulders tense as I start scrolling through my mental checklist, trying to remember if I asked the housekeeper to get the guestrooms ready for Freddie's former bandmates. I'm sure I didn't, so...does that mean I dropped the ball somehow? Forgot to make the arrangements?

"Relax," Freddie says as if sensing my unease. "They asked if they could come early, so I reached out to the house-keeper and asked her to prep the rooms. It's taken care of."

I sink back into my chair, relieved that I didn't actually forget but all too aware that before all of this happened, Freddie would never have reached out to the housekeeper himself. He would have asked me to do it.

I can't decide how it makes me feel that he didn't. But maybe it's better this way. Right now, my brain is so full of Freddie, it's a wonder I'm able to accomplish anything at all. It was all I could do just to make it through the conversation with Sloane and Kat, pretending like I was, one, in complete control of myself, making mental notes of all the details they were giving us, and two, perfectly chill and motivated to tackle a fake relationship with Freddie with professionalism and efficiency.

If they could have seen what the inside of my brain looked like, they probably would have been searching for my replacement on craigslist. Putting out ads for women of medium height with stupidly curly hair and at least two brain cells, seeing as how that's two more than I'm currently operating with.

"Um, the guys?" Carina whispers from beside me. "Does he mean the other members of Midnight Rush?"

Freddie must hear her, despite her whispering, because he turns and offers her his most charming smile. "I hope you don't mind sharing the house with them too. Well, at least with Adam and Jace. Leo's local, but he'll still be hanging out a lot this week. Since we aren't all together very often."

Carina reaches over and grips my arm. "Please say I can stay," she says. "Just for a few days. Please, please?"

I look at Freddie and he shrugs like it's not a big deal at all. "I don't mind if you don't."

I think through the logistics. Usually, Freddie's six-bedroom house would be plenty big enough for Carina to have her own room, but considering all his other guests, she'll have to stay with me. The other rooms will be occupied by Jace and his mom, who is traveling with him to help with his kids, plus an additional one for the kids, then one for Adam and Laney. Still, my bedroom was meant to be a mother-in-law suite, so it's more like a studio apartment. It has a tiny kitchenette, plus a sitting area, a king-size bed, and an outside entrance. There's plenty of room.

"Fine," I finally relent. "You can stay. But you'll have to stay in my bedroom with me." I bite back a request for Carina to be on her best behavior. That's the kind of thing I *used* to say, and it feels like a small victory that I've managed to stop myself this time.

Carina lets out a squeal. "Yay! Sleepover! Thank you, thank you, thank you!" She leans over and gives me a side hug that triggers an unexpected flood of love for my little sister.

I can't believe I'm even thinking it, but maybe it wouldn't be so bad to have her in Nashville full time. If I can figure out how to stop thinking of her as my responsibility, I might actually enjoy her company.

"If you want, you can also come to the Voltage party tomorrow night," I say, surprising myself as much as I surprise Carina.

But she only considers for a moment before she holds up

her hands. "I appreciate you offering," she says, "but I think I'm due for a break from partying."

"Really?"

Her expression shifts as she shrugs her shoulders. "It's only been a couple of days, but I like the person I am with you so much more than the one I am with Margot. I need a reset. This feels like a good time to have one."

I lean over and hug her again, a real one this time instead of the one-armed side hug she gave me. "Okay, well, if you just want to go inside and head straight to bed, I'm sure the rest of Midnight Rush will understand."

She leans back and looks at me, eyebrows lifted. "I said a break from *partying*. Not a break from *living*."

When we make it inside, Leo, Jace, Adam, and Adam's fiancée, Laney, are standing around the island in Freddie's expansive kitchen eating chips and salsa and what looks like very delicious homemade guacamole.

An older woman I'm guessing is Jace's mother sits at the table with a baby on her lap and a toddler strapped into a highchair beside her.

"You're home!" Leo says, stepping forward to give Freddie a hug. "How did the road treat you?"

"About as well as you'd expect," Freddie says.

Leo and Freddie are probably the closest of the four former band members, mostly because he also lives in Nashville, which means he's the one I know best. I've known him from almost the beginning, while I only met Adam and Jace last year when the band got back together for a one-time reunion show.

But after all the time we spent together leading up to the concert, rehearsing and promoting and getting things ready, I would consider all of them friends.

Leo makes eye contact over Freddie's shoulder and offers me a warm smile. His dark hair is longer than it was the last time I saw him. It's still short on the sides, but it's flopping over his forehead in a way that suits him.

Adam steps up next. He's grown his beard back in, and he has a baseball cap pulled low on his face. I swear, the man can hide in plain sight better than anyone I know. With a beard, he looks like a totally different person than clean-shaven Deke, which is the stage name he used when the band was still together.

Finally, it's Jace's turn for a hug. He looks tired—dark circles visible under his blue eyes despite the California tan he brought with him to Tennessee. I guess it makes sense. His baby is only four months old, and from what Freddie tells me, Jace is a very hands-on dad. After his wife walked out and moved halfway around the world to pursue her modeling career, he probably could have hired a nanny. Outsourced the bulk of his parenting responsibility. He definitely has the money for it. But so far, he only has his mom help when he travels. Which means he has to be exhausted.

Freddie leans back and looks at Jace, his hands on his shoulders. He asks him something that I can't hear, and Jace nods.

I will never get tired of seeing these four men embracing, honoring the friendship they built in the years they were making music together.

Even though they are all in entirely different places now—and none of them have a career like Freddie's—when they're together, that never seems to matter. They've had their moments, but I genuinely believe that at their core, these men want what's best for each other. And they aren't afraid to say it out loud.

After the men finish up their hugs and backslaps, Jace introduces his mom and his kids, Annie and Eli, then Freddie introduces Carina.

While she gets hello hugs from each of them, Laney moves over to me. She hugs me hello and asks me about our flight, but then she loops her arms through mine and gives me a knowing look. "Honestly," she says, leaning close, "I wasn't at all surprised when I heard the news. I'm genuinely so happy for you two."

I freeze, confused by her words. "Happy for who?"

Laney furrows her brow, like *my* confusion has confused *her*. "For you and Freddie," she says, and understanding hits me like a bucket of cold water.

These people—Freddie's closest friends—all think we're dating for *real*.

"That's right," Adam says, clearly picking up on our conversation. "Congrats to both of you."

My stomach sinks as I make eye contact with Freddie. I assumed he would tell his friends the truth, though I'm not at all surprised he hasn't had the time to do it yet. We've barely had time to process things ourselves.

But I really, *really* wish I didn't have to be here for the conversation. I don't know why, exactly. Maybe because I don't want anyone's pity. And in my head, that's what people will feel when they find out I'm *not* dating one of the world's most beloved music artists.

They'll feel sorry for me.

Freddie lifts a hand to the back of his neck. "Yeah, about that," he says, looking at each of his friends. "We aren't actually dating."

I'm standing closest to Laney, so it's impossible to miss the flash of disappointment in her eyes as Freddie tells the story of what happened at Margot's and how one impulsive kiss landed us in the middle of an unintentional publicity stunt.

"And you're okay with all this?" Laney asks, her voice low enough that only I can hear.

I swallow against the sudden knot in my throat and do my best to feign indifference. "Why wouldn't I be?"

In a different setting, I would probably tell Laney everything. We spent a lot of time together last year, and we've been texting ever since. Not all the time, but enough for me to know her concern—her friendship—is genuine.

But I can't have this conversation right now.

I can't unpack my heart and explain how complicated my feelings are. Not when Freddie and his three closest friends are standing on the other side of the room.

Laney nods, but she hardly looks convinced.

"It's just the nature of the industry," Freddie says. "But we're handling it. Ivy is being a very good sport."

"I should say so," Leo says. "Putting up with your ugly face." He turns and looks at me. "What are you getting out of the deal, Ivy?"

I think of the demand I made—my insistence that I would help Freddie if he would help me land a job with his label. It was an impulsive request when I made it. A desperate attempt at self-preservation. As if I sensed that if I *did* go through with the fake relationship, escaping might be my only means of survival.

But standing here among Freddie's closest friends, it almost feels heartless to declare my only motivation for agreeing to the scheme was *leaving* Freddie and working somewhere else. "Oh, um..."

"We're still working out the details," Freddie says, saving

me from having to answer. "Now." He claps Jace on the back. "Do I get to hold the baby? Or is that against the rules?"

It's an obvious deflection, one that makes my shoulders sag with relief. The conversation shifts to Jace and his kids, but I feel Freddie's focus on me, making my skin hum with quiet energy. When I look up to meet his gaze, I can practically hear his voice in my head.

Are you okay?

I nod once, hoping he senses my gratitude. His mouth lifts into a small smile, then his attention is pulled away when Jace lowers baby Eli into his arms.

Freddie's eyes brighten, his delight utterly unabashed as he smiles at Eli, who reaches up and pats Freddie's cheeks, then smiles in return.

Oh. Oh, this is not good.

Freddie holding a baby? What sort of inexplicable torture is this? I've always been one to scoff at talk of biological clocks, but my body is having a visceral reaction right now, like my ovaries are ringing some sort of bell announcing their approval.

When I was little, my mother had a pair of peafowl on her rescue farm. At first, I didn't understand what triggered the peacock to lift his feathers, to unfurl the shimmering hues of turquoise and blue. Then my mother explained the mating ritual, the peacock's desire to impress his peahen with all that gorgeous plumage. I'm not sure I fully understood then, but I definitely do now.

Mom's peahen needed fancy blue feathers and an elaborate mating dance. Apparently, I just need to see Freddie Ridgefield holding a blond-haired baby with big blue eyes and a dimple in his left cheek.

"You okay?" Laney asks. She tugs her arm gently, and I

look down only to realize I've been squeezing her elbow with a vise-like grip. I quickly let go, smoothing my palms down the sides of my jeans.

"Sorry," I quickly say. "I don't..." My words trail off, eyes still glued to Freddie as he bounces Eli and makes him laugh.

"Girl, I get it," Laney says, breathing out a sigh. Jace has his daughter, Annie, in his arms, and Adam is playing a game with her, making her giggle. "Watching handsome men play with babies is its own kind of drug."

The kids only last a few more minutes before Jace's mom comes and takes them upstairs to get ready for bed. But it's not long before the rest of us are ready to call it a night too. Freddie makes plans to head to the studio with the guys early the next morning, and I hang around, wondering if he'll want me to go with him. It's the kind of thing I normally *would* do, but I have no idea how to handle my regular work responsibilities now that I'm *also* pretending to be his girlfriend. Not that we're pretending here, when we're in his house with only friends and family surrounding us, but it still feels like something has shifted.

I don't want to let Freddie down, so I swallow against the knot in my throat and stop him before he disappears into his bedroom for the night.

"Hey, you got a sec?" I ask.

He turns, halfway through a yawn. "Always for you," he says. "What's up?"

There are only two bedrooms on the main floor of Freddie's house—his and mine. Everyone else has gone upstairs, and Carina is already in my room taking a shower, so it's just the two of us in the small alcove outside his bedroom door.

He leans against the wall and runs his hands through his

hair, leaving it completely askew, pointing in a dozen different directions. His hairstyle is naturally a little messy, but this looks more like bedhead than the artfully mussed look he usually wears.

Not in a bad way, though. In a *sexy* way. Here, in his house, he's a little undone, a little less polished. And I get to see him that way. I get to stand here and look into his green eyes and be the last person he talks to before he goes to sleep.

"What are you smiling about?" he says, his tone light, almost teasing.

I let out a little chuckle and lift my hand to his hair, smoothing down the wildest parts. "You just made your hair completely ridiculous."

He grins. "I did it for you. Just to entertain you."

His eyes close, and he slumps against the wall a little, like my fingers in his hair might lull him to sleep right here in the hallway.

It's all I can do to *stop* touching him, but once his hair is tamed again, I let my hand fall. Before everything happened, I might not have stopped. But now, I'm weighing every action, wondering if he'll read into things differently. It's exhausting. And silly, really. If anything, faking gives me an excuse to touch him *more*.

But my feelings are too close to the surface. Every inch I give him, the more worried I am that he'll see through the facade and recognize this *isn't* fake to me. When I touch him, take care of him, it's because I want to.

"So, I'm wondering how things are going to look the next few days," I finally manage to ask.

He opens his eyes. "What do you mean?"

"Work-wise, I guess. Like, do you want me to go to the

studio with you tomorrow? I only ask because you reached out to the housekeeper about the guys coming early, and that's something I would normally do. I don't want you to think I can't do my job just because we're...also doing this other thing."

He nods, like he fully understands my question. "Yeah, not gonna lie. It feels weird to ask you to do stuff now. Bossing you around—I don't know. I don't want to take advantage of you."

"But I'm not your real girlfriend, Freddie. And I'm still getting paid, so I shouldn't stop doing what I usually do. Besides, you never boss me around. You ask me to do stuff, and you always ask nicely. That's different. Honestly, most of the time, I'm the one bossing *you* around."

He chuckles, then his voice drops deliciously low when he says, "I like it when you boss me around."

Heat flushes my skin, coiling low in my belly, and I clench my fists, willing my body not to respond. I drop my eyes and force a slow, steadying breath.

How does he do this to me with just a few words? The man will be my undoing.

"Sorry," he says. "That probably sounded—"

"It's fine," I say, waving a hand dismissively. "I know what you meant."

I'm not sure I really do, but I'll happily change the subject if it will distract him from noticing the warmth I can still feel in my cheeks.

"So...tomorrow?" I say.

"Right. Tomorrow." He studies me for a long moment. "What do you want to do? Do you want to come to the studio?"

I bite my lip. Of course I want to go. But it's probably the last thing I need. Watching him work is almost as addictive as watching him snuggle babies.

"I'll absolutely be there if you think you'll need me," I say. "But if not, it might be nice to spend some time with Carina."

"You should do that, then," Freddie says.

"I can still take care of stuff," I quickly say. "I'll stay on top of texts and emails and everything else. And if you need anything while you're there, you can just call—"

"Hey," he says, cutting me off. "It'll be fine. You never take time off. You should."

I nod, feeling both relieved and disappointed at the same time.

"Okay," I say. "I will, then."

He yawns and rubs his eyes, but he makes no move to leave. Instead, he crosses his arms over his chest and leans against the wall, closing his eyes.

"Freddie," I say through a chuckle. "Go to bed."

He smiles without moving. "I like standing here with you."

My traitorous heart thumps in response. "But I need to go to bed too," I say. I push him gently toward his door. "Come on. I'll see you in the morning."

He finally stands upright, stretching his arms high over his head. His shirt lifts, and his pants are low enough on his hips that I catch another glimpse of the tattoo just by his hip bone—the one I'm certain is mystery tattoo number eighteen.

He must understand my staring because he asks, "Do you want to see it?"

My gaze darts up to meet his. "That's number eighteen?"

He nods. "The only one my fans haven't mapped." His

tone is perfunctory, matter-of-fact, and it makes me think of the woman who came to his concert with half of his tattoos already inked onto her body. It's not a wonder he keeps this one secret.

"Can you show me without taking off your pants?" I ask. Because I do want to see it. But I can only stand so close to the edge of a cliff before self-preservation kicks in. And seeing Freddie sans pants would definitely knock me clean into the canyon.

Freddie rolls his eyes and reaches for the waistband of his pants, his eyes dancing as he says, "Yes, Ivy. I'm not suggesting I strip for you. Do you think I would have offered otherwise?"

I lift my hands. "Sorry. I was just making sure. I didn't want to be accidentally scarred."

"Wow," Freddie says. "Scarred? Hit me where it hurts."

It feels good to be bantering like this, a little bit like we're back to our old selves again, except right now, there's a tension buzzing between us that feels thick enough to cut. Then Freddie shimmies the waist of his pants low enough for me to see his secret tattoo, and my throat goes dry.

He's fully decent—I'm only seeing skin—but it's *not* skin I usually see. He could be standing here in a swimsuit, otherwise unclothed, and it would still feel less scandalous than this.

I force myself to focus on the ink instead of the jut of his hipbone or the light dusting of hair on his abdomen.

"It's a maple leaf," I say. "Are you secretly Canadian?"

He chuckles. "No. But my grandparents had a big-leaf maple tree in their backyard. It had these huge leaves that turned bright yellow every fall. Whenever my parents didn't know what to do with me, how to *handle* me, I guess, they would send me down the street to my grandparents' house." He shifts his pants back up, covering the tattoo, and lets his shirt fall back down. "My grandfather is the one who taught me how to play guitar. When the weather was good, we would sit outside under the maple tree and play until it was too dark to see."

"You've never told me that," I say. "About your grandfather."

"I should tell you more about him. Best man I've ever known."

I fold my arms across my chest and lean against the wall, mirroring Freddie's pose. Even though I already told him to go to bed, I like to hear him talk about his family. At least his grandparents. His parents drive me crazy, with the way they seem to express only mild appreciation for his chosen career. And his brother is no better. But whenever he mentions his grandparents, they seem like people I would have liked.

"He died when?" I say, speaking of his grandfather. "How old were you?"

"Nineteen," he says. "Then twenty when Grandma died."

"So they got to see you in Midnight Rush."

Freddie smiles, his expression a little wistful. "Yeah. They did. We did a show in Seattle, and they were able to come and watch from a private balcony. That was a great night."

"I bet they were so proud of you."

He shrugs. "It's not quite a PhD in mathematics, but yeah. They were proud."

I cock my head, studying his face, searching for any hint of malice or hurt. But there isn't any. If there was ever hurt over his parents' disinterest in his career, I don't think it's still there. There was a tiny bit of sarcasm in his tone, but it didn't seem deeply rooted.

"When did you stop trying to impress them?" I ask, and Freddie lifts his eyebrows.

"My parents?"

I nod.

He considers my question for so long, I wonder if I shouldn't have asked. But then he says, "Honestly, I don't know that I've *ever* tried to impress them. They never understood me, really. And I got that when I was a little kid. Six or seven, even. I knew I was different. That what mattered to them was never going to matter to me." He runs a hand across his face. "I don't know. It didn't feel like a painful thing. Just a part of my reality. And I can't really complain, right? They supported me when I wanted to try out for Midnight Rush, then when I moved to Nashville. They didn't stand in my way. But that doesn't mean they're going to enjoy my music just because it's mine."

His patience with his parents does him credit, but it also makes me want to take him home to *my* parents, just so they can gush over him like I know they would. Mom would sit him down at her kitchen table and fill him with homemade peach pie and ask him a thousand questions about his music and touring and his favorite cities and his favorite songs and then she would let him name one of her rescue donkeys and promise every time she said its name, she'd think of Freddie.

That's just how my parents are. Fully invested. The world's greatest cheerleaders.

"They *should* enjoy your music because it's yours," I say. "But also because it's brilliant."

"Wait, hold on," Freddie says, reaching for his phone.

"Can you say that one more time? I'd like to record Ivy Conway saying I'm brilliant."

I roll my eyes. "Okay. Now it's really time for bed." I push away from the wall, but Freddie catches my wrist.

"Wait," he says.

I pause, turning back, eyes snagging on the way he's holding me, his thumb just over the pulse point on the inside of my arm. I wonder if he can feel how quickly the blood is racing through my veins. His thumb moves the slightest bit, tracing a tiny circle across my skin.

He licks his lips, and for a split second, I could swear his gaze drops to *my* lips. There's something in his gaze I've never seen before—something weighty and intentional that sends awareness skittering over my skin. I lean forward the slightest bit, yielding to the magnetic pull of his presence. But then his hand slides down to mine, and he gives it a quick squeeze before letting me go and taking a step backward.

"Good night, Ivy," he says softly. Then he turns and slips into his bedroom without glancing back.

I sag against the wall and close my eyes, heart still pounding.

It wasn't much. Just a whisper of a touch across my wrist. That isn't enough to justify feeling any kind of hope. But I can't help it. When I walk across the kitchen to my own room, I can't help but feel like I'm floating.

CHAPTER SIXTEEN

Ivy

T HE NEXT FEW DAYS PASS UNEVENTFULLY.

Well, mostly.

Freddie spends a lot of time in the studio, each day coming home a little more invigorated than he was the day before. And I spend a lot of time with Carina. Her recently graduated and currently unemployed status means she doesn't have to hurry to get back to Knoxville, and I'm enjoying her company, so we aren't in any rush to take her home. We watch movies, go to the spa to get massages, and tour the Country Music Hall of Fame. We go shopping and to the Johnny Cash Museum, and we wander up and down Broadway, visiting different music venues and sampling overpriced mocktails.

At first, I wasn't sure about going out, afraid people might recognize me, but without Freddie beside me, it's easy to fly under the radar. I wear a hat, sunglasses, and no makeup, intentionally dressing myself down, and it works. Aside from two teenage girls who eye me in a record store, whispering behind their hands, no one else pays me much notice. At first, it's slightly awkward having Jason, a member of Wayne's security team, following behind us—Freddie insisted, just in case—but after the first outing, we get really good at ignoring him.

At home, we bake cookies and make our favorite meals, and while I keep up with what little work Freddie is still letting me do, Carina spends a good chunk of each day playing with Jace's kids. Jace's mom, Shay, is incredible—she reminds me a lot of our mom—and she's mothering us as much as she's mothering her grandkids.

Annie, who is only three and a half, talks like a tiny adult and has learned how to roll her eyes in a way that I'm sure will frustrate her father in a few years. But for right now, it's so completely adorable that Carina keeps coming up with ways to trigger it.

Shay thinks it's hilarious, but I should probably apologize to Jace before he flies back to California. It's possible Carina has accidentally taught Annie how to be a drama queen.

As a couple, Freddie and I go out together twice. Once as a group because Freddie wants to take the other members of Midnight Rush out to dinner. And once for lunch, just the two of us, because Sloane texts and suggests we make an appearance at an upscale restaurant where paparazzi are known to hang out, hoping to spot celebrities. The paparazzi scene in Nashville is nothing like it is in LA, but there's enough country music royalty living in the city that there are always photographers around trying to grab relevant shots.

Both times, Freddie keeps me close, holding my hand,

keeping his arm around me. He is attentive and thoughtful and basically the perfect boyfriend.

Perfect *fake* boyfriend, anyway.

But he is also intentional. Measured in a way that makes me think he's being careful with me. He was unguarded that first night home, when I talked to him outside his bedroom, but he hasn't been since then.

I can appreciate his efforts to be cautious—I'm sure he doesn't want to take advantage—but I also *hate* his efforts to be cautious. Because they are constant reminders that all of this is fake.

When we hold hands on our way into the restaurant or he guides me through the dining room with his hand on the small of my back, it's fake.

When we stand at the curb, waiting for the car, and he wraps his arm around me, pressing a kiss against my temple—also fake. Even if the way his lips make me feel is anything but.

Still, our efforts are paying off. The public is eating up any scrap of information about our new relationship, and the buzz is having a noticeable impact. Freddie's numbers are up across all platforms, and everyone is talking about the new album, speculating about when the first single will drop. His label is happy, his agent is happy, and now, Freddie is finally writing again, so he's happy too.

That makes *me* happy, but I still feel like I'm holding my breath. Like we're building a house out of straw, and when the whole thing collapses, I'll be the one standing in the middle of the wreckage.

On the morning of the party at Voltage Records, I stretch across the foot of my bed while Carina goes through my clothes, trying to find something for me to wear.

"Are these seriously your only options?" she asks. She steps out of my closet holding all three of the only dresses I actually own. "None of these will work. They're all too casual."

"The party *is* casual," I say.

"No," Carina says. "The party isn't *formal*. That doesn't mean you can wear jeans and a t-shirt." She moves back into the closet and hangs up the dresses. "Why have we not talked about this? We could have bought something this week. We went shopping multiple times."

"Shopping for *you*," I say. "Which is different. I hate shopping for me." I reach for the black dress hanging in the middle. "I'll just wear this one. I pair it with my red leather jacket and my boots. It's a great outfit."

Carina props her hands on her hips. "It's eighty-five degrees out. You can't wear leather to this party." She starts pacing across the wood floor of my bedroom, reaching the plush rug that sits under my bed before turning and heading back to the closet.

"Just the dress, then," I say. "It'll be fine. I managed to dress myself the other two times I went out with Freddie this week. And nobody said anything about my clothes."

"But this is different," Carina says. "This isn't a small, private gathering. This is a party where the goal is to see and be seen. Not to mention the fact that the party is at Voltage Records. That means you'll have the opportunity to network, to meet people who you hope you'll be working for when all of this is over."

My gut tightens the slightest bit. I hadn't thought about networking, but Carina is right. If that's what I want, the party really could be an opportunity to nurture some connections. But *is it* what I want?

Finding clarity on that point is basically impossible considering my present circumstances. It hurts to think about not working for Freddie, but I'm not entirely sure if that's because I don't want to leave my job or I just don't want to leave him. Either way, making a little extra effort tonight can't hurt.

"Right. Networking," I say. "So I need something that's both professional enough to be taken seriously but also fabulous enough to look like I belong on the arm of the world's biggest popstar. I guess we *should* have gone shopping."

"Shopping for what?"

I look up to see Freddie standing in my open bedroom doorway, his long arms lifted over his head and his hands grasping the door frame.

"An outfit for Ivy to wear to the party tonight," Carina answers for me. "Please tell her she can't wear her plain black dress that she's already worn a million trillion times."

Freddie's eyes shift to me before he says, "I love her black dress. But also, that's why I'm here."

I sit up. "It is?"

"I promised I would help you pick out something for the movie premiere, so I thought we could do that today. Then Natasha can help you choose something for tonight too."

"Yes!" Carina says. "Perfect. Wait. Who's Natasha?"

"My stylist," Freddie says. "And she just pulled up with a van full of clothes. Should I tell her to set up in here?"

Carina spins to look at me. "The shopping comes to you? This is incredible." She spins and races from the room, likely to watch Natasha and her team bring everything inside.

This is less overwhelming for me because I've seen her

do this for Freddie. But it does feel weird to know it's me who will be trying on the clothes this time.

"Wren's here too," Freddie says, finally coming into the room. "When she heard it was *you* getting styled, she didn't want to miss out on the action."

When Wren isn't on tour with Freddie, handling his wardrobe needs for his shows, she works out of Natasha's studio. It'll be good to see her again, though I can already imagine her *I told you so* face. She was relentless in her teasing during the last few tour stops before the break. Every time Freddie and I were in the same room, she was shooting me knowing looks and raising her eyebrows suggestively.

It was always good-natured and completely harmless. But that doesn't mean she won't gloat.

Freddie sits down on the bench at the foot of my bed. "I hope this isn't too much," he says, a hint of vulnerability in his tone. "I just thought you deserved the whole experience. Natasha has someone coming for hair and makeup too—tonight, then again for the premiere. But you don't have to do that part if you don't want to. I'm not saying you *need* hair and makeup. Just that it's available if you *do* want it." He rubs his palms down his thighs like he's nervous. Which—*is* he nervous? I don't know why he would be.

"It isn't too much," I say. "It's amazing. And the hair and makeup is great too. I'll take all the help I can get."

He lets out a disbelieving laugh. "You don't need any help."

My heart flutters in my chest. "I don't?"

Freddie holds my gaze for a long moment. "You're beautiful exactly as you are." His voice is low, his tone sincere, giving his words a weight that assures me he isn't feeding me a line. He really thinks I'm beautiful. Which. Maybe he's just making an objective observation. It doesn't have to mean anything.

Before I can respond, Carina bursts back into the room, pulling a rolling cart full of shoeboxes in behind her. I breathe out a sigh of relief as Natasha appears in the doorway.

"Have I found the right room?" she asks.

"This is it!" Carina says, then she turns and says to me, "I'm so excited!"

The next few minutes are a whirlwind as Wren and Natasha take over my bedroom. They have everything. A three-way mirror. A changing screen. And clothing racks full of dresses in every imaginable color.

"This is so much more than you ever bring for Freddie," I say as Natasha ushers me toward the changing screen.

"Because I've never done this for you before," she says. "I have no idea what you're going to like. Also, dresses are just so much fun!"

My stomach tightens. Dresses *should* be fun. But even just looking at the sequins and sparkles and shimmering fabrics is making my anxiety spike. The dress on the end of the rack is the same turquoise blue that Daphne wore the night she died, and it sends my mind back in time to the Saturday afternoon the two of us went shopping together to buy our dresses.

We begged Mom to let us go without her, because we wanted to feel grown up and responsible, and she relented. I've never had so much fun in a mall. We probably tried on fifty dresses, some boring, some beautiful, and some so completely ridiculous they made us laugh until we cried. Then we fell in love with the same dress. Daphne tried it on first, but she saw the way I was eyeing it and insisted I try it on too.

It was perfect, and even though I know Daphne loved it too, she made a show of picking out a blue one instead, fawning over it like it was *so much better* than the one I picked.

I knew she was lying. But she wouldn't back down. Even when I argued it was her senior prom, and I could even wear the dress next year when it was *my* senior prom.

She wanted me to wear the dress. That's just the kind of sister she was.

"Maybe not that one," Carina says, pulling my attention back into the present moment. She points to the turquoise one on the end, then whispers something to Wren, who quickly puts the dress inside a garment bag and tucks it out of sight.

Carina looks at me, her eyes full of understanding. "Are you okay?"

Before responding, my gaze slides over to Freddie, who is sitting on the other side of the room in one of the armchairs in front of my window. He's leaning forward, arms propped on his knees. Our gazes catch, and though he doesn't say anything, somehow, it feels like we're talking anyway. In a split second of eye contact, whole sentences pass between us. Entire paragraphs of encouragement and calming reassurances are somehow bundled into the warmth radiating from his gaze.

When it reaches me, it spreads through my chest like a warm, weighted blanket. It's the anchor I didn't know I needed, and I feel myself relax the slightest bit.

Still, there is resolve in his expression.

I *need* to do this. I know I do. It's a silly mental block, and it's time to push through it.

Freddie knows that too. I love that he isn't coddling me. He knows what I want, and he's helping me do it.

"I'm okay," I say, giving Carina a nod. "And maybe I *can* try the turquoise dress. I want to try them all." I look at Freddie one more time. "Thank you," I mouth, and he smiles, sending a shot of dopamine right into my heart. "Okay. Let's do this."

Overall, it's not a terrible way to shop. Wren stays with me, helping me in and out of dresses, Natasha chooses what I try next, adjusting her picks according to how I feel about each thing I put on, and Carina and Freddie are a captive audience, offering opinions about what they like most.

We tackle tonight's event first, and it only takes a couple of outfits for me to fall in love with a blue silk halter dress that makes my shoulders look amazing. The back plunges low to the small of my back with a series of crisscrossing straps that more than make up for the otherwise simple silhouette.

Then we move on to formalwear.

I do not enjoy myself like I did when I was trying on dresses with Daphne, but I can tell Freddie and Carina are working overtime to keep me happy and distracted. After ten dresses that are pretty enough but not quite right, Wren helps me into a black A-line dress with a strapless neckline and a high slit on the right thigh.

"Girl," she says softly. "I think you found your dress."

I slide my hands down the front of the skirt, then make my way out to the three-way mirror. It really is a beautiful dress. Contrast stitching swirls down the front, accentuating my waist, and the slit hits at a spot that feels sexy without being *too* sexy.

I can't keep myself from smiling as I turn to face Freddie and Carina, but then I see Freddie's face.

He's leaning forward in his chair, body tense like he might jump up at any moment. And his expression—I'm not sure I've ever seen him look at me like this. Like he wants to...*devour* me.

I lick my lips, suddenly nervous. "What do you think?" I ask.

It's Carina who answers. "You know who would love that dress?" she asks, her voice soft.

Freddie's intense focus temporarily distracted me, but I know the answer to Carina's question as soon as it's out of her mouth.

"Daphne would love it," I answer. Because it's true. Had *this* been the prom dress she found first, she never would have given it up. And that makes me want to wear it even more.

I close my eyes and think of my sister, and for a split second, a warmth settles across my shoulders, and the anxiety I've been battling since this whole try-on-a-thon started calms and settles.

I can practically hear Daphne's voice in my head. *You're right. I would have worn that dress. Which is why you should wear it now. Wear it for me.*

I take a deep breath and open my eyes, then lift my fingers to catch a tear brimming over on one side.

"Are you sure this is okay?" I say to Carina, my voice cracking on the words.

She stands and walks toward me, pulling me into a hug. "Of course it's okay. You know she would want you to be happy. To live your life and wear the dress and do the things." She pulls back so she can look me in the eyes but keeps her hands on my shoulders. "Refusing to do those things won't bring her back. All it does is make your life small."

I'm not sure she means for me to, but I easily sense the double meaning in Carina's words. Because being overprotective only makes *her* life small. And that's not what I want for her any more than Daphne would want it for me.

"When did you get so smart?" I ask, and she grins.

"Rude," she says playfully. "You know I came this way." She tilts her head toward Freddie. "I think he likes it too."

I finally look back at Freddie, who is still studying me. His gaze is softer now, the fire from moments before banked and controlled.

"What do you think?" I ask.

He licks his lips. "You look beautiful," he says. "That's definitely my favorite." He stands and moves toward the door. "I think..." He clears his throat. "That is, if we're done here, I have some...something. To do."

I furrow my brows, surprised by his sudden departure. Then again, he's already stayed longer than I thought he would, so I quickly nod. "Okay. Thanks for your help. And thank you for..." I wave my hands to encompass the entire room. "All of this."

"You deserve it," he says simply. Then he turns and disappears through the door, shutting it softly behind him.

"I think you flustered the poor man," Natasha says, kneeling at my feet and messing with the hem of the dress. "Not that I'm surprised. The dress really is perfect. We'll probably need to have it hemmed for you, but let's pick your shoes first."

As soon as I have the right shoes, a pair that is miraculously comfortable despite the four-inch heel, Natasha drops back to the floor in front of me with a pin cushion and adjusts the hem of the skirt. "I can't tell you how happy I was when Freddie called," she says. "Almost as happy as I was when I saw the news that you two were finally together. It seemed like it was all anyone was talking about, but it still meant more to hear the news directly from Freddie. And then to have him ask for all this. 'Spare no cost,' he told me. 'Whatever she wants, I want her to have it.'"

My heart climbs into my throat. "He really said that?"

"Is this the part where I get to say *I told you so*?" Wren says. "Because I totally saw this coming, and *you* tried to tell me it was nothing."

Natasha laughs. "I think we *all* saw this coming."

"Definitely," Carina adds, shooting me a pointed look. "Even the fans agree. They literally love you so much. There's an entire Reddit thread dedicated to stories from fans who had backstage passes or tickets to a meet-and-greet at one of Freddie's shows, and it's all about how perfect you are together."

"What? Are you being serious?"

Carina clears her throat, then holds up her phone and reads from the screen. "They basically finish each other's sentences. And once, a woman in front of me in line tried to push Ivy out of the way so she could get closer to Freddie, and he immediately activated beast mode, pulling Ivy behind his body and very firmly telling the woman to keep her hands to herself. I knew then they had to be a couple, so this news doesn't surprise me at all."

Even though my job has usually included keeping an eye

on Freddie's online presence, I've been almost entirely offline this week, outside of text and email.

Right before we landed on the flight home to Nashville, Kat pulled me aside for a private conversation, one in which she reminded me of all the reasons why I should stay off social media now that I'm also in the spotlight.

"There will be a lot of people who love you simply because they believe *he* loves you," she said. "But there will also be people who say horrible things. Those things will not be true, but that won't stop people from saying them. They will make things up, they will criticize you, they will be unkind and unjust and irredeemably rude."

"I understand," I told her, even as I swallowed against the lump forming in my throat. "I've seen the same things happen to Freddie over and over again. I know how to ignore it."

She shook her head. "This isn't the same thing. It's different when it's about you. Please trust me on this. Don't go online. I have a whole team of social media interns monitoring everything that's said about either one of you. If anything worrisome comes up, we'll let you know. In the meantime, your job is to stay off the internet."

I know Carina wouldn't share even if she *did* happen across any of the negative stuff, but it does feel good to know that most people seem to be happy for us.

But does their happiness even count if none of this is real?

Natasha and Wren and Carina, and apparently a million of Freddie's fans, all think they saw this coming, but really enthusiastic cheerleaders can only do so much to help a team win. At the end of the day, Freddie and I are the only two people who matter—and we've decided we're just pretending. That after his album releases, all of this will end.

I have to be okay with that.

But the way he just looked at me. I don't think I made it up. Something is shifting between us. I don't know what it is. And I definitely don't know what it means. But I know he's never looked at me like that before.

Is it possible I'm *not* the only one feeling something?

A new feeling simmers in the tiniest corner of my heart, something warm and bright and fluttery. Something that feels a lot like *hope*.

CHAPTER SEVENTEEN

Ivy

AT LEAST ONE GOOD THING ABOUT THE VOLTAGE PARTY IS THAT with more than half their artist roster in attendance, the room is so full of famous people that Freddie doesn't really stand out.

After stopping on our way in for photographs, Freddie makes the rounds, shaking hands and networking with the label's executives, meeting the teenage daughter of one investor and the daughter-in-law of another. Since this is the first album he's done with the label, the faces are all mostly new to me, people whose names I've heard and seen copied in emails but I've never actually met in person.

Freddie makes a point of introducing me by name to every single executive, talking me up, mentioning the many ways in which I keep his career running smoothly. Eventually, we run into the artist relations manager who's been working with Freddie, a woman named Danica Smith. She's someone I *have* met in person, when Freddie first signed his contract, but we haven't had much interaction since then.

With Danica, Freddie lays it on thick, even going so far as to mention my music business degree from Belmont. Danica ends up offering me her card and tells me she's always looking to expand her team if I'd ever be interested in working for Voltage Records.

"See?" Freddie says as I tuck her card into my clutch. "Easy as that."

"Easy when I have you talking me up," I say. "You're a very convincing salesman."

"You're the one who makes it easy," he says. "I didn't say anything that wasn't true."

My heart squeezes, and I second-guess—for about the billionth time—my decision to work somewhere else. When Freddie looks at me like he is now, I don't want to be *anywhere* but right here. Right beside him. Even if he never loves me back.

Okay, *fine.* That last part is probably just my hormones talking. But *gah,* the man is not making it easy to keep my head on straight.

After Freddie and I have talked and smiled and posed for at least two dozen photographs, we finally sync up with Leo, Jace, Adam, and Laney. We find a couple of couches arranged around a low coffee table near the back of the event space and mostly keep to ourselves.

Freddie lifts his arm and puts it around my shoulders, pulling me close enough for him to ask, "Do you think Jace has a new girlfriend?"

I ignore the goosebumps triggered by his touch and force my attention across the small space to Jace, who is typing out a text. "I doubt it," I say. "I bet he's just texting his mom about his kids."

"Nah," Freddie says. "With that level of focus?"

I shoot him a look. "Have you *seen* the way he dotes on those kids?" I put a hand on Freddie's knee and use it to push myself up, then move around the coffee table and sit down next to Jace.

"Are the kids okay?" I ask.

Jace looks over, expression sheepish as he pockets his phone. "They are. Mom says your sister is hanging out with them and just made everyone homemade hot chocolate. Now she's watching a movie with Annie while my mom gets Eli to bed."

"Hot chocolate is one of our mother's specialties," I say. "And I'm sure Carina is happy to be spending time with Annie."

He nods. "I'm sure Mom appreciates the help."

I glance back at Freddie, giving him a look that says I was *absolutely* right, and he smiles and shakes his head. But then Sloane shows up, pulling him into a conversation, so I sit back, content to talk to Jace as long as Freddie is occupied.

"Freddie thought you might have a girlfriend," I say, and Jace chuckles.

"Nooo, absolutely not. I'm nowhere near ready for that."

"Do your kids always travel with you?" I ask.

"This is the first time I've gone anywhere since Eli was born. Mom would have just stayed with them. But Annie has had such a hard time since her mom left. She doesn't do well when we're apart—even for a couple of nights. So they go where I go, at least for now."

"You're a good dad, Jace."

He runs a hand through his wavy blond hair. "I don't

know about that," he says, vulnerability flashing in his blue eyes. "But thank you anyway." He looks up, and his gaze narrows. "Hey, who do you think Leo is staring at?"

I look to the couch opposite us to see Leo staring across the room, brow furrowed. I follow his gaze to a cluster of women standing near the entrance and let out a little gasp. "Is that Dolly Parton?"

"Hey," Jace says, calling to Leo. "Respect the legend, man. Stop staring at Dolly."

Leo gives his head a little shake. "I'm not staring at her. I'm trying to figure out who's standing beside her. Why do I feel like I know her? Is she an artist?"

I look back at the group of women. "The blond one?"

Leo nods.

"That's Claire McKenzie," I say. "She's an actress."

"An actress?" Without another word, Leo stands and strides across the room directly toward the woman.

"Wow," Jace says. "I don't know if I've ever seen him look so intense."

"What did I miss?" Freddie asks, then he looks at me. "Sloane thinks we should dance. She says we have to stop hiding."

"We think Leo has a crush," Jace says, and Freddie turns and looks to where Leo is now hovering beside the group of women.

"Don't we all?" Freddie says. "Dolly is amazing."

"Not on Dolly," I say. "On Claire McKenzie. The actress."

"She was in a movie with Flint, wasn't she?" Freddie asks. He holds out his hand. "What do you say? Dance with me?"

"We'll dance too," Laney says, standing and holding her hand out to Adam. "But not you, Jace. You'll make the rest of us look bad."

We all laugh at Laney's comment, but nobody disputes. Jace was the best dancer in Midnight Rush by far. He really would make the rest of the guys look bad.

He grins. "Your egos are safe. I'm going to step outside so I can say good night to Annie."

Freddie and I follow Laney and Adam to the dance floor. The music is louder and faster than I would like, and I'm not a particularly skilled dancer, but Freddie keeps his eyes on me, one hand resting gently on my hip, and I do my best to settle into the rhythm of the bass reverberating through my body.

Freddie pulls me closer, moving his mouth to my ear where he says, "You look really great tonight. Did I tell you that? I like your hair up."

It took some convincing from the stylist Natasha brought along—I really like wearing my curls down—but I have to be grateful now. My hair would be a riotous mess were I dancing like this with it down.

It's too loud and Freddie is too tall for me to just talk and trust that he'll hear me, so I reach a hand up, looping it around the back of his neck and pulling him down so I can whisper back, "You aren't so bad yourself."

His green eyes dance as we continue to move, our bodies in sync, his smile wide, his focus wholly on me.

The party is packed with people, but the longer we dance, the more it starts to feel like Freddie and I are tuned into a frequency that's only ours.

He guides my movements with gentle touches, pulling me close, then nudging me back again, eyes on me the whole time. I've never danced with Freddie, never had him look at me like this, and the effect is dizzying. I could do this all night. Stand here with him, stare at him *all. night. long.*

But then Freddie reaches up and tugs on his earlobe, and I'm jolted back into reality. This is what we talked about. The sign he would give me if he thought we should kiss. It's a painful reminder that we aren't just here to have fun.

We're here to sell a story. And if he wants to kiss me, it must be because someone is watching.

My heart starts pounding.

I could shake my head no. Tell him I don't want to, and I know he'd respect it.

But I *do* want to. That's the trouble. I want it so much I don't even care that every time I give in, I'm aiming an arrow at my future self. At the woman who's going to have to get over being this close to something she wanted so badly when it was never truly hers to have.

I lean forward the slightest bit, tilting my head up so Freddie knows I'm game. We made a deal, and I'm willing if he is.

He lifts one hand to my jaw, sliding it back so his long fingers are wrapped around the back of my neck, then he tugs me forward and lowers his head. His eyes are open, watching me, like he's gauging my reaction as he brushes his nose against mine, then he pulls back and holds my gaze for a long moment. He smiles the slightest bit, and I'm not sure what to make of it.

Is he acknowledging that we're in on this together—like, ha-ha, look at how well we're fooling everyone? Or is he just genuinely enjoying the moment?

I'm thinking too much, and the anticipation is practically killing me, so I take matters into my own hands and push up on my toes, finally pressing my lips against his.

The last time Freddie kissed me, I was so surprised, I

didn't have time to anticipate. But now, I'm hyperaware, every sense tuned to every single place our bodies are touching. The hand that wraps around my waist to the small of my back. The heat of every single fingertip as it presses through the thin fabric of my dress. My hands on his chest, the way I can feel his heart pounding through my palm. The taste of him as his lips part and he deepens the kiss.

Somewhere in the back of my mind, I know we're standing in a room full of people. That I'm *kissing* Freddie Ridgefield in a room full of people. But it doesn't feel like it.

It feels like it's just us. Like he's the only person in the world who matters.

He has to feel this too. The electricity. The fire coursing through my veins. He has to know this matters so much more than a publicity stunt.

I push up on my toes, feeling a sudden need to be even closer. Freddie responds, his hands lifting to my face as the kiss shifts to something more intense. Lips parting. Hands grasping. Hearts pounding. The brush of his tongue. The graze of my teeth across his bottom lip.

The stubble on Freddie's cheeks is rough under my palms as I ask for more, tasting him, savoring the contact. But then he wraps his hands around my wrists and gives them a gentle squeeze before finally pulling back, chest heaving as his breath slows. The fire in his expression turns my insides molten, but there's something else there too. A question I can't read.

Panic floods my brain. Was I the one pushing the kiss? Asking for more? Was it too much and now he's wondering what could possibly have come over me?

I lick my lips and drop my hands, taking a step backward.

"That should do it, I think," I say. I pat Freddie on the chest with an awkwardness that even makes *me* cringe. "I think we definitely convinced everyone."

Even me, I think.

Then I turn and make a run for the bathroom.

I STAND at the sink and stare at my reflection, hands pressed into the cool marble countertop. My dress is speckled with the water I just splashed on my neck and cheeks, but I hardly care. As far as I'm concerned, I'll spend the rest of the night in here anyway.

I definitely can't go back out there.

When the bathroom door swings open, I start to panic, but then Laney slips into the room, locking the door behind her. She makes quick work of checking the stalls to make sure we're alone, then she moves in beside me, leaning against the counter so she can face me.

"So," she says gently. "Should we talk about that kiss?"

I breathe out a sigh. Even though I haven't known Laney very long, when we met last year, we had an instant kinship that made her feel like an immediate friend. Whenever we see each other, our relationship feels easy and natural, like we're picking up exactly where we left off, so I'm not at all taken aback by her question.

And truthfully, I'm glad she showed up to ask about it because if I *don't* talk about it, I might explode.

"It was obvious, wasn't it?" I ask. I turn on the tap and hold my hands under the cold water, then lift them to my neck a second time.

"Obvious that you two are into each other?" she asks.

I look up sharply. "No! That *I'm* into him. That was me, Laney. I was driving that kiss. I lost control. Stopped thinking. He probably thinks I..." I turn off the water and reach for some paper towels, fighting the urge to flee.

Maybe the bathroom isn't far enough. I need to leave Nashville altogether.

"Ivy," Laney says gently. "I know I'm just one person, but from what I saw, you were *not* the only person enjoying that kiss."

I prop my hands on my hips. "Sure. Kissing is fun. I'm sure he enjoyed himself. But that doesn't mean he wanted whatever that turned into. It doesn't mean he has real feelings."

Her eyebrows lift, then her expression softens. "But you *do* have real feelings."

I almost laugh at how easily she calls me out. For years I kept my feelings hidden, and now it seems like someone only has to look at me to know the truth. "I should just write it on my forehead in Sharpie," I say. "Apparently, I'm that bad at hiding it."

"I mean, to be fair," Laney says, "you aren't exactly being chill right now. Without all the bathroom drama, I might not have made the leap."

I give her a pointed look, and she winces.

"Okay, fine. Without the kiss and all the bathroom drama, I might not have made the leap. But that's a good thing, right? You guys want people to think you're together for real. Well, mission accomplished. That was some kiss."

"I'm not worried about what people think. I'm worried about what Freddie thinks. I'm worried about him realizing I wasn't faking."

"You could just tell him," she says gently. "Maybe he feels the same way."

I scoff. "He does not feel the same way."

"I'm sorry, were you out there just now—when he was kissing you like his life literally depended on it?"

"That was just a kiss. It's not the same thing. I've worked for him for years, Laney. Years when he could have made a move, when he could have seen me differently. And he never has."

She bites her lip like she's considering, her arms wrapped around her middle. Then she lifts her shoulders in a gentle shrug. "Maybe something changed for him. It's not always just about the person. It can also be about timing, about what someone is looking for, what they're ready for."

I take a deep breath, wanting to believe she's right. But I don't know how to let go of my fear, my desperation to keep my secret safe from Freddie.

Laney lets out a little chuckle. "You know, last year when Freddie showed up in Lawson Cove, Adam said he had a whole list of 'normal person' things he wanted to do. Go through a drive-thru. Shop for his own groceries. He even wanted to help clean the kennels out in the dog barn. Adam thought he was ridiculous, but I think sometimes we take for granted what it means to have that kind of freedom. There aren't many places Freddie can go by himself. Not without compromising his safety."

"Yeah. He hates complaining about his fame, but I've seen his frustration over the limitations it brings."

She nods. "I also wonder if the fame has impacted how he approaches relationships. He was, what, sixteen when Midnight Rush took off?"

"Fifteen," I say. "He was the youngest of the four."

"Which means he's probably never had a relationship where his fame wasn't a factor."

"Okay. But...what does that have to do with me?"

"Maybe nothing," Laney says. "But it could mean he doesn't really know what a normal relationship is supposed to look like. Or how to make a move without violating all kinds of rules about power dynamics and bosses hitting on their assistants."

I shake my head. "There's a power dynamic on paper, but it doesn't feel like it in person. He treats me like an equal. I run his life, Laney. I know everything there is to know about him."

"Okay. But that sounds like it could *also* make things complicated when it comes to feelings."

I turn and slump against the counter beside her. "Complicated is a good word."

She's quiet for a beat before she says, "I think you should still tell him how you feel."

I'm shaking my head before she even finishes the sentence. "I can't."

"Why not?"

"Because he's Freddie freaking Ridgefield."

"Not to you, he's not. He's just Freddie."

"But he isn't," I say. "His life, everything that comes with his fame. It's a lot, Laney. I know it's a lot because I've been watching him live it for years."

"So what? You can handle a lot. You *have* been handling a lot because you've been living that life with him. You're capable, practical, level-headed. That sounds like the perfect combination to handle a more serious relationship, despite the complications of his fame."

"You're making it sound way too easy."

"Hi. Do you remember what I do for a living? A small-town veterinarian is probably the last person cut out to be the girlfriend of a former popstar. And now I'm engaged to one. We figured it out."

"But Adam lives in your hometown. You have privacy, a life that isn't *just* about his fame."

She's quiet for a long moment. "Yeah. I get that. It definitely matters. And we don't have to deal with Freddie's level of fame. But I still don't think that's a reason *not* to tell him how you feel. After everything you've seen about his life, you still feel the way you feel. That has to mean you'd be up for the challenge."

"I can't. At least not until after all this faking is behind us."

"Why not?"

"Because if he doesn't feel the same way, there's no way I can *keep* faking. I have to walk the red carpet with him at a movie premiere next week."

"You don't *have* to do anything," Laney says. "I remind Adam of that all the time. There are always expectations, but his peace is more important than anything else. More than Midnight Rush. More than recording contracts or the expectations of his fans. If it's true for him, it's true for you too. Freddie would understand."

"I know. I know he would. But we have a plan. And the positive press is really helping him right now. I don't want to back out now."

"Okay. I get it." We're quiet for a beat, but then she nudges my shoulder with hers. "I recognize the many, *many* layers of complications here," she says, "but you have to at least tell me one thing. Was that kiss as good as it looked?"

My skin flushes as I think of Freddie's hands sliding up my arms, his fingers pressing into the base of my scalp as his mouth devoured mine.

I breathe out a sigh.

"It wasn't," I finally say. "It was better."

CHAPTER EIGHTEEN

Freddie

I CAN'T DECIDE IF I'M FRUSTRATED OR RELIEVED THAT AFTER the kiss to rival all kisses, Ivy decides to avoid me. She eventually comes back out to the party, but she stays close to Laney and does her level best to avoid eye contact.

When we get back to the house, she makes a vague comment about being tired and disappears into her bedroom before we have the chance to talk.

I leave for the studio the next morning before she wakes up, and by the time I come home, she's watching a movie with her sister and doesn't do more than wave to me from her corner of the couch where she's burrowed into a nest of blankets. I'm exhausted after working all day, so I crash before the movie is over.

Which is how I wind up in my kitchen the following morning, nearly thirty-six hours after the kiss, still having not had a conversation with Ivy.

The good news is my time in the studio was *very* productive. Working with Leo has been amazing, and having Jace and Adam around to lend their expertise has made everything feel easier.

But it's more than that. This thing with Ivy has woken me up. Broken through whatever logjam was keeping my brain from working—from *writing*.

The bad news is I can't stop thinking about that kiss.

I shouldn't be surprised that Ivy thinks we were only doing it because someone was watching. That was the plan. The agreement we made. And maybe I *did* recognize an entertainment reporter watching us from the edge of the dance floor before we kissed.

But that isn't why I wanted to kiss her. Or why I've been thinking about it ever since.

When she pulled away, the expression on her face looked an awful lot like regret. But then she ran, and I lost the opportunity to talk to her. To ask if I pushed too far. Made her uncomfortable.

She kissed me back. I *know* she kissed me back, and it felt like she was aware of the same current, the same fire, that I was.

But I can't be sure I didn't read everything wrong. That my own desire didn't cloud my judgment and make me see and sense things that weren't really there.

And don't even get me started on the spiral that starts whenever I think about what would happen if Ivy *does* have feelings for me.

What would it look like?

Would she have to stop working for me? It might not matter, since she's already planning to leave. But if things didn't work out, would that mean she wouldn't be in my life at all?

I don't know how to quiet the questions. To make any kind of sense of my jumbled thoughts.

I turn my phone face down next to my empty coffee cup and drop my head onto my arms, resting them on the cool kitchen countertop. I didn't get enough sleep last night, but Leo's expecting me in the studio again in a couple hours, and I'd like to see Ivy before I go.

I wish I could ask her to come with me, but I already told her she could take some time off to spend with her sister. She's still been doing a lot—honestly, things would probably fall apart if she didn't—but she's doing it from her corner of the house without ever venturing into mine.

I don't like spending less time together. If we were in a real relationship, we would be spending *more* time together.

Which is what I want.

I *think* it's what I want?

We at least have the movie premiere tonight, so we'll be together for that. I have all kinds of feelings about the event. I'm excited to see Ivy in the dress she picked out, but I'm also nervous about her getting through the night without too much emotional trauma.

It means a lot that she's doing this for me. That she's tackling something personal just to help me, and she's doing so in an incredibly public way.

My relationship history is woefully underdeveloped, but every woman I've dated has also been a celebrity. Walking the red carpet would just be another day at work for any of them. But the stakes feel a lot higher with Ivy. Because she's Ivy, obviously, but because she also has so much more to lose by being with me.

Either way, I don't think I can even suggest the possibility when I'm not sure it's also what *she* wants.

"You're up early."

I lift my head to see Ivy at the foot of the stairs, still in pajamas, her hair pulled back from her face. She looks beautiful, fresh-faced and well-rested, and I'm suddenly grateful she's taken some time off. We rarely get a full night's sleep when we're on the road.

I run a hand through my hair, wishing I'd at least looked in the mirror before stumbling into my kitchen for coffee. "Hey."

"Fancy meeting you here," she says as she moves into the kitchen and pulls a mug out of the cabinet. "Seems like we keep missing each other."

"Yeah," I agree. "Yesterday was a long day at the studio."

Ivy moves to the espresso machine at the end of the counter. It's fancy and expensive, and I still haven't figured out how to use it, but Ivy has a cappuccino every morning we're home, so I can't regret the purchase.

"How has it been?" she asks. "Are you making good progress?"

"Surprisingly good," I say. "We're working on several new songs, and I really like them all."

"I'm sure you're so relieved," she says. "Any idea what changed?"

I hold her gaze.

I changed. We kissed outside Margot's beach house, and something turned over inside my brain. I'd been stuck, mired in the monotony of touring and traveling, uncertain that I was even living a life I still wanted, and then we kissed and suddenly, there was something else to think about. Something else to *feel*.

But I'm not sure I can say that yet. Not when I suspect she spent the last day and a half avoiding me.

I shrug my shoulders. "I know better than to question when or why inspiration strikes." It's not the full truth, but it isn't a lie either, so that's good enough for now. "How's your time with Carina been?"

Ivy blows on her cappuccino, holding the mug close to her face. "Really good. Better than I expected it to be."

"So a vacation with Margot was temporary insanity?"

She shrugs. "Or a desperate plea to her family to stop treating her like she's made out of porcelain. Mom and I both probably need to let her live her life without so much hovering and worrying."

"I'm sure that's easier said than done."

"Do you ever worry about your brother?" she asks, and I immediately scoff.

"No. I really don't."

"Why not? He's younger than you, right?"

"Technically, yes. But he's the oldest twenty-five-year-old I've ever met. He doesn't need anyone to worry about him."

She takes a tentative sip of her drink. "Has he finished his PhD yet?"

"Next spring," I say.

Then he'll be Dr. Ridgefield just like my parents. A perfectly matched trio of doctorate degrees in mathematics. I couldn't fit in *less* if I tried.

"I'm sure your parents will be so proud," she says, her voice dripping with a disdain that immediately makes me smile. Ivy is my parents' worst critic, often grumbling about how little they seem to care about everything I've accomplished. I'm a little more forgiving. If I thought my parents had the capacity to express more enthusiasm, I might expect more. But they've always been exactly how they are. I can't do anything about that.

I chuckle at Ivy's comment, but I don't say anything else, and the silence quickly turns awkward.

We should talk about the kiss, but how do I bring it up? How do I ask her if it meant as much to her as it did to me? My brain pulls up the image of her running away seconds after we kissed, and I force myself to swallow the question.

"Are you ready for tonight?" Ivy asks, and I nod, happy to accept the subject change.

"Are *you*?"

She looks up at the ceiling. "Uh, let's go with yes? I'm nervous, I think. But also a little excited? And I think that must be a good thing."

"Remember our signal," I say. "If you need to get out of there, one squeeze on my elbow. That's all it'll take."

She nods, the gratitude in her expression making my heart stretch.

What would it be like to have her look at me like that all the time? To spend every day trying my hardest to make her life easier, better?

Ivy lowers her cup into the sink and backs away from the counter. "I should..." She tilts her head toward the stairs. "Carina and I are going to get pedicures this morning."

"I hope you have a good time."

She bites her lip. "So I'll see you tonight?"

I nod. "Car will be here at seven to pick us up."

I watch as she nods, then disappears up the stairs.

A part of me thinks tonight can't get here fast enough. But another part feels like I'm careening toward heartbreak, and I have no idea how to put on the brakes.

Every moment I spend with Ivy, the stakes raise a little bit higher. I've been taking risks all my life.

But I've never felt like I have this much to lose.

AFTER A FEW MORE HOURS AT the studio with Leo, I'm back home and ready to go, pacing the entryway as I wait for Ivy. Natasha has me in a dressed-down tuxedo, no tie or cummerbund, just a black dress shirt open at the neck, a black jacket, and black pants. It's a simpler look than she'd usually style for me, but she said the outfit is a nice complement to Ivy's dress, so she didn't get any complaints from me.

Adam and Laney show up in the entryway first, then Jace, who is carrying Eli. He's brave to carry the baby when he's already dressed and ready to go, but he doesn't seem to be worried.

Annie is beside him, something clutched in her hands. She looks up at her dad, and he nods his encouragement. "Go ahead," he says softly.

To my surprise, Annie walks over to me.

I crouch down so we're eye to eye. "Hey, Annie," I say.

She blinks at me with wide blue eyes, a matched set to her dad's. "I made this for you," she says, then she holds up a bracelet with chunky red beads. "For you to wear."

"Tonight?" I say, smiling as I take the bracelet. "Annie, this is the coolest thing I've ever worn!" I loop it over my wrist, holding it out for Annie to see. "It makes the whole outfit."

She surprises me when she throws herself against me, her tiny arms wrapping around my neck. "Bye, Uncle Freddie." She runs back to her dad, who runs a hand over her head and smiles at her, then bends down and kisses her on the forehead before handing Eli to his mom, who is standing nearby. She takes both kids into the kitchen, and Jace makes his way over to me.

He's wearing a bracelet just like mine, except the beads on his are blue and green. "Her mom would never wear them," he explains. "You don't have to keep it on after we leave, but thanks for putting it on for her."

I reach out and squeeze Jace's shoulder. "Are you kidding? She just called me Uncle Freddie. I won't take it off all night."

Adam and Laney raise their clasped hands, both of them wearing matching bright pink bracelets. "We won't either," Laney says.

Jace nods, gratitude making his expression soft. "Thanks, guys."

When movement across the entryway catches my eye, I turn to see Ivy at the edge of the space, and all the air escapes out of my lungs.

She looks incredible. *Beautiful.* More beautiful than she's ever looked before, which is saying something because she always looks amazing.

Jace clears his throat. "Breathe, man," he says, and I take a stuttering breath, quickly crossing to where she's standing.

"You look..." My voice cracks, and I swallow, trying again. "Wow. You're beautiful."

She offers me a hesitant smile, and I reach forward, threading her fingers through mine.

"Are you feeling okay?"

"I think so. Carina and I had a good cry this morning while we were getting our toes done, then we imagined all the things Daphne would have to say about her sister fake-dating a popstar and walking the red carpet at a movie premiere. It was surprisingly cathartic."

I lift my eyebrows. "What's the verdict? Would she have approved?"

"Of what we're doing?" Ivy says. "Absolutely not. But she would have loved you anyway."

"I'm sure I would have loved her too."

She drops my hand and lifts her wrist, showing off a red bracelet just like mine. "I see that Annie gave you your gift."

"Look at that. We match."

"I helped her make them this afternoon," she says. "I hope you like red."

"I love red," I say. "Red is perfect."

She's perfect.

"Cars are here," Wayne says from the doorway.

"And they already picked up Leo?" Ivy asks, and Wayne nods.

"He's in the car and waiting," he says.

"Good," Ivy says. "Then we're right on schedule."

I wrap an arm around her back and guide her toward the door. "Stop working," I say under my breath.

"Not until you hire my replacement," she says, and a knot tightens in the pit of my stomach.

It's still months away, but hiring Ivy's replacement is the *last* thing I want to do—and not because she's so good at her job. I push the thought out of my mind and force myself to be present, to focus on the night ahead.

Ivy and I climb into the SUV with Leo, while Wayne slides into the front seat, then Laney, Adam, and Jace get into the second car idling behind us.

Ivy is quiet as we drive over to the theater, but halfway

there, she reaches over and laces her fingers through mine, giving my hand an almost painful squeeze.

I lean toward her. "Did I tell you about the windmill I ran into the other day?"

She looks at me, brows drawn in confusion. "What?"

I nod. "Yeah. Looked right at me and said, 'I'm a big fan.'"

"Oh, that's bad," Leo says from the other side of Ivy, but it makes her smile, so I have zero regrets.

"Tell me another one," she says, her voice soft, her hand still gripping mine.

"Okay. How does an elephant hide in a cherry tree?"

"How?" she says.

"It paints its toenails red. Have you ever seen an elephant in a cherry tree?"

She chuckles. "Nope."

"Amazing how well it works."

Her shoulders lift in laughter, and satisfaction makes my heart stretch.

"That one is better," Leo says. "But you still shouldn't quit your day job."

"Don't make him stop," Ivy says to Leo. "He's distracting me. And it's exactly what I need right now." She takes a deep breath and leans into me, looping her arm through mine. "Thank you," she says softly, and I lean down and press a kiss to her forehead.

The action feels more like a reflex than a conscious choice, and I pause, holding my breath to see how she'll react. Did I cross a line? We aren't exactly pretending here, when everyone in the car already knows the truth.

But Ivy doesn't flinch. She just snuggles a little closer, relaxing into me as she takes a few slow, even breaths.

I don't have time to think about what her actions might

mean because we've just pulled up in front of the theater. Leo will get out first, then a few minutes later, Ivy and I will follow, giving the photographers lining the red carpet long enough to grab any shots they need. Once we've all walked the carpet, we'll pose at the end, just the four band members, then I'll reunite with Ivy, and we'll head toward the line of press doing interviews. Kat sent over the names of the journalists hoping to get a few minutes with me, but I'm welcome to stop and talk to anyone else if I'm feeling good.

For me, it will be about whether Ivy feels good.

For years, events like this one have been easy. The spotlight is easy for me. I'm good at thinking on my feet, at putting people at ease. All things that make interviews and red carpets easy.

But tonight, Ivy's my focus. And that changes things.

Not in a bad way. It feels good to be thinking about something besides my own image. It feels good to feel like I'm living for something bigger. For *her* comfort. *Her* well-being.

I don't know where the thought comes from, but the image of my grandfather pops into my head.

The first time he ever saw me perform with Midnight Rush, the band was back in Seattle, performing in the football stadium of the high school I attended before moving to Nashville. It was just a few days before my sixteenth birthday, and my grandfather came backstage to see me and give me my birthday present.

To my surprise, the gift was his guitar, the same vintage Gibson I have tattooed on my torso and the one I still play with whenever I have the option. He'd never let me play it before—he taught me to play on something much less expensive—so it was significant that he decided to give it to me then.

"You're growing up, Freddie," he said after I opened the case and pulled out the guitar. "Now get out there and make me proud."

I like to think that if he could, he'd say the same to me tonight. *You're growing up, Freddie.*

I hope I'm still making him proud.

CHAPTER NINETEEN

Freddie

"Just follow my lead," I whisper to Ivy as I help her out of the car. Even though she's watched me do this a million times from the outside, it's a different experience when all the cameras are aimed at you. I think back to the morning after the kiss at Margot's, when we'd just barely decided to keep up the facade of our relationship. I climbed out of the car, not unlike I'm doing now, turned, and helped Ivy out.

But tonight feels so much bigger than that first moment. It's not just fans watching. It's media. Press. Dozens of photographers with zoom lenses and prepared questions.

But my feelings are bigger too. I'm more sure of what they are, even if I do still have questions, which makes the stakes feel so much higher.

Ivy nods as we make our way forward, her hand looped through my arm. And then we're in it. Posing, smiling, looking this way and that.

People know who she is—they're calling her name as

often as they're calling mine. She handles herself like a pro, but I take every chance I get to lean down and whisper encouragement into her ear, to press a firm hand to the small of her back so she doesn't forget I'm right beside her.

It doesn't take long to make it down the length of the carpet, where Ivy steps to the side long enough for me to pose for a few photos with the rest of Midnight Rush.

"Can we get Freddie in the middle?" a photographer calls out.

"Is there a middle when there are four of us?" Jace asks as he and I switch places so I'm no longer standing on the outside.

"Maybe he should stand in the front with the rest of us in a row behind him," Leo jokes.

"Stop," I say, wrapping an arm around Leo's shoulder. "Just smile so we can get this over with."

"The faster the better," Adam says.

"Great. Thanks, guys," an event organizer says, motioning for us to move forward. I hold out a hand to Ivy, and she joins me from where she and Laney were standing off to the side. We walk toward Vivica Rose, an entertainment reporter who's smiling wide, microphone at the ready. I've met her before, so I greet her by name and introduce Ivy, then she comments on our matching bracelets.

"These were made by Jace's daughter, Annie," I say, holding up my wrist. "I think she's got a future in fashion."

"It must be so special to be here with the rest of the band members from Midnight Rush," Vivica says to me. "And, of course, with the new love in your life. Congratulations, by the way. I want to talk about romance in just a moment, but first, can you tell me a little about what it's like to be with your bandmates again?"

Ivy squeezes my hand once, and I squeeze it back.

"It's great," I answer. "Jace, Leo, Adam—they're my best friends in the world. Whenever we're together, we just fall back into it. I wouldn't trade that for anything. Even though we aren't making music together regularly, over the past year, we've been talking or texting almost every day. And we're proud of the song that's a part of this incredible movie we're all celebrating. So, yeah. It's amazing to be here and to share the evening with them."

"Good answer," Ivy whispers. "You make this look easy."

"And it must also be special to have Ivy with you," Vivica says, shifting the microphone to Ivy. "Is this overwhelming for you?"

I drop her hand and slip my arm around her, resting my palm on the small of her back.

"It's definitely a different experience being on this side of things as opposed to behind the scenes," she says, "but I'm proud of Freddie and just happy to be here with him, soaking it all in."

I look down at her and grin. She thinks I make this look easy? She's a natural.

"Okay, I've got a very specific question, if you don't mind me getting personal."

I expect Vivica to turn the microphone back to me, but she keeps it in front of Ivy.

"You've worked with Freddie for a number of years, but as far as I understand it, the romantic part of your relationship is relatively new. Was there a specific moment when you realized your feelings for him had shifted into something more?"

I'm about to tell Ivy she doesn't have to answer, but then she nods.

"I actually remember the exact moment," she says. "We were on tour—which, we're almost *always* on tour—and we got word from security that a mom and daughter outside the gates had a problem with their tickets and couldn't get in. I don't remember what happened—something about the ticket account having been hacked and their seats transferred to someone else. Whatever the reason, they couldn't get in, and the daughter was completely devastated."

I remember the concert Ivy is talking about, and I'm impressed with her quick thinking. That she was able to recall a memory so easily.

"So the security team messaged us to see if there was anything we could do," Ivy continues. "I told Freddie about it, and he immediately popped up off the couch in his dressing room, grabbed a couple of security guys, and went in search of them. It was a nightmare for security. He literally just ran through the crowds like it was no big deal, and everyone was watching and freaking out. But then he found this mom and her kid, and he crouched down in front of the little girl—she was probably eleven or twelve?—and told her he'd love for her to be his special guest at the concert." Ivy looks up at me one more time, the gold in her eyes brighter than usual as she says, "I respected Freddie from day one. He makes that very easy because he's genuinely a good man. But that day—" She licks her lips and something in her expression shifts. "That's when I realized I was in love with him. That's when everything changed."

Ivy's words wash over me, sending a wave of heat pushing out to my fingertips and down to my toes. I know she's pretending, playing it up for the narrative we're trying to sell, but her words land like truth, and I have no idea what to do with that possibility.

Except her words *can't* be true, because the experience she's talking about happened well over three years ago. It wasn't even the same tour we're on now.

If she's telling the truth, does that mean...?

Is it possible she's had feelings for me all this time?

The yearning that swells in my chest is almost painful.

I *want* her to be telling the truth.

Desperately.

Beside me, Ivy clears her throat, elbowing me gently in the ribs, and brings my focus back to the present. Clearly, Vivica has asked me a question, and I completely missed it.

"Sorry, I—" I look down at Ivy. "You've never told me that."

She shrugs her shoulders like it's no big deal. "You never asked."

Vivica repeats her last question for me, something about the new album and when fans can expect an update, then we say goodbye and we're ushered to the next interview.

No one digs quite as deeply as Vivica did, keeping things relatively surface level, which is good for me. Because in my mind, I'm thinking through countless interactions with Ivy in a new light.

Has she truly been standing right in front of me all this time, hiding feelings I didn't know she had—and I've never noticed? Over the past couple of weeks, so many things have come into focus for me. Ivy's brilliance, her sharp wit, her unending loyalty. How incredibly beautiful she is, like she is tonight, red-carpet ready, but also at home in her pajamas with her curls piled on top of her head and an oversized hoodie hiding everything from her shoulders down to her knees.

But Ivy has *always* been all of those things. She hasn't changed, so how did I miss them for so long?

It's no wonder she wants to work somewhere else.

Her boss is a colossal idiot.

"Hey," Ivy says, and I look down at her. "Where is your brain?" she asks. "I'm trying to give you a signal here."

My eyes shift to where her hand is tugging on her earlobe. She tilts her head toward a set of temporary bleachers directly across from the entrance to the movie theater where fans have gathered to watch us walk the red carpet.

"Fans are watching," she whispers. "You should kiss me."

I don't want this to be a kiss like the one we shared at the Voltage party, where she runs away and avoids me for a day. But I also don't want to miss the opportunity to kiss her again.

When I finally press my lips to hers, fire floods my veins, and I forget to be scared. I forget to worry that this might not last. That she's leaving me to work somewhere else. I just melt into the kiss and breathe her in.

Somewhere beyond us, cheers erupt and multiple cameras click, flashes popping. But I don't care about any of it.

I'm too consumed with the softness of her lips, with the scent of her as I lean close, the look in her eyes when I finally pull away.

"What's gotten into you?" she says, her tone playful, and I almost ask her. Right there with everyone watching.

I almost ask if she was telling the truth. And if she'll ever forgive me for taking so long to realize what was standing in front of me all this time.

But I can't do it. I can't because if she says no, then I'll be the one having to squeeze her elbow looking for a way to escape.

"Nothing. I'm good," I finally say. "Just really glad you're here with me tonight."

She pushes up on her toes and kisses me one more time. "Me too," she says as my hands slide to her hips. I give them a squeeze.

"Have I told you how incredible you look?" I ask.

"You have," she says. "But I don't mind you telling me again."

"You do," I say. "You look like you belong out here."

She playfully rolls her eyes. "Ugh, don't wish it on me. I like it much better behind the scenes. I can't stop wondering if I have something in my teeth, which is stupid because I haven't eaten since I left the house. But all this attention is messing with my head. I can't believe how easy you make this seem."

"I got used to it," I say. "Then the whole world shared a video of me looking like I was picking my nose seventeen million times, and I just stopped caring."

"Did you *really* stop caring?" she teases. "Because you still seem a little salty."

"I had an itch," I say. "My nose itched! I did not deserve to be maligned so brutally."

Ivy laughs. "Whatever you have to tell yourself."

I silence her laughter with one more kiss, chasing the impulse to be as close to her as possible. I'm too aware of our surroundings to let go like I did at the Voltage party, but as simple as it is, this kiss almost feels more intense. Because I'm kissing her with a sense of possibility that I didn't feel before.

When Ivy pulls back, there's a question in her eyes, and

for once, I don't filter what I'm thinking. I look at her like I want her, like I'm ready for this thing between us to be real.

"If you kids are done making out with your eyes, it's time to go inside," Leo says, stepping up beside us. He drops an arm around my shoulder, and another cheer erupts from the watching crowd. Leo lifts his hand and waves. "You guys gave them quite a show."

I smile, eyes still on Ivy. "I forgot they were even there."

LATE THAT NIGHT, after we've watched the movie and gone to an afterparty that kept us out until close to two a.m. and answered a phone call from Sloane saying Ivy and I basically broke the internet with our public displays of affection, a knock sounds on my bedroom door. I'm half undressed, down to my suit pants and socks, but I answer anyway, expecting it to be Wayne with some sort of security update. He lives in the pool house, but he has access to the entire property, and he's the only one who ever needs anything this late.

But it isn't Wayne.

It's Ivy. She's changed into tiny sleep shorts and a *Living Out Loud* tour hoodie. Her hair is up, and her face is bare, and she looks perfect.

"Hey."

Her eyes travel over my naked torso. "Hey," she says back.

I wait for her to say something else, but she just stands there, so I eventually ask, "Is everything okay?"

"Do you want to go to Knoxville with me?" she blurts in response. "To take Carina home?" She shifts on her feet, her hands hooked around the hem of her sweatshirt. "I thought you might want to see the farm. And..." She hesitates, then licks her lips. "And meet my parents."

There is a weight to her words, and I immediately sense the significance of what she's asking me. This isn't about a random trip to Knoxville. This is about going to Knoxville *with her*. To meet her family. To see where she grew up.

So far, the significant moments that Ivy and I have shared have been orchestrated. Appearances for the press. Kisses for the fans. Holding hands to show the world that we're together.

But this. Going to Knoxville doesn't have anything to do with any of that. This isn't part of an act. If I go, it's going to be because I want to.

And I really, *really* do.

"Yes," I say without hesitation. "I would love to."

Her face relaxes the slightest bit, and her lips lift into a small smile. "Good." She holds my gaze for a long moment. "I'm glad."

"Tomorrow?" I ask, and she shakes her head.

"I was thinking the day after? You'd have to miss a couple days of studio time, so I totally get it if you'd rather—"

"I don't care about the studio time," I say, cutting her off. Because I don't. At this point, I'd record the rest of the album on my phone in a bus stop bathroom if it meant getting to spend more time with her. "Seriously. I think a break would be good for me."

She smiles one more time. "Okay."

"Okay," I repeat.

She backs up a few steps without breaking my gaze. "Good night, Freddie," she finally says. Then she turns and darts down the hall, disappearing into the darkness.

Taking my heart with her.

CHAPTER TWENTY

Freddie

CONSIDERING HOW LATE WE WERE UP THE NIGHT BEFORE, I don't expect to make it to Leo's studio until after lunch. But when he texts me just past ten and says I'm welcome to show up whenever, I don't waste any time getting there.

I've had lyrics running through my brain all morning, and I'd love to get it down on paper.

As soon as we show up, Wayne heads to the lounge area at the back of the rehearsal space while I unpack my guitar.

Leo looks up from where he's sitting at the piano and immediately grins.

"What has you smiling?"

I shrug as I connect to Leo's amp. "Nothing. Just happy to be here. Ready to make some music."

"I don't believe you," Leo says.

"Why don't we believe him?" Adam says as he and Jace walk into the room from the booth situated opposite the sound stage.

"Because he's got a weird grin on his face," Leo says. He plays a few chords of the song we worked on the last time we were here, and goosebumps break out across my skin. Sometimes when a melody finds me, something happens on a visceral level, some recognition of a good, true, creative thing.

I can't explain it, and I don't always find it. But knowing it's out there—it's enough to keep me chasing it every time I write.

"That's why I'm grinning," I say to Leo. "We wrote a good song."

When Leo bought the space that now houses South Hollow Sound, it was a crumbling shell of a building, the former location of Lamplight Studios. Lamplight was a Nashville icon back in the sixties, with some of country music's greatest artists coming through to record. But then it went bankrupt in the early nineties, and the building was shuttered and probably would have been condemned and torn down had Leo not stepped in when he did. He had to basically gut the entire space and start over to make it functional and up to code—new wiring, new plumbing, that sort of thing—but it's obvious he worked hard to honor the vibe of the original studio. There are two isolation booths at the back, plus a state-of-the-art control room with everything Leo needs to mix and master tracks like the professional he's become.

I could work with just about anyone in the industry, but using Leo to produce my albums is an easy choice.

"You wrote it," Leo says. "I've just been your sounding board. Either way, I still think there's something else making you happy."

"Maybe *someone* else?" Jace says, and I roll my eyes.

"Stop." I lift the strap of my guitar over my head and position myself on my stool. "Are we working or what?"

Adam pulls up a seat next to the piano. "You're working. We're just here to watch."

"And make fun of you," Jace adds as he sits down beside Adam.

"That's why I'm here too," Wayne says from the opposite side of the room.

I roll my eyes one more time. "Fine. I get it. So happy to be your entertainment." I strum my guitar and reach for the tuning pegs. "Give me an E?" I say to Leo.

The last time we were together, we worked on two different songs. One is mostly finished but the other still needs a chorus and everything past the first verse. For all their talk of only being around to watch, Adam and Jace were genuinely helpful the last time we were here. They probably deserve a writing credit as much as Leo does.

We didn't do much writing when we were Midnight Rush. Not at first. We were too curated, too much a product of a record label who picked us individually to turn us into their vision of what a boyband should be.

But we've come a long way since then. And I'd argue we're writing better music than anything the label executives picked for us when they were in charge.

"Which one are we doing first?" Leo asks. "You want to pick up where we left off last time?"

"Let's play through 'Golden Eyes' first," I say. "I was messing around with the bridge last night, and I think it'll work better in a minor key. And I wrote a final verse too, so, let's start there."

Leo nods and plays through the opening chords. I sing through the first verse. When I hit the chorus, Jace starts humming a harmony line that sounds really great, so I motion for him to keep it up, and he joins in, singing through the rest of the chorus with me.

"That sounds good," I say. "You know the second verse?"

Leo lifts one hand off the keyboard and slides a sheet of paper across the top of the piano toward Jace. "If you can read his handwriting," Leo says.

Jace picks up the paper and nods. "Geez, man," he says and Adam leans over his shoulder to look.

"Does that say heart or herd?"

"Or head?" Jace asks.

"Come on," I say. "Context clues."

"I guess a pounding head would be a very different kind of song," Adam says dryly.

"I want to hear the bridge," Leo says, hands still playing through the interlude between verses. "Are we doing this?"

I wait another measure, then I join in with the second verse, and by the end of the first line, Jace is singing too. After the second verse, we sing the chorus again, then I sing the bridge, followed by a key change that circles us back to the chorus a third time. By the time we finish, my instincts are telling me I've got a hit on my hands, and it's making me buzz with a new kind of energy.

Sometimes writing feels like work. Sometimes it feels like magic. And this song—it's magic. I can tell by the look on Leo's face that he feels it too.

"Okay, this is where it changes," I say.

"You lead and I'll follow," Leo says.

He pauses as I shift my hands and change keys, then he jumps in. "Yes," he says, nodding his head. "That's it."

"And then the lyrics," I say, pausing before singing,

"There's no thunder, no big sign,

Just the slow undoing of the lines—
Where one thing ends
And something else begins—
Something better wins."

We play through the chorus one more time, and I lean into the lyrics about a woman with gold in her eyes and a promise in her smile and a shifting world I'm seeing for the first time.

It's good. I *know* it's good. So when the song ends and I look at my friends, I can't figure out why they're all staring at me. Maybe it's *not* good? Maybe I've forgotten how to make music and I need to find a new job?

But then Leo mutters a quiet, "*Damn,* Freddie," and I let out the breath I'm holding.

"It's good, right?" I say, and he nods.

"It's better than good."

Adam clears his throat. "I just have one question."

I run a hand through my hair. "Okay."

"Are you going to tell Ivy it's about her? Or just let her figure it out on her own."

I frown. "It isn't about Ivy."

"Come on," Jace says. "You know it is."

"It's not," I repeat.

Leo lifts an eyebrow. "Freddie." He reaches for the sheet of paper I used to write out the lyrics the last time I was here, then reads, "You laugh, and I forget my name. Same joke, but it doesn't land the same. The truth was there but too close to see, you've rewritten my world and set me free?"

"It's about *finding* love generally," I argue. "It isn't about Ivy."

"Because Ivy *doesn't* have gold in her eyes?" Jace asks.

Adam reaches for the paper. "And you aren't slowly

undoing the lines where friendship ends and something better begins?"

I don't answer. I *can't* answer. I didn't intentionally set out to write a song about Ivy, but when I close my eyes, it's definitely *her* eyes I see when I'm singing.

I lean to the side and prop my guitar against a nearby stand, then drop my elbows onto my knees and stare at the floor.

"We're not saying it's a bad thing," Adam says.

"We like Ivy," Jace adds.

"Honestly, we weren't surprised when we heard the news you were together. It was *more* surprising when you told us it was a publicity stunt. We all kinda assumed this is where you were headed."

I finally look up. "Really? You all thought that?"

They nod in unison.

"You're good together," Adam says. "And she's great."

I let out a little chuckle, thinking about our interview at the premiere last night and the way things seemed to shift after that. "She, uh..." I hesitate, suddenly unsure if I want to relay the entire story she told to Vivica Rose last night. "Last night she answered an interview question about when she knew I was the one for her. And she told a story from a long time ago. Like, three years long."

"Was she pretending?" Leo asks. "Like, just making it up for the sake of the interview?"

"That's what I thought at first," I say. "But it didn't really seem like it. I know Ivy. And there was something about her tone. It felt like she was telling the truth."

"How do you feel about that?" Jace asks.

"Like an idiot," I say. "Like I've been missing out on

something amazing because I couldn't see past the nose on my own face."

"So you want a relationship that's real," Leo says, matter-of-factly, and I nod.

"Yeah. I do."

Wayne coughs on the other side of the room. I can't be sure, but the cough sounds an awfully lot like the words, *I told you so.*

"Then why not tell her?" Jace asks.

I lean back and run a hand through my hair. "I want to. I'm going to Knoxville with her tomorrow," I say. "I just have to figure out how."

"You could just play her the song," Adam suggests.

I nod. It's not a terrible idea, now that I realize it's about her. Which, honestly, I don't know how I *didn't* notice. I was too close to the process, maybe.

"I just don't want to screw things up," I say. "I don't have a ton of experience with *real* relationships. If I do this thing with Ivy, I want to do it right. But what does right even look like when my life is...what it is?"

"Because of the fame?" Adam asks.

"The fame. The paparazzi. The never-ending scrutiny. Why would anyone want any of that?"

"But Ivy already knows all that. She's been working with you for years," Leo says.

"Just tell her, man," Adam says. "Give her the opportunity to decide for herself."

"You don't think I should wait until all this faking stuff is behind us?" I ask. "I don't want her to question my motives. Or feel trapped—like she has to go along with it even if she doesn't feel the same way just because of all the publicity stuff."

"Uh, have you *met* Ivy?" Leo says. "She won't go along with *anything* unless she wants to."

I chuckle, and my heart expands the slightest bit. That's one of the things I love most about Ivy. She knows her mind, and she definitely won't let anyone push her around. Especially me.

"That's fair," I say. "But...what if she doesn't feel the same way? What if I tell her and ruin everything, and then we can't even be friends anymore?"

"What if you never tell her, and then you never know and you miss out on the opportunity to love her?" Adam shoots back.

Of the four of us, he's the only one in a committed relationship, so he's probably the most qualified to ask the question.

But then Jace adds, "Sometimes you have to take the risk and hope for the best. If we only focused on the worst thing that could happen, we'd never do anything. Take my marriage, for example. It ended. And it sucked. But I still don't regret it. I have my kids, and I learned a lot about what I want my next relationship to look like."

In every other aspect of my life, I'd fully embrace Jace's philosophy. It's a huge part of why I've built the career that I have. Sometimes making it in this business means acting first and thinking later. But this thing with Ivy—there's so much at stake if it doesn't work out.

"Listen," Adam says, running a hand over his beard. "I'm not saying I know something. If I *did* know something, it would be wrong for me to say something, especially if someone asked me not to." He looks at me pointedly, and I get the sense he *does* know something and he's trying his hardest to talk around it. "But in this hypothetical situation where I am not betraying anyone's trust, if I thought you were going to get yourself hurt by admitting your feelings, I would definitely figure out a way to warn you."

I narrow my gaze at him. "But you *aren't* warning me now?"

"I'm not doing anything now," he says. "Because I'm a man of my word."

I smile and let the hope growing in my chest shoot out a few more roots.

Tomorrow, I think, then I tap the side of my guitar. "All right. Let's do it again."

CHAPTER TWENTY-ONE

Ivy

By nine a.m. the next morning, Freddie is in the front seat of my car, Carina is in the back, and we are ready to leave for Knoxville.

I am nervous for so many reasons, I can't even begin to list them all. But I'm excited too. And there's a strange, buzzy energy around Freddie that makes me think he feels the same way, which weirdly helps me feel better.

A tiny voice in the back of my head keeps suggesting I'm making things up, but I don't actually think that's true.

Not anymore.

Wayne begrudgingly gave us permission to travel without him, but it was no small feat to convince him. We're allowed to spend one night at my parents' house, then we're driving straight home. No stops on the way there or the way back. No snack breaks or bathroom breaks, even for emergencies.

Wayne made me promise on that last point, which felt

absolutely ridiculous, but then he blocked the front door and scowled until we all went to the bathroom before we left the house, so I don't doubt his seriousness. It wouldn't surprise me if he tracks Freddie's phone the entire time and calls us the second we veer off course.

"Your tires look good," Wayne says through my open window. "But if anything happens, you *only* call me. Understood?"

"Yes, Dad," I say, and he scowls one more time.

"Bye, Wayne," Freddie says, leaning across me to make eye contact with his head of security. "Enjoy a couple days off. You deserve it."

He mumbles something incoherent, then finally steps away from the car.

I start down Freddie's long, winding driveway, but I haven't made it a hundred feet before Carina leans up from the backseat and grabs my phone.

"Hey," I say, meeting her gaze through the rearview mirror.

"If I don't get the front seat, I at least get to control the music," she says.

"I don't mind if you sit in the front," Freddie says, but I quickly shake my head.

"Don't let her guilt you," I say. "You're six feet tall. You get to sit in the front." I look at Carina one more time. "Just don't pick anything stupid."

The touchscreen on the car flickers to life and shows the connection to my phone. Then Midnight Rush's first album blasts through the speakers, Freddie's very young, very high, barely pubescent voice on lead vocals.

He winces, then groans. "Geez. I don't think I can hit any of those notes anymore."

Carina laughs. "I'm not even sure *I* can hit those notes."

"We don't have to listen to this if you don't want to," I say, but Freddie only grins.

"Nah. It's fun. We can see how many of the words I remember."

Turns out that number is impressively high. He sings pretty much every word, making it easy for Carina and me to join in.

When we reach the end of the album, he looks over at me and grins. "Not a fan, huh? Isn't that what you told me when we met?"

Heat climbs up my cheeks. "What? Why do you say that?"

"This is old music, Ivy. And you know it."

"Just because I wasn't a fan doesn't mean I lived under a rock."

"You just sang every single word of every single song," he says. "That doesn't happen without some effort."

"I did not sing every word," I practically huff.

"Yeah, you did," Carina says. "When did that happen? You really weren't a fan when we were kids."

"See?" I say to Freddie. "I didn't lie to you."

"So, you've been listening to Midnight Rush since then?" he asks. The amusement in his voice makes me want to punch him directly in the nose. Except his nose is far too pretty to risk breaking it, so maybe a punch in the gut would be better. But *then* I would feel his abs, and that feels more dangerous, so maybe I *should* break his nose.

"Your silence is telling, Ivy," Freddie says. "I think I figured you out. You started listening to my music *after* we met. Was I really that charming?"

My eyes dart to his for a split second, and they are practically *dancing*. He is enjoying himself way too much.

"Shut up," I tease. "You were insufferable. But I wanted to be good at my job, and I figured that meant I needed to understand your catalog. So I listened. It's not a big deal."

"You listened...enough to learn *all* the lyrics. That's dedication."

"I take my work responsibilities very seriously."

"Right. But I'm not *in* Midnight Rush anymore, so..."

I breathe out an exasperated sigh. "Fine. It started as research, but then I ended up liking the music, and it was basically all I listened to for three solid months. Is that what you want me to admit?"

He chuckles. "Exactly that."

"You're horrible."

"I think what you mean to say is that I'm the lead singer of your favorite band," he says with a smirk.

He and Carina pass the phone back and forth for the next couple of hours, taking us on a musical journey from the wildly popular to the completely obscure.

We laugh, we joke, and I mostly forget to be tense around Freddie. To wonder if he's thinking about the kisses we've shared as much as I am. I just have fun. It feels really good. And serves as a reminder of why I like him so much.

But then Freddie turns on another Midnight Rush song, this one from the last album they released before the band split up. He's singing lead vocals, as always, and both his voice and the lyrics are more mature than the band's earlier stuff.

I grip the steering wheel as the opening verse plays over the speakers. For once, Freddie isn't singing along, and when I glance over at him, he's studying me closely.

At the line *You've given me the kiss I can't forget, You'll always be the one I won't regret*, I force my gaze back to the road.

Did he pick this song on purpose? Is that why he's watching me so closely?

It could just be a coincidence, but it's been almost an hour since any Midnight Rush music has played. Why this one?

"You wrote this one, didn't you?" Carina asks from the back seat, and Freddie clears his throat.

"Yeah, I did," he says.

Carina leans up, tugging her seatbelt forward so her face is hovering in between us. "About who? Was there someone special who really *did* give you the kiss you couldn't forget?"

Oh, I am going to murder my little sister. What is she doing? Is she *trying* to make me miserable?

"Absolutely *not* someone special," Freddie says through a chuckle. "I mostly write about ideas more than specific people or situations."

Carina meets my gaze through the rearview mirror, and I scowl at her, hoping she senses how much I really, *really* want her to change the subject.

She wrinkles her forehead like she has no clue what I'm talking about and lifts her shoulders into a shrug.

"That doesn't feel nearly as romantic as you writing a song for someone specific," Carina says. "Have you ever done it that way? Written a song about an actual person?"

I can't keep myself from looking over at Freddie one more time. He meets my gaze, his expression pointed and intentional.

"Yeah," he finally says as I force my eyes back to the road. "I have, actually. But not until recently."

Oh. Oh, man. Is he saying what I think he's saying?

I don't want to jump to conclusions. Recently could mean anytime in the last year. Or the last *three* years. It doesn't have to mean *now*. And he only said *someone* and someone could be *anyone*.

But the way he just looked at me. It *felt* like he was telling me something, like he was willing me to read between the lines.

I'm *deep* into existential pondering about what life will be like if Freddie really *has* written a song about me when my phone buzzes with a text. With the music turned off, Siri decides to read the message out loud.

"Message from Laney," Siri says. "How's the trip going? Have you told him yet?"

I scramble to grab my phone and turn on Do Not Disturb mode just in case Laney texts again, then I let out a nervous laugh. "Ha. She's probably talking about my dad. Just the other night I was...telling her all about his recent...tree thing."

Carina leans forward and slips a hand around my arm before whispering, "It's only going to get worse if you keep talking."

Her whisper is *definitely* loud enough for Freddie to hear, and his shoulders start shaking from the passenger seat, but she's right. Laney could have been talking about anyone, but my weird reaction made it perfectly clear she was talking about Freddie.

Now he's going to spend the rest of our trip wondering what it is I'm supposed to tell him and why I haven't yet.

"Stop laughing," I say, though now my nerves are making me laugh too. "It's not funny."

He looks over at me, warmth and humor in his eyes. "I mean, it's a little funny."

Carina at least has the sense to keep her mouth closed. For once.

"Come on," Freddie says. "What is it? What are you supposed to tell me?"

"Absolutely nothing," I say. "Because look." I motion toward the enormous wooden sign on the side of the road that reads Conway Nursery. "We're here."

Freddie's eyes are glued to the surrounding landscape as I turn onto the dusty gravel road that leads to my parents' farm. On either side of the road, rows and rows of Dad's field-grown trees cut through the hillside. Behind the house, several large greenhouses hold the smaller varieties he cultivates in pots and larger containers, but out here, maple, cypress, redbud, dogwood, and so many others grow for five, even ten years before they're ready to sell.

"This is all your family's?" Freddie asks, his eyes taking it all in.

I nod, happy to have a distraction that can pull us away from our previous conversation. I'm keenly aware that it's time to tell Freddie how I feel, even without Laney's gentle prompting. But I've had enough conversations with Carina or Wayne or the entire freaking internet watching or listening in. Privacy with Freddie is hard to come by, but for this conversation, it's worth waiting for.

Or so I tell myself to justify my procrastination.

I point across the field to our right. "There's a swimming hole over in that cluster of trees," I say. "We used to spend all summer out there."

"Especially when the Benson brothers were home," Carina says from the back seat.

"Who are the Benson brothers?" Freddie asks, and I grin, loving how jealous he sounds.

"Will, Brady, and Chad," I say. "They grew up about a mile down the road."

"And they *loved* to swim," Carina adds.

"I'm sure they did," Freddie says dryly, and I laugh.

"Will was my first kiss," I say, watching Freddie's reaction. "Brady was my second."

His eyes widen. "Two brothers?" He's smiling, despite his indignant tone.

"What?" I say innocently. "Will went off to college. His brother was absolutely fair game."

"You should have waited around for Chad," Carina says. "He was *my* first kiss, and it was epic."

"I think I draw the line at kissing more than *two* brothers," I say, and Freddie scowls, looking undeniably grumpy about the idea.

"Someone looks jealous," Carina singsongs from the back, and Freddie huffs.

"I'm indignant," he says. "That's different."

What he *doesn't* do is protest. Act like he wouldn't have reason to be jealous or indignant. And that realization makes me smile all the way to the end of my parents' driveway.

When we finally reach the house, I shift into park, but Carina stops me before I can open my door.

"Wait," she says. "What are we telling Mom and Dad?"

"About what?" I ask.

She scoffs like I've asked the stupidest question, then motions between me and Freddie. "About the two of you. They think you're together for real, right? Are you going to tell them differently, or are we all pretending?"

I've been so focused on how and when I'm going to tell Freddie the truth, I honestly haven't even thought about what my parents think. But Carina's question is a valid one.

I look over at Freddie. "What do you think?"

"I think...I'm happy to let your parents think we're together," he says slowly. Even *carefully*. Like his words were chosen intentionally.

It's an interesting way to respond. He doesn't say we should keep faking or that he's happy to pretend. He says he's *happy* for them to think we're together.

Because he wants us to be together for real?

"I vote you don't say anything," Carina says. "Daddy would hate the lying."

It's the same thought I had when I decided not to tell my parents the truth, so it's validating to hear Carina echo my concerns. But *continuing* to lie feels just as bad as *telling* him we've *been* lying. I don't really want to do either one.

"If he hates lies, then we shouldn't tell any," Freddie says, eyeing me.

"Right. Good," I say, though I have no idea what he's suggesting. "So that means we just..."

"Be ourselves," Freddie says, filling in the blank. "No more lies."

I don't have time to ask exactly what that means because my mother is already on the front porch with a wide smile on her face.

But *no more lies* can really only mean one thing, right? It means however we act around each other will be truthful. A reflection of how we *really* feel.

I can't decide if I'm more excited or terrified to see what that looks like.

CHAPTER TWENTY-TWO

Ivy

Mom is wearing jeans and a faded t-shirt, just like always, her short hair swept off her face in a way I've always loved. My mother has always been effortlessly cool. Comfortable in her own skin, and so beautiful, with an unassuming confidence that makes her easy to be around.

Freddie steps up beside me as she descends the stairs. "I'm nervous. Should I be nervous?" he asks.

"Absolutely not. Just be yourself. They're going to love you."

Mom finally reaches the car and pulls me into a hug first.

"Hi, Mom," I say, sinking into the embrace. It's been too long since I came home, and being here, feeling the certainty of her love, soothes the frayed edges of my heart. There are a lot of things I *don't* know right now.

But for a split second, with the weight of Mom's arms around me, none of that really matters. Because no matter what happens, even if my heart gets broken and my professional life falls apart, I'll still have this. I'll have a home where I'm welcome and loved and seen. And that's no small thing.

Mom leans back and cups my face with her palms. "Look at you," she says. "Beautiful as ever."

"I've missed you," I say, and her eyes turn a little misty.

She kisses my forehead. "You have no idea."

She approaches Carina next, their prolonged eye contact suggesting they'll have a conversation later, but then she pulls her youngest daughter into a hug, the relief on her face so obvious, it makes my chest ache.

Finally, she turns to Freddie. She props her hands on her hips and looks him up and down. "Well, if it isn't the famous Freddie Ridgefield."

Freddie extends his hand, looking adorably sheepish. "Nice to finally meet you in person."

She waves away the handshake and pulls him into a hug. "Likewise. I hope you're taking care of my girl."

Freddie glances over at me. "I'm doing my best," he says, and my heart climbs into my throat.

"How was the drive?" Mom asks.

"Entertaining," he says, and she chuckles.

"I expect it would be, with these two in the car."

"Where's Daddy?" Carina asks.

"Out in the greenhouse. But he'll come in if someone runs out and tells him it's time to eat. Are y'all hungry?"

I glance at my watch. It's only three-thirty, but we didn't stop for lunch, so when I catch a whiff of fried chicken floating out the front door, my eyes widen.

"You made chicken?" I ask, my mouth already watering.

"And biscuits," Mom says. "And potato salad."

"With the tiny pickles?"

She smiles. "You and your pickles. Yes, with the tiny pickles. We can wait until it's closer to dinner time, but it's ready now if you didn't have lunch."

"We didn't stop, and I'm starving," I say.

"I can always eat," Freddie adds.

Carina drops her bag. "I'll go find Dad."

I should not be surprised at how easily Freddie folds into our family. My parents are easy to love. Warm and accepting, always leading with empathy and compassion. Even when they worry about us, it comes from a place of concern, not judgment, which is something I've learned never to take for granted.

They ask Freddie a lot of questions, but very few of them have anything to do with his career. They ask about his family, his life growing up, his siblings. My dad, who has three tattoos of his own, asks Freddie about the ink that's visible on his arms and the little bit of chest exposed at his collar, and Freddie explains their meaning, then listens while my dad does the same.

After we eat, the five of us walk outside to the greenhouse and look at Dad's newly planted Japanese maple seedlings. Freddie seems to enjoy the greenhouse and asks my dad question after question. *Good* questions. Curious questions that I can tell impress my dad. He keeps grinning at me over Freddie's shoulder, which makes me fight to keep from giggling.

Poor Dad. Surrounded by daughters for so long. He's probably thrilled at the prospect of having another guy in the family.

Afterward, Dad and Carina head back inside, but Mom takes Freddie and me to the rescue barn to meet Pirate and the new foal born just a couple of days ago. If I thought

Freddie liked the greenhouse, here he might as well be seven years old and visiting the zoo for the very first time.

I'm not sure I have ever seen him smile as much as he does when he meets the one-eyed donkey he's been following through pictures for weeks. "Hi, Pirate," Freddie says, scratching the donkey's long ears. "Wicked eye patch, man. You're really selling it." He holds out his phone. "Here. Take a picture of us? I want to send it to the guys."

He poses beside Pirate, smiling wider than I've ever seen him smile, and I snap a few shots for him. "You look good out here," I say as I hand his phone back. "Happy."

"I *am* happy," he says. "Happy is easy out here. This is a great place."

I lean against the fence post, propping one foot up on a hay bale. "Yeah. A little hot, though. It's a shame we can't go swimming."

His eyebrows lift. "Why can't we?"

"Because I didn't pack a swimsuit, and I'm guessing you didn't either," I say.

"No, but I am wearing a pair of black boxer briefs that have doubled as a swimsuit before."

I think about the blush pink bra and underwear I'm wearing. "Yeah. That's not an option that will work for me."

Freddie's eyes drop to my torso, his eyes flickering with a hunger that makes my skin flush with heat. "Okay, but you grew up here. There has to be something in that house you can wear. Or you could borrow something from your sister."

I bite my lip, considering. I *could* borrow something from Carina. Her boobs are half the size of mine, but she probably has something I could make work. Besides, it's hot and muggy and the sun probably won't set for another three hours, and now that I've *thought* about swimming with Freddie, I don't think I'll be able to let the idea go.

"Fine," I say. "But I'm just warning you. This is a cold mountain river we'll be swimming in. Like, steal-your-breath, make-your-teeth-chatter cold."

"Consider me warned. I still want to go."

"Go where?" Mom says as she returns from the barn.

"Just to the swimming hole," I say.

"Good idea," Mom says. "But you should meet this sweet baby first."

"Wait, how is it so small?" Freddie asks as we take in the baby donkey in Mom's arms. It's less than half the size of Pirate, and Pirate already looks pretty small.

"She's miniature," Mom says. She motions for Freddie to sit on the hay bale beside us, then she lowers the donkey into his arms. "She'll always be small. No more than three feet at the withers, even when she's full grown."

I have seen a lot of cute things in my life. But Freddie Ridgefield snuggling a newborn donkey might be the cutest of all.

"This is the happiest day of my life," he says, voice serious, and Mom laughs.

"I'm glad you're enjoying yourself," she says. "Why don't you give her a name? I've been trying, but I haven't come up with anything that fits."

Freddie's eyes widen. "For real?"

"Sure. Give it your best shot."

Freddie runs a hand down the donkey's neck. "I think we should call her...Louise," he finally says.

Mom looks up to meet my gaze, a question in her eyes.

"Louise?" I ask, because he has to be kidding. Who names a donkey Louise?

But Freddie nods. "Sure. Look in her eyes and try to tell me it doesn't fit."

I crouch down beside him and let the donkey nuzzle my palm as I stare into her enormous brown eyes. "Louise," I say again, and she lets out a tiny bray.

"See?" Freddie says. "She likes it."

"Louise," Mom repeats. "I guess that's it, then."

AN HOUR LATER, I'm wearing one of Carina's bikinis under a pair of cutoffs and my high school swim team t-shirt, leading Freddie down the wooded trail that leads to the swimming hole.

I haven't walked this trail in years, and it's a little more overgrown than it was when I was a teenager, but it's still easy to follow, familiar in all the ways that matter most.

"I really like your family," Freddie says, and I turn and meet his gaze over my shoulder. The trail is too narrow for us to walk side by side, so I appreciate a reason to turn and take him in. He's changed into a pair of black shorts and a plain white t-shirt, and he has our towels draped around his neck, his hands hanging onto them on either side. He looks relaxed and happy and not at all like a rockstar, despite the plethora of tattoos visible on his body.

"Yeah, they're pretty great," I say. We reach a spot on the trail that descends steeply, and I make quick work of using a nearby tree to steady myself as I hop down. When I reach the bottom, I turn and offer Freddie a hand.

"Show off," he says as he takes my hand, bracing himself against it as he makes the same jump I did.

"Not showing off," I say as I turn back around. "I'm just in my natural habitat."

He chuckles. "I like you in your natural habitat. I like everything about this place."

As soon as we round the next bend, the sound of rushing water reaches us, infusing me with a sense of place and permanence that I haven't felt in a long time. Touring with Freddie means sleeping in a different city every night, places that blend together into a constantly shifting blur. But this place is rooted deep in my heart. No matter how far I go or how far I travel, nothing will ever stop it from feeling like home.

I smile back at Freddie and point to my ears. "That's how we know we're close!"

Minutes later, we're standing on the edge of a rock looking out over the river. It flows toward us, cascading over a waterfall into the deep green water below. At the base of the falls, the swimming hole is wide and deep, perfect for swimming. "We jump from here," I say, looking over the edge of the rock to the water below. It's only a five-foot drop—an easy jump—but Freddie's eyeing it like he's second-guessing his decision to come.

"You sure about this?" I say. I tug my t-shirt over my head and drop it onto the rock behind me.

His eyes move over my body, and he grins, unabashed appreciation in his gaze. "If you're getting in, I'm getting in with you."

"Better hurry, then," I say. Then I kick off my shorts and run to the edge of the rock, hurling myself into the water below.

The cold mountain water steals my breath just like I warned Freddie it would, so I'm gasping when I reach the surface, pushing my hair away from my face. I let out a *whoop* because I can't *not*—it really is that cold—and I look up to where Freddie is still standing on the rock.

He's stripped down to his boxer briefs, and I relish the chance to study him so openly, to take in the sight of his long, lean frame. I really *do* love his tattoos—every single one of them.

"Having second thoughts?" I yell up at him, treading water to keep myself afloat.

"It looks cold," he calls back.

"It *is* cold. Now get in!"

I will never forget the scream Freddie lets out when he hits the water, or the way he's smiling when he pops back up through the surface.

I laugh and flick a little water into his face. "I think you found your soprano notes," I say playfully.

He swims over to me, wrapping his arms around my middle and tugs me down until we're both under the water. We both come up laughing and splashing, water dripping off our eyelashes and down the ends of our noses.

"Okay, you're right," Freddie says. "It does feel good."

"See?" I say. "I told you it would."

We're maybe two feet apart, both of us treading water, just staring at each other.

There are so many things I want to say to Freddie. Things I need to tell him. But for right now, it feels good to just be with him. To relax without having to talk about anything big.

I turn and swim toward an enormous boulder on the other side of the river. It's wide and flat, with a low lip that makes it easy to climb on.

I push myself up and onto the edge, turning so I can sit

with my legs still dangling, my feet and calves fully submerged in the water.

Freddie swims over and hooks his hands onto the rock on either side of my knees so I'm sitting inside the circle of his arms. I am *not* unhappy with this development, with how easy he's making it to be close to him.

"You're a good swimmer," he says. Water beads up on his eyelashes, and I'm struck by how impossibly long they look. His eyes are the same mossy green as the river.

"East Tennessee regional champ," I say. "Two-hundred-meter freestyle."

"Really? How did I not know that?"

I shrug. "It's a very small claim to fame."

"There is no such thing," he says. "Tell me something else."

"Like what?"

"Anything," he says. "What were you like in high school?"

I smirk, then lean back on the flat rock, stretching my arms over my head. "You mean, when I wasn't making out with one of the Benson brothers?"

He scowls, then ducks under the surface, but then he shoots out lightning fast, darting sideways and hoisting himself out of the water. He comes down right next to me and leans over my body, cold water dripping onto my chest and stomach. He reaches up and takes my hands, pinning them over my head, his grip firm but still gentle enough that I could tug away easily if I wanted to. Then he shakes his head like he's a shaggy dog, sending drops of icy water all over me.

I squeal and laugh, squeezing my eyes closed until he

stops. When I open them, he's hovering over me, green eyes wide, a smile playing on his lips.

"What's it going to take to banish all thoughts of the Benson brothers from your mind?" he asks.

A bead of water drips off the end of his hair and lands on my collarbone. "Probably..." I say, "I'm going to need to replace my old memories with new ones."

He leans down and brushes the tip of his nose against mine. "Memories of swimming hole kisses?" he asks, mouth so close, I can almost feel the movement of his lips as he speaks.

"Mm-hmm," I say, tilting my face up, the anticipation practically killing me.

"Ivy, is this okay?" he whispers, lips still torturously close. "We've never..."

He doesn't have to finish the sentence because I know what he's asking.

We've never kissed with no one watching.

Even if we've wanted it, there has always been some ulterior motive, some extra reason the kiss seems necessary. The press or the paparazzi, even just his fans.

But we're utterly alone now. If we kiss, it will only be because we want to.

Because we want it for us.

For each other.

"It's more than okay," I whisper. "It's exactly what I want."

His mouth crashes onto mine with a fervency that's been absent in all our other kisses. Even the one at Voltage, when we both got lost in the moment, pales in comparison to this. At Voltage, and every other time we've kissed, Freddie's fame has been woven into the moment. I was always kissing the famous Freddie Ridgefield.

But out here, I'm just kissing Freddie.

He's just a guy, kissing me at the swimming hole because he can. Because he *wants* to.

And he does want to. I feel his desire with every brush of his lips, with every slide of his tongue as he takes my mouth over and over again.

Freddie wraps a hand around the curve of my waist, his long fingers splaying against my water-chilled skin. His thumb brushes across my ribs, and I suck in a breath, every spot he touches burning with new awareness. I want more of this, more of him, and a deep yearning pushes through my chest, then expands outward, filling me with peaceful certainty.

I love him. I love him and I'm *always* going to love him.

"Ivy," Freddie says against my mouth.

I lean up and kiss him before he can move away, not yet ready to give him up. "Mmm?"

"This rock"—I interrupt him with a kiss—"is really uncomfortable."

I laugh and finally let Freddie go, then use my hands to push myself up so I'm sitting. The sun has already fallen below the tree line, and a cool breeze blows across the water, making my skin break out in goosebumps. I glance at my watch. It's just past seven, so we have a few hours before the sun sets completely, but the longer we're here, the colder the water is going to feel.

Freddie must be thinking the same because he turns to look at me. "I'm suddenly realizing we have to get *back* in the water to get *out* of the water," he says.

"Not unless we want to go on a really long hike," I say. I nudge his leg with mine. "Come on. It's like ripping off a Band-Aid. The longer we stall, the worse it's going to be."

Once we cross the river and make it out of the water, we make quick work of drying off and getting back into our clothes.

"From about two to four o'clock every afternoon in the summer, this entire rock is in full sunlight," I say as I slip on my Birkenstocks. "We used to swim until we were nearly blue, then climb up here and stretch out on our towels and read while the sun warmed us back up again."

"Sounds pretty magical," Freddie says.

We head up the path, slowly making our way back to the house. Freddie is quieter than I expect him to be, and I start to worry, to wonder if he regrets the way he kissed me in the river.

It's probably a stupid worry. But this is still so new, and we still haven't talked about anything yet. I don't know that I'll stop second-guessing until we've talked about where we stand.

"Did I ever tell you I set up a retirement fund for my parents?" Freddie asks.

We step out of the woods and onto a wider path that cuts through the east field, so I pause my steps, waiting for Freddie to catch up so we can walk side by side.

"I don't think so," I say. "When?"

"Years ago. Right after my first solo album went triple platinum." His eyes shift, looking out across the field to the mountains melting into the horizon. This late in the day, the fading blue of the sky makes it hard to see where mountains stop and sky begins.

I walk slowly, waiting for Freddie to continue, sensing that he has more to say but might need time to say it.

In another hour, this field will be full of fireflies dancing among the redbud trees. It'll be beautiful, almost magical, so if we have to walk around this field until then, you won't hear me complain.

"I paid off their house," Freddie says. "Bought them a car. And put enough money into an account that they could've retired right then if they'd wanted to."

I reach over and slip my arm through his. "What did they say? Surely they were grateful."

He lets out a little chuckle. "They definitely were. They said thank you. But then I suggested they use the money to travel. To come see me perform if they want or, I don't know, go literally anywhere in the world that isn't inside the fifty square miles outside their neighborhood. And you know what my mother said?"

"Tell me," I say softly.

"She reached over and squeezed my hand before saying, 'Thank you, dear. But our life isn't small because it has to be. It's small because we *want* it to be.'"

"Wow," I say. "You really aren't anything like them."

Freddie lets out a humorless laugh. "I'm definitely more my grandfather's son than either of my parents. The point is, I've thought about that a lot over the years. About not wanting a small life. And I thought the only way I could do that was to have the opposite. So I chased it. Fame. Fortune. Stadiums full of fans who were only there because of me. I built a really big life." He shakes his head and lets out a little chuckle. "Because I was so afraid to wind up like them. To be *small*."

"I don't think that's a bad thing, Freddie."

"Maybe not. Trouble is, it wasn't making me happy. That's why I couldn't write. Because everything felt hollow. Big and meaningless? That's not a better option."

I resist the urge to tell him that nothing about his life is meaningless. But I can only offer him words, and I don't want them to seem like empty platitudes when they contradict how *he* feels.

So I just wait. I wait and listen and let him talk.

"So I've been thinking lately that maybe it isn't about living big or living small. It's more about living with people where you belong. I've never felt that with my parents. Not ever. So I think I was chasing what I thought I needed. A big, important, impressive life. But I don't think it has anything to do with that. I think I just want to belong somewhere." He lifts his shoulders into a shrug and offers me a sheepish grin. "Is it too soon to say I feel like I belong here?"

He reaches out and takes my hand, rubbing his thumb across the back of my palm. "Here with your family because I really liked naming one of your mom's donkeys. And I could talk to your dad about trees all day. And after the car ride today, I've even developed an appreciation for Carina's taste in music."

I laugh at this and roll my eyes. "Please don't ever let her hear you say that."

"I also mean here with *you*," he says, his lips lifting into a tiny grin. "Because I really liked kissing you at the swimming hole." He tugs me forward and lifts my hand, pressing it against his chest just over his heart. "But I also mean *here* with you. Because I'm not sure belonging is a place so much as it's a person. I'm pretty sure I can feel at home anywhere, as long as I'm with you."

I close my eyes, breath caught in my throat as I replay his words over and over. As long as he's with me. *Me.*

I have loved Freddie from a distance for so long, agonized over my feelings, willed myself to get over him, to just freaking move on.

But I couldn't quit him. No matter how hard I tried, I could never shake the hope that somehow, some way, he would eventually see me like I see him.

And now we're here.

Standing in the middle of a field full of redbud trees, and he's telling me I'm his *home*.

I open my eyes to see him searching my gaze, hope clear in his expression.

"Freddie, are you telling me what I think you're telling me?" I ask, not even trying to hide the tremble in my voice.

He offers me a sheepish, lopsided smile. "That I'm in love with you?" he asks, and all the air whooshes out of my lungs. "Yeah," he says softly. "That's what I'm telling you."

CHAPTER TWENTY-THREE

Ivy

OVER THE PAST FIVE YEARS, I HAVE IMAGINED FREDDIE Ridgefield telling me he loves me countless times. What did not happen in *any* of those fantasy versions of our declarations of love was my dad showing up right in time to spoil the moment.

But that's what's happening now.

Freddie said I'm in love with you.

Then I said nothing.

Then Dad showed up and asked if Freddie would like to see the irrigation system he uses to water his redbud trees, and we took a walk to the edge of the field to study the setup Dad designed himself and really, *really* likes to show off.

Freddie glances at me over his shoulder and smiles, then looks back at the pump my dad is pointing out. "Very cool," Freddie says, and I gotta say, his tone is *convincing*.

Surely he knows that I love him too.

I didn't *say* it. But only because I didn't have time. It's a lot to process, learning that someone is in love with you.

Especially when that someone is your boss.

Who is also a wildly famous rockstar.

Whom you have loved, *desperately,* for almost as many years as you have known him.

"Anyway, that's how it works," Dad says. "The upgrade to the pump really made all the difference."

"Yeah, I bet," Freddie says. "It's amazing you can reach the entire field with just one system."

Dad claps him on the back. "If you have time before y'all leave tomorrow, I'll take you out to see the junipers. It's a little too far for walking, but we can take the four-wheelers." He holds up a finger. "You have to wear a helmet though."

"Um, that sounds amazing," Freddie says. "I would love to see the junipers."

I'm betting he'll really just love the four-wheeling, but I'm not about to burst Dad's bubble if Freddie isn't.

Dad finally turns to me. "Your mother sent me out to see if y'all want any peach pie for dessert. It's fresh out of the oven, and you know your mother thinks it's best when it's hot enough to melt the ice cream." He looks from me, then over to Freddie. "Are you coming in soon? Or should I tell her not to wait?"

I exchange a glance with Freddie, and he shrugs, offering me the tiniest of nods. "I like the sound of peach pie."

"We're coming in right now," I say to Dad. "We'll be right behind you."

Dad moves toward the house, and Freddie and I follow, but I slow my steps, hoping for a few more moments of privacy before we get to the house.

I reach over and take Freddie's hand, and he looks at me,

his expression warm and sincere. "I'm sorry we were inter-rupted," I say.

"Nah, it's fine. I like your dad a lot."

"Me too. But his timing was terrible."

Freddie chuckles, then he stops walking altogether and turns to face me, a new vulnerability in his eyes. "What would you have said if your dad hadn't interrupted?"

I look into the green eyes I've grown to know so well. "I would have said I'm really, *really* in love with you too."

———

AFTER DESSERT and a shower to wash off the river, I find Freddie in the kitchen doing dishes with my mom. He's also managed to sneak in a shower, and he looks perfect, wearing dark jeans and a plain black henley, the sleeves pushed up to his elbows, and my mom's bright pink rubber gloves.

He's elbow deep in suds when I walk over, so I duck into the space between him and the sink and turn to face him, arms wrapped around his torso.

"Hi," I say, and he grins.

"Hi."

"You smell good."

"I showered. Carina let me use her bathroom. She said I'd have to wait forever if I planned to use yours."

I scowl. "Carina is judgy and mean."

"I heard that," Carina yells from the living room.

Mom chuckles from where she's unloading the dish-washer. "Your father was looking for you earlier, Ivy. He's got something he wants to show you."

"Does he? What is it?"

"You'll have to go see for yourself," she says. "He's waiting for you on the back porch."

I nod, then look up at Freddie. "Will you be okay here?"

"Absolutely," he says. "Your mom already promised me albums full of your baby pictures if I finish the rest of the dishes."

"See, you expect me to complain about that, but I was a very cute baby. So go ahead. Knock yourself out." I lean up on my toes and press a quick kiss to his lips. "I'll be back soon."

Something flickers in his eyes. "When you are, I *also* have something I want to show you. Or...play for you, actually. If you're up for it."

I think about the moment in the car when he told Carina he'd never written a song about someone specific until recently.

I've never been a fangirl. It's not really my nature or my personality to freak out over artists or authors or any other kind of celebrity.

But the thought of Freddie Ridgefield singing a song that he wrote *about* me...*to me*...that probably deserves a *tiny* bit of fangirling.

"I take it you won't give me any clues either?" I ask.

"Not a one," he says. But he does give me one more kiss before I go.

As promised, Dad is waiting for me at the base of the back steps. It's already after nine, and the farm is bathed in the soft moonlight of a summer night, the stars twinkling overhead.

Dad doesn't say anything as we cut across the back lawn, which isn't typical for him. Even if he's just talking about farming, he's usually got something to talk about, some new improvement in the greenhouse or a new tractor he loves more than all the others.

His silence makes me wonder if he's nervous about something, and it piques my curiosity.

When we reach the edge of the grass, we turn to the right, moving away from the commercial operations of the nursery. The greenhouses, the employee parking lot, the tractors and mowers and other machinery used for everything from seeding to harvesting.

Once, when I was in middle school, I asked Dad if he wanted me to help him run the nursery one day. It was a much smaller operation back then, half what it is now. I remember he'd just purchased a second delivery truck, the Conway Nursery logo painted onto the side.

"I want you to grow up and do whatever you want," he said, like it was the easiest answer in the world.

"But what will you do if I don't? Or if Daphne and Carina don't want to either?"

He shrugged. "I'll sell it all and move to the beach."

When we pass the firepit, I finally realize where Dad is taking me. There's a small workshop on this side of the property, one of the only places that doesn't have anything to do with Dad's business.

He's always enjoyed a little bit of wood carving, and the workshop is where he keeps all his tools.

Somewhere in the house, in the boxes of things I left at home when I moved out but didn't want to throw away, I have at least a dozen tiny animals my dad carved for me over the years. Donkeys and goats and bears and rabbits. Even an octopus, because I watched a documentary about one and became fully obsessed for six solid months.

His carvings are good enough that he could sell them if

he wanted to, but he's always said that selling them would ruin the fun. That he'd rather not turn his hobby into a job because then it would be a job, and then what would he have as a hobby?

Hard to argue with that kind of logic.

We finally reach the workshop, and Dad pauses before opening the door. He turns to look at me, his expression a little sheepish, then he clears his throat. "So, your mother was cleaning out one of the closets upstairs, the one in Daphne's room, and she came across a box of Daphne's things. I don't know how we missed it before, but it had a notebook in it that seemed to be ideas for a wedding. Pictures of flowers, dresses, that sort of thing."

"Daphne's perfect wedding," I say. "I remember. It was one of those black and white composition books, right? And she glued in pictures of what she liked."

"That's it exactly," Dad says.

"Oh my gosh. I haven't thought about that thing in years. We were in middle school when she made it."

"I'm surprised it wasn't you who made one," Dad says. "You were always more of a planner."

"True. But Daphne was the romantic one."

Dad chuckles. "Yeah, I guess you're right about that. Either way, there were several pictures of these wooden arbors, the kind you might stand under when you're exchanging vows, and it just got me thinking…"

I suck in a breath. "Daddy. Did you build one?"

He smiles, then he turns and opens the workshop doors and flips on the light. "The learning curve was pretty steep," he says. "I've never carved anything this big before, and you probably shouldn't look too closely because I'm not as precise when I'm working on larger pieces of wood. But I don't know. I think it turned out all right."

His modesty is compelling but entirely unnecessary. The arbor is beautiful. There are four posts, two on each side, with a gently sloped arch overhead. The entire thing is covered in carved vines, in tiny leaves that wrap and swirl. I've seen arbors where the point is to cover them with flowers. They're structural—a medium for decoration. But this is artwork all on its own.

"Dad," I say, my voice soft. "It's so beautiful."

"You think?"

"Are you kidding? I've never seen anything like it."

"That's what your mother said you would say."

"It's what *anyone* would say." I run a hand down the post closest to me. The wood is sanded and smooth. "Truly. It's amazing."

He pushes his hands into his pockets. "Your mother *also* said I shouldn't show this to you now, since Freddie came home with you. She didn't want it to seem like now that you're dating someone, we're trying to marry you off. But you're here, and you don't come home all that often, so I'm showing you anyway and just trusting you to know I would have shown you even if you hadn't brought Freddie along." He takes a deep breath. "And maybe you won't even get married, and that would be okay too. But if you do, I just thought—I know it was Daphne's idea to have one of these. But I thought it might be a nice way to have her with us."

Understanding finally dawns. This might have been Daphne's idea, her dream, but Dad built this for me.

For *my* wedding.

"You don't have to use it," Dad quickly says. "I thought I could build a bench to go under it, and it could sit out front near your mother's rose bushes. If it isn't what you had in mind, it doesn't have to be your dream just because it was Daphne's. I just thought…"

"Dad," I say, stopping his nervous rambling. "I love it so much. I have no idea when I'll get married, but I would love to use it."

He smiles with obvious relief. "I know Freddie can afford anything. You might not want something so simple."

"You're that sure I'm going to marry Freddie?"

He shrugs. "Of course you will. I've seen the way he looks at you."

My heart squeezes in my chest, but his words don't surprise me like they might have a week ago. Because now, I've seen the way Freddie looks at me too.

"Does it scare you a little?" Dad asks. "How famous he is?"

"I've gotten used to it," I say. "It's just a different kind of normal. We do stay off the internet, though. At least when it comes to stuff about the two of us."

He nods, then pulls a couple of stools away from his work bench, offering one to me.

"I'm glad you found each other," he says as he lowers himself to sit.

I smile. "Yeah. Me too. Took us long enough to figure things out. But sometimes it happens that way, I guess."

Dad's expression turns thoughtful. "For a long time," he starts, "I worried that losing Daphne would keep you and Carina from really spreading your wings. That you might live scared." He pauses and wipes a hand across his face. "It makes me happy to see you finally putting yourself out there. Taking risks."

"You sound like Carina. She said the same thing."

"Yeah. We had a conversation this afternoon about healthy risks...and not so healthy ones."

"I'm trying to be better about not worrying so much," I say. "About *her,* specifically. But I think it's hard-wired into my DNA."

"It's not your job, honey. Let us worry about her. That's something your mother and I have talked about too. We've probably relied on you too much. You can worry about her. That's just being a sister. But it isn't your job to protect her. She's her own woman. And she's going to be okay."

I nod, appreciating the validation. "You know what's funny?" I ask. "I've never thought of myself as risk-averse. But I'm recognizing now that my need to plan and be in control—that's what I've been doing. Trying to keep myself safe."

Dad smiles. "Sitting on feelings for years definitely feels like playing it safe."

"Seriously? Did *everyone* know how I feel about him?"

"Well, *he* didn't, so at least you managed to convince somebody. But we know you, Ivy. We've heard the way you talk about him."

It occurs to me that so many things about a relationship with Freddie will be different because of his fame. And it probably won't always be easy. There will be ripple effects that impact my family, no matter how much I try to keep them out of the limelight.

Freddie's family is annoyed by his fame. They see it as a nuisance. As noise. And they're missing out on having a relationship with someone really incredible because of it.

It makes me grateful to know it doesn't matter to my parents. They'll love him because I do. But also because they'll see how amazing he is.

"I really love him, Daddy," I say, and he smiles.

He stands and moves over to where I'm sitting and wraps his arms around me. "I'm happy for you, Ivy. Also, he asks really good questions about my trees."

I let out a little chuckle. "You're gonna turn him into a farmer."

"You think he'd give up singing to move out here and work with me?"

I think of the way Freddie lights up on stage. "Not a chance," I say. "But maybe when he retires?"

Dad grins. "I'll hold out hope for that."

CHAPTER TWENTY-FOUR

Freddie

"AND THIS IS DAPHNE HERE?" I ASK, POINTING TO A LITTLE girl in the photo album spread out in front of me. She has her arm looped over Ivy's shoulders, and she's smiling wide. Ivy is easy to spot. Her wild curls were even wilder when she was a kid.

"Yeah. That was Ivy's seventh birthday party," Mrs. Conway says.

"Seems like they were really good friends," I say as I turn another page.

Ivy was right—she really was a cute baby. A cute kid too. But the photo albums I'm looking through tell me something much more important. They draw a clear picture of a family who has always had fun together. A lot of the pictures are totally random. Unposed, candid shots that aren't great quality but still seem to tell a big story. The girls in the backyard or riding on a tractor or feeding the animals in their mom's rescue. There aren't a lot of posed photos, which is what you see in photo albums at my house. Professional quality photos of the four of us posing behind birthday cakes, posture rigid, fake smiles on our faces.

Those photos were important to my mom, and I don't fault her for wanting to document our lives. But I get the sense Ivy's family has so much fun on Christmas morning, they forget to take any pictures at all.

"So, Freddie," Mrs. Conway says. "I have a question for you."

I close the album and look up at her. Ivy might have her Dad's curly hair, but she has her mom's eyes.

"Okay. Shoot."

"Now, I want to preface this by saying I don't want to take advantage. I imagine you have people asking for things all the time. And that's not what I'm trying to do here. But, well, not everyone gets the chance to have dinner with someone of your level of influence. So I'm shooting my shot."

"Okay. Noted," I say, more than a little intrigued by where this conversation might be going.

She takes a deep breath. "The other day, I came across an article about you and Ivy and your newly discovered romance..." She hesitates. "And it mentioned Daphne's accident."

My stomach drops into my shoes. "That shouldn't have happened," I say. "I have a publicist who is supposed to keep an eye on things—who should have—"

She lifts a hand, cutting off my words. "I didn't mention it to upset you. Or to complain. It was bound to happen eventually, and the article didn't say anything that wasn't true. They included a picture of the vehicle—they probably found that from the news articles that ran right after it happened—and that was pretty much it."

"Still, it had to be jarring to see it when you weren't expecting to."

Her expression softens. "It's not how I like to remember Daphne, that's for sure," Mrs. Conway says. "But it did get me thinking. We've been talking for years about doing something in Daphne's name. A foundation of some sort to promote education and awareness. I don't want teenagers to drink. Ever. But if they're going to anyway, I'd like them to understand how it impacts their body. Daphne was smart. She wouldn't have climbed into that car if she'd thought she was in danger. So she must have believed she was safe. That her boyfriend hadn't had enough to drink for it to matter. What if I'd sat her down and been more straightforward? Told her what signs to look for. Insisted that *any* amount when you're only eighteen is enough to make you a risk." She shrugs her shoulders. "I can't bring Daphne back. But I can talk about her. I can educate. I also thought I could provide support for other families who have been through what we've been through."

"I think that's an amazing idea," I say.

"I also thought if people are going to be digging up things about her accident now that you and Ivy are together, maybe if we're the ones talking about it, then we get to control the narrative. It can't be a scandalous story if we're the ones telling it."

When Ivy asked me to kiss her outside Margot's beach house, that's exactly what she was thinking about. The importance of controlling the narrative.

"Now," Mrs. Conway continues, "we've set a little money aside, so I'm not asking for financial support. But would it be shameless of me to ask for a little celebrity endorsement?"

My heart expands, and I almost get choked up. After so

many years of feeling disdain from my own family, to feel like my chosen career path has only ever given them reasons to keep their distance, to have the Conways ask for help with something so personal means a lot.

They aren't looking at me like I'm a liability—a reason their privacy will be violated. They're seeing my platform as a benefit—a help to the good they want to accomplish.

"I would be honored to help," I say. "Truly. Financially. Logistically. I have a lot of resources and an incredible team of attorneys and public relations people and marketing people. Anything you need—I probably have a connection to someone who could help."

She smiles. "That would be amazing. Carina has a degree in nonprofit management, so I'm hoping she'll eventually be able to help. As soon as we can afford to pay her something. But however much you want to be involved, we'd love to have your help too."

We chat for a few more minutes about her vision for the foundation, then she gives me a huge hug, tells me how grateful she is to have me in her home, and sends me outside to wait for Ivy. I stop on my way and grab my guitar from where I left it in the entryway.

Even though Mrs. Conway didn't think it was cause for concern, I still search for the news article that mentioned Daphne and forward it to Kat so she can be aware. Mentally, I need to expand the circle of people who I think about when it comes to how and when I market my career. Ivy belongs in that circle, but if this relationship goes somewhere, and every instinct tells me she's who I want to spend the rest of my life with, her family needs to be in that inner circle too.

I pull my grandfather's guitar out of its case and settle

onto the wicker couch along the back wall of the screened-in porch.

This might be my new favorite place to sit. The furniture is worn and comfortable, the mountain air is cool and crisp even though it's still technically summer, and the cicadas' song is rolling through the trees like an undulating wave.

I love being at Conway Nursery as much as I've ever loved being anywhere, even after one afternoon. Maybe because I see Ivy in every part of this place.

I want it to be a part of me like it's a part of her. I want to joke with her parents and hang out with her sister and kiss Ivy at the swimming hole a thousand more times.

But mostly I just want her.

I want her to be the first person I see when I wake up in the morning, and the last person I see before I go to sleep. I want to text her for no reason and kiss her because I can and insert the image of her into every love song I ever sing again.

I play through a few measures of "Golden Eyes," nervous energy buzzing under my skin. When Ivy left with her dad, she went out this way, so I assume she'll come back this way too.

I finish the song, then start another, this one a little less polished than "Golden Eyes," but still mostly finished. It'll take a few more weeks of work to lay down the final tracks, but I'm happy with where we're headed. And it's finally feeling fun again—easy in the best way possible.

When Ivy finally appears at the edge of the porch, my heart rate spikes and my hands start to tremble, fingers slipping off the guitar strings and making my next note falter.

She climbs the steps, then sits on the wicker couch across from me. "Something new?" she asks, tilting her head toward my guitar.

I play a few more measures. "Yeah. You like it?"

"I really do. Does it have words?"

"Some," I say. "It isn't finished yet."

"It's not the one you want to play for me?" she asks, and nerves make my stomach tighten.

"Nah, that one *is* finished."

She bites her lip. "You gonna keep me in suspense?"

"Yes," I say easily as I set down my guitar. I lean forward and prop my elbows on my knees.

She chuckles. "Why?"

I look up and meet her gaze. "Because I'm nervous. And I'd like you to tell me about your conversation with your dad."

"Freddie Ridgefield is nervous?" she jokes. "I didn't think that was possible."

She's not wrong. It's been years since I've felt anything but adrenaline pumping through my veins when I perform. But this is different.

I offer her a pleading expression. "Please?"

She finally relents and spends a few minutes telling me about her conversation with her dad, about the arbor he built for her and how he hopes it will remind her of Daphne when she gets married.

Then I tell her about my conversation with her mom and her parents' idea to start a foundation. This makes her cry a little, especially when I mention the part about Carina helping to run it.

"That would be so good for her," Ivy says.

I nod. "I was thinking if I made a donation big enough to help cover employment expenses for the first couple of years, they could hire Carina sooner. I wanted to run that by you first, though. I didn't mention it to your mom."

Ivy nods, her expression shifting in a way that tells me she's puzzling through something logistical. I know that look well.

"We'd have to hire someone else too. Someone to train her and help her gain some on-the-ground experience. But I think it's a brilliant idea." She studies me closely. "Freddie, I'm sure Mom meant what she said about not needing any money. Are you sure you want to be a part of this?"

I lift my shoulders into a shrug. "I want to be a part of all of this. This place. Your family. Does that...overwhelm you?"

She leans over and cups a hand around my cheek, pressing a quick kiss to my lips. "You never have been a man to do anything by halves. Now, sing to me. Please?"

I reach for my guitar, mostly because I doubt she'll let me kiss her again if I don't.

"So the arbor your dad built," I ask as I tune up. "Does he anticipate you getting married anytime soon?"

I really like the fact that the question makes her cheeks redden. "I—no," she quickly says. "He does not have a time-frame. Just thought the arbor would be nice to use when I *do* get married. Assuming I want to get married on the farm."

"This would be a really beautiful place to get married," I say, and her gaze locks on mine.

"You think so?"

"Absolutely." We're quiet for a beat before I say, "Your mom showed me a lot of pictures. A lot of you and Daphne. I wish I'd met her."

Ivy's smile softens. "Yeah. Me too. But she would have been tough on you."

"For more than just the fake dating thing? I thought you said she would have loved me."

"She would have. But she would have teased you about

your fame. Definitely about your tattoos. And about the picture of you that was used for all the merch on your first solo tour."

I groan. "You wound me. You know how much I hated that photo. But what's wrong with my tattoos?"

"I love your tattoos," she says, and my heart flips over. "But Daphne would have had questions. She would have made you explain your reasons behind every single one to prove you didn't get them just to look more like a rockstar."

"I mean, they don't exactly *hurt* my image."

Ivy grins. "You're shameless."

"Unfortunately, that's part of my job description."

"Is singing a part of your job description, because it seems like you're stalling," Ivy teases.

I scowl at her, but she's right. My guitar has never been so perfectly in tune.

"All right, so this one will go on the new album. It's probably the first single, actually."

She nods and pulls her legs onto her chair, wrapping her arms around her knees.

I blow out a steadying breath, glance up at her one more time, then I start to play. I repeat the first few measures of the song, waiting to settle into the rhythm, the feel of it. Once I do, I start to sing.

About noticing the gold in her eyes for the first time. About a relationship that shifted and changed without me realizing, turning into something so much better than what it was before.

When I finish the song, Ivy doesn't say anything. She just looks at me, her body so still, my nerves ratchet back up, and I start rambling to fill the silence.

"So anyway, that's the song. I didn't add the key change until right at the end, and I wasn't sure about it at first, but Leo said it was good, and I think it fits with the vibe, but if there's anything you don't like about it, you can absolutely still tell me..."

My words trail off when Ivy stands and moves around the small wicker coffee table, stopping in front of me. She lifts my guitar out of my arms and sets it in the chair she just vacated, gently leaning it against the seatback. Then she kneels on the couch beside me and lifts her hands to my face.

"The song is perfect," she says. She presses a kiss to my lips. "The key change is perfect." Another kiss. "I love every single thing about it. Every word."

I lean up to capture her mouth one more time, feeling an impulsive need to keep her right here, right next to me forever. It's illogical to crave something so much, but this, the taste of her, the feel of her skin—I could do this every day and still not feel like it's enough.

"I don't know what to do with this feeling," I say in between kisses, my words brushing against her mouth. "I feel like I'm on fire. You *consume* me, Ivy. I can't stop kicking myself for how long it took me to recognize—but I'm so glad I did. I'm so glad you didn't give up on me."

She pulls back, a smile in her eyes. "You're doing a lot of talking right now," she says, and I grin.

"I process verbally."

She climbs onto my lap, her knees on either side of my thighs, and brushes her nose against mine. "Process this, then."

Her kisses are slow, languid as she moves from my mouth across my jaw to the spot just below my ear. I am lost in how good she smells, in the way her hands are cradling my face, the way her lips feel against my skin.

But mostly I'm overwhelmed with a crystal-clear certainty that no emotion I've ever experienced compares to this. It feels good to be loved by my fans. To win awards. Receive the accolades.

But this is so much better—so much *more*. This is permanence. Acceptance. The *belonging* I didn't know I needed until I found it.

Ivy deepens the kiss, her tongue brushing against mine, and I move my hands to her waist, my fingers slipping under the hem of her t-shirt until they're pressed against her warm skin, just above the waist of her jeans. She feels like silk, and I'm suddenly aware of where we are—out here on her parents' porch—where any member of her family might find us at any moment.

I shift my hands out to her hips and give them a squeeze, breaking the kiss, but then a sound escapes the back of her throat that weakens my resolve, and I'm lost in her mouth again.

Finally, she pulls away, brown eyes sparkling as she grins. "Okay," she whispers, humor in her tone. "You can talk again."

I smile and shake my head, closing my eyes. "No words."

She presses one more kiss against my lips, then climbs off my lap so she's sitting beside me.

I tilt my head, following her movements with my eyes, then hold out my hand.

She threads her fingers through mine.

"Can I ask you a question?"

She nods. "Of course. Ask me anything."

"Do you promise you'll tell me the truth?"

She wrinkles her nose. "You want me to promise before you ask me the question?"

I nod. "No secrets. No lies. That's what I want with you."

She takes a deep breath. "Okay. I promise."

"When Vivica Rose asked you when you fell in love with me, did you tell her the truth?"

She closes her eyes, her face scrunching up. "Don't make me answer that."

"You promised," I remind her. "Please, Ivy."

She sighs and opens her eyes. "Fine. No. I didn't tell her the truth."

I frown. I did *not* expect her answer to be no. "You didn't," I say, a statement more than a question.

"No," she says gently. "But only because I knew I was in love with you long before then."

A sense of relief washes over me, a peace and purpose settling into my heart at the sound of her words. *I knew I was in love with you.*

"Do you remember that time you got the flu?" she asks. "At the beginning of your Heartbeats tour?"

"Vaguely?" I've been sick more than once on tour, so I don't know exactly which time she's referencing. But I know that *all times* have been terrible.

"We were on the bus, and you wouldn't let me into your room because you didn't want me to get sick, but you also didn't want to be alone."

"So I made a bed on the floor next to my door, and you sat on the other side," I say, remembering that night, how much of a comfort it was to know she was close.

"That's when I knew," she says. "Up until then, you'd been this larger-than-life rockstar, but that night, you were just a guy. We talked for hours, and you were either high on your meds or high from your fever because you were so incredibly honest. And vulnerable about stuff that made you seem so normal." She shrugs. "I was cramped and uncomfortable and desperate for sleep and I still didn't want to be anywhere else. I figured that could only mean one thing."

"I guess you didn't want to tell *that* story to Vivica Rose."

She leans over and gives me a quick kiss. "I do like having some things that only belong to us."

I nod, agreeing with her, but I'm still struggling to wrap my head around her having feelings for so long without telling me. "That was still years ago, Ivy. Why didn't you ever say anything?"

"Because when you hired me, I promised I wouldn't fall in love with you. And I wanted to take my job seriously, and it just felt like such a clichéd thing to do. Falling in love with my rockstar boss."

"It would not have been a cliché," I argue. "I would have..." My words trail off because honestly, I'm not sure *what* I would have done.

"See?" she says gently, calling me out. "I might have been pining away all this time, but your feelings are relatively new, right? Had I said something sooner, we might not be here right now."

"I like to think I would have wanted to try," I say. "That it would have woken me up sooner."

She shrugs. "Maybe. But maybe not. And for that reason, I'm okay with how things have played out now." She nudges my leg with her knee, which she has pulled up under her. "No regrets. We're here now. That's all that matters."

She's right. I know she's right. "So, speaking of your employment. I know you mentioned wanting a job with Voltage Records, and I'm still happy to write you the best recommendation in the world. But I've also been thinking about the changes to your employment package that come with being my manager. And before you make any final decisions, I was hoping you'd hear me out?"

She grins. "Are you trying to woo me into not quitting?"

"Yes," I say without hesitation. "Unabashedly."

"Okay. Give it your best shot," she says. "But I'm not making any promises."

"So, the downside is you're going to lose your salary," I say. "The upside is that instead, you'll get twenty percent of gross artist revenue."

Her eyes widen. "Freddie, that's…"

"I know," I say. "You're worth it."

She clears her throat. "Okay, well…that's definitely something to consider."

"I was also thinking we'd have to do something about your sleeping arrangements on the bus. That little bunk—it's too small for a manager."

She lifts her eyebrows, a smile playing around her lips. "Is it now?"

"Definitely," I say, keeping my tone serious. I lean over and kiss her, my lips hovering over hers when I say, "The bed in *my* room, however…"

She laughs and pushes against my chest. "You really *are* insufferable."

I capture her hand, weaving our fingers together and pull it close to my chest, holding it there as I look at her. "I will support you if you want to work somewhere else. But I also don't want to tour without you. I want you close. I want every opportunity to build on this." I motion between us. "On us."

"I want that too," she says, and my heart expands enough to fill the entire back porch. "Honestly, Freddie, half the reason I wanted to quit was so I could figure out how to fall out of love with you."

"That sounds horrible," I say, and she grins.

"Well *now* it does," she says through a chuckle. "I don't want to quit. But we have to hire you another assistant. My job is too much for one person."

"So maybe we need to hire *you* an assistant," I say.

"How about *an* assistant that does whatever we need?"

I squeeze her hand. "Good plan. We can start looking as soon as we're back in Nashville."

She holds my gaze. "I love you."

I kiss her one more time. "I love you too."

"When did you know?" she asks, her mouth still close to mine. "That you loved me?"

I think back over the last couple of weeks. It feels like so much more time has passed since I kissed Ivy outside of Margot's beach house, but that probably has everything to do with the intensity of what I'm feeling.

Then again, those feelings have probably been building for years. I just didn't recognize them until now.

"I don't think I can pinpoint a single moment," I say. "It feels more like I just...woke up. Like the feelings were already there, but the room was dark so I couldn't see them. Then the light turned on and...there you were."

"Cool, cool," she says, her tone glib. "So instead of suffering in silence for *four years,* I could have just turned on the light. So good to know."

I smirk. "Had you just kissed me, Conway, we could have started this so much sooner."

"Don't you dare pin this on me," she says, laughter in her tone. "You're the clueless one."

I lift our clasped hands and tug them to my mouth,

kissing the back of her palm. "True. And I'll never stop trying to make it up to you."

"Good," she says. "Because the number of times I had to listen to you profess your fake love to me and ignore your marriage proposals when I remembered your dinner order was the worst kind of torture. You definitely owe me."

I groan. "I'm really the worst, aren't I? I asked you to marry me all the time."

"You did," she says. "And my heart broke a little every time."

I lean over and cradle her face in my hands, pressing a long kiss to her lips. "I'm sorry I was such an idiot. I'm sorry it took me so long to catch up."

I hold her gaze. I could almost ask her to marry me right now. That's how sure I am of this—*of her*. But I settle for making a promise I know I'll be able to keep.

"The next time I ask you," I say, "I promise I'll be asking for real."

EPILOGUE

Ivy

The energy at the Nashville show is *electric*.

Freddie is on fire—he usually is when he's back on stage after a long break—and the fans are giving him some serious love. In a private box on the other side of the stadium, my parents are watching the concert with Carina and a collection of aunts and uncles who were thrilled to receive VIP invitations to the show.

We all had dinner at Freddie's house last night, and he kept telling me how exciting it was to have so much family in his house. *Family.*

I'll never get tired of thinking of him that way.

Freddie's tour manager steps up beside me backstage, his arms folded over his chest just below the end of his bolo tie. "I'm just saying," he says in his usual dry tone. "I'm glad you'll still be with us when we hit the road next week."

I look up and smile. "Thanks, Seth."

"Also, Eric is doing fine, but could you please tell him he

doesn't have to respond to every one of my texts with 'Yes, sir, thank you, sir?'"

I stifle a grin. Freddie's new assistant is incredibly competent and so nice. But he's a little eager to please.

"A thumbs up would do just fine," Seth continues.

"I'll see if I can find a time to mention…" My words trail off because Adam, Leo, and Jace appear on the other side of Seth.

"Oh my gosh!" I step around Seth to give Adam and Jace hugs, since I don't see them nearly as frequently as I do Leo. It feels especially significant to see Jace since he lives in California and has the kids to think about. He was *just* here last month. And now he's here again. "What are you guys doing here?"

It's a dumb question because it's clear what they're doing here. The stage manager is currently checking their wireless mics like they're about to go on stage.

"Wait. You guys are singing?"

The members of Midnight Rush haven't performed together in public since their reunion show last year.

Leo smiles. "Freddie wasn't sure he'd be able to keep it a secret from you."

"*That's* why he didn't want me around for soundcheck," I say.

On stage, Freddie finishes a song, then waits for the cheers to quiet. "Thank you," he says. "I always appreciate the love. Nashville has been my home for the past decade, which is why I wanted to do something special for you all tonight. So I've invited a few friends—" Freddie has to pause because the cheer that erupts through the stadium is practically deafening. "A few friends," he finally continues, "to sing a very special song with me. You haven't heard this one, but it'll be on the next album. And it was inspired by someone very special to me."

I lift a hand to my chest. I had no idea he was going to debut the song tonight, and the thought of hearing him sing it live has my heart in my throat.

"Please welcome to the stage the men who helped me become who I am today—Midnight Rush!"

I hold my breath as the guys run onstage. Leo sits down at the piano, and Adam and Jace settle onto stools on either side of Freddie while a roadie hands Freddie his guitar.

"This song is called 'Golden Eyes,'" Freddie says. Then he looks off stage in my direction. "Ivy—you know it's for you."

I'm not sure I breathe for the entire song. By the time Freddie finishes, tears are streaming down my face, and I'm overwhelmed with a desperate need to kiss him. To let him see how much that song means to me.

So I do something I never thought I would do.

I hand Seth my iPad, then I run onto the stage.

Freddie doesn't see me at first, but his fans do, and their cheers immediately intensify. Freddie looks around, like he knows something is up, then he sees me coming. He smiles wide, handing his guitar to Adam just in time to catch me when I launch myself into his arms.

He laughs as he hugs me to his chest. Whoever is running sound for the concert is thinking on their feet, because when Freddie looks down at me and says, "What are you doing?" I'm the only one who can hear him.

"I just wanted to say I love you," I say. "And I love that song."

He leans down and kisses me, eliciting another round of cheers. "I'll write you a thousand more." He tilts his head toward the audience. "But I've kind of got a show to finish."

I laugh, then push up on my toes to kiss him one more time. "Sorry. I'm going now. Love you."

Freddie turns back to the audience. "Well, that was fun," he says, and everyone laughs and cheers again.

He and the rest of the guys sing a few more Midnight Rush songs, then he goes back to his regular set. Eventually, I make my way up to the box to watch the end of the show with my family. I rarely get to see Freddie perform from this vantage point—I'm always backstage—so it's a treat to see the full scope of his performance. The close-up camera shots that do such an incredible job of capturing his magnetism, his incredible talent.

I sit down next to Carina, and she loops her arm through mine. "Do you ever watch him performing and think 'I get to make out with that man anytime I want'?"

I laugh. "This is the first time I've seen him perform since we got together, but yeah. I'm definitely thinking it now."

"Oh! I wanted to show you something," Carina says. She pulls out her phone. "Look who texted me today."

I take her phone and read the message across the screen. It's from Margot Valemont, of all people.

It's brief. But it's very clearly an apology. With a last line that reads *Please tell Ivy and Freddie I'm happy for them and I wish them well.*

"Wow," I say. "I guess people change."

Carina takes her phone and slips it back into her bag. "I read an article that says she's going to rehab. I hope things get better for her."

"Yeah," I say. "Me too."

I stay in the private box until the end of the show, then

text Freddie, letting him know I'm riding back to the house with my family, and I'll see him at home. He has one final post-concert meet-and-greet with a collection of VIP fans who won a promotional thing through a local radio station, so it'll be a while before he's finished, and since my parents are leaving first thing in the morning, I want to soak up as much time with them as possible.

He gives my message a thumbs up, then sends a reply.

FREDDIE

Can we eat together when I get back?

IVY

Sure. Thai food?

FREDDIE

I'm craving cheese curds.

IVY

On it.

Practically speaking, I could let Freddie's new assistant pick up two mushroom and Swiss burgers with fries and extra sides of cheese curds. But sometimes, it's fun to do it just because I can.

Because taking care of Freddie makes me happy.

Because he's mine to take care of in the first place.

Once we're back at the house, I put Freddie's food in the warming oven, then change into pajamas. My parents try to wait up for him, but they've got an early drive in the morning, so they head to bed, and Carina does the same.

When Freddie finally makes it home, I'm the only one still up, sitting at the kitchen island reading a book.

He leans down and presses a kiss to my lips. "Hi."

He must have showered at the venue, because he's clean

and in fresh clothes. "Hi," I say. "Are you hungry?" I stand, motioning for him to take my barstool, then I move around the island to retrieve our food.

I slide his across to him, then retrieve a water bottle from the fridge, opening it for him just like I always have in the past. I move around the island so I can sit down beside him, and he holds his hand up to take the bottle, like we're doing a dance we've done a thousand times before.

As soon as the bottle is in his hands, he looks at me over his shoulder. "Marry me?" he says.

My first impulse is to roll my eyes. How many times has Freddie made this joke? But then I see his expression, and I freeze.

"What?"

He puts his water bottle down and spins to face me. "Marry me," he says, his voice low.

I swallow against the knot forming in my throat. "Are you serious?"

He shrugs. "I *did* say the next time I asked you, I'd be asking for real."

I take a steadying breath. "Freddie, it hasn't even been two months since we made things official."

"I know. But we've been working together—living together—for five years. We know everything there is to possibly know about each other. And we're in love. What else do we need to know?"

I lift my hands to my cheeks and look into his eyes. The logical side of my brain wants to protest. But he's right. We probably know each other better than most couples do when they get engaged. This new part of our relationship doesn't feel new so much as it feels like we finally clicked into what we were always meant to be.

"I can't believe I'm going to say yes," I whisper. "But okay. Let's get married."

He grins and tugs me forward, pulling me into his arms, where he kisses me long and slow.

"Did you plan this proposal?" I ask when he finally pulls away. "That's why you asked for a burger? Because it's your favorite thing to eat on the road?"

"I absolutely did."

"What would you have done if I'd gone to bed and just left your food for you?"

He wrinkles his forehead like that's the stupidest thing he's ever heard. "The night I sing your song in front of a hundred thousand people, I felt pretty confident you wouldn't just *go to bed.*"

"So much confidence," I say, sliding my hands up to his face. He's still sitting, and I'm standing in the circle of his arms, bracketed by his legs on either side of me, so for once, I'm a little taller than he is. "When?" I ask.

He shrugs. "After the tour, so...next fall, maybe? When the weather is cool at the farm."

"Because you want to get married at the farm?" I ask.

"I want to *be* the farm. You know how much I love that place."

I do know, because in the last month, he's convinced me to make the drive with him two more times. He's different there. More at peace. More connected to his music. I haven't minded the extra time at home. It's been nice to spend time with Carina, and we've had some great planning conversations about the foundation.

I lean down to kiss him again just because I can. "You should eat your food," I whisper against his lips.

"I have one more thing to show you first," he says. "I don't have a ring for you yet, because I know you, and I know you'll want to pick it out. But I wanted to do something to honor the commitment I feel to you, so..." He puts his hands on my hips and shifts me forward, then tugs his t-shirt over his head.

It takes me a minute to find the new tattoo. When I find it, I gasp. The skin is still a little red, so he must have gotten it today—maybe yesterday. I lift a hand to the ivy vine that starts at his heart and trace it up and over the top of his shoulder to where it ends in between his shoulder blades.

"Freddie, it's beautiful," I say. The artwork really *is* exquisite. Perfectly shaded with just enough detail.

"It's yours," he says. He puts a hand over his heart. "*This* is yours."

All those years ago, when I randomly ran into Freddie Ridgefield in the women's bathroom of his record label, I would have laughed at the suggestion that one day, I might find myself in Freddie Ridgefield's kitchen, kissing him after accepting his perfectly delivered marriage proposal.

But here we are.

There are probably all kinds of reasons to consider this a risk.

But that's just love, isn't it?

As I stand in Freddie's arms and feel the certainty of his kiss, the confidence of his embrace as he holds me, I know with perfect clarity.

For him, this risk will always be worth it.

For a One More Made Up Love Song Bonus Epilogue, please visit www.jennyproctor.com and click on Bonus Content.

ACKNOWLEDGMENTS

Several years ago, I attended a Harry Styles concert with my oldest daughter. She was sixteen or seventeen at the time, and she saved her money for months to be able to purchase a very expensive front row seat. I sat in the nosebleeds—I didn't need the experience quite like she did—but I still loved every minute of the concert. Harry Styles was charismatic and charming and his performance was outstanding. I didn't truly base Freddie on Harry, despite the old-fashioned names and tattoos they have in common. Mostly because I don't know Harry Styles personally. I have no idea what he's like while I know everything there is to know about Freddie. But I can't say I didn't think of Harry *a little*, when I was crafting the general idea of Freddie's image, so, to Harry Styles, I say thank you for being a rockstar charming enough to inspire (a very little bit) the talented Freddie Ridgefield.

As for Ivy, I borrowed her name from my youngest daughter, another Ivy Clare who shares her strength and fortitude with the fictional Ivy. Ivy, you are always one of my biggest cheerleaders, and I love, *love* being your mom.

There's a line in this book where Freddie is talking about writing music. He says that sometimes writing feels like work, and sometimes it feels like magic. This is definitely the case for me. I've written books where every page felt like a struggle, like I was wrestling with the story to make it what it needed to be. Fortunately, it isn't always like that. Sometimes, writing a book feels like magic. And this book was like that for me. I was so burned out after my last project that it took me a long time to start this one. But once I *did* start, it was so deliciously fun. Exactly the kind of escape I needed to remind myself why I love to write in the first place. This is a gentle story, but I think that's what I needed it to be. I hope you enjoyed it, and I thank you for being on this journey with me. My readers mean the world.

Kiki, as always, the only thing more valuable than having you as a critique partner is having you as a friend. Thanks for always reading and cheering me on.

Brittany, I loved having your help on this book. You're brilliant.

Emily, thank you for fixing all my commas and deleting all my crutch phrases and saving me from myself, really, pretty much, definitely, just about all the time.

Kristina, I don't know how I ever did my job without you. Thank you for all your help and for sending me so many adorable pictures of your girls. I hope we work together forever, but if we don't, you better never stop sending them!

Josh, and the rest of my family, I love you guys. Even you, Henry. One day I'll convince you to read one of my books. Just skip the kisses if they weird you out!

ABOUT THE AUTHOR

Jenny Proctor is an award-winning author of more than fourteen romantic comedies and an Amazon bestseller.

She began her career in publishing in 2013; her writing has been a constant since then and is now her full-time focus, but in the past, she spent several years as the owner and managing editor of Midnight Owl Editors and as the chair of the Storymakers Conference.

Wired for relationships, Jenny loves public speaking, teaching, and building lasting connections.

Jenny was born in the mountains of Western North Carolina, a place she considers one of the loveliest on earth. She loves to hike with her family and spend time outdoors, but she also adores lounging around her home, reading great books or watching great movies and, when she's lucky, eating delicious food she did not have to prepare herself.

Jenny currently resides with her husband and children in the Charleston, South Carolina area. To learn more, find Jenny online at www.jennyproctor.com.

ALSO BY JENNY PROCTOR

The Midnight Rush Romance Series

Once Upon a Boyband

The Appies Hockey Romance Series

Absolutely Not in Love

Romancing the Grump

When Alec Met Evie

How to Kiss a Hawthorne Brother Series

How to Kiss Your Best Friend

How to Kiss Your Grumpy Boss

How to Kiss Your Enemy

How to Kiss a Movie Star

The Some Kind of Love Series

Love Redesigned

Love Unexpected

Love Off-Limits

Love in Bloom

The Oakley Island Romcom Series

Eloise and the Grump Next Door

Merritt and Her Childhood Crush

Sadie and the Badboy Billionaire

Other Novels

* 9 7 8 1 9 6 7 5 0 0 0 1 7 *